DEMON

DEMON

A Novel

ERIK WILLIAMS

HARPER
VOYAGER
IMPULSE

An Imprint of HarperCollins*Publishers*

EPub Edition SEPTEMBER 2014 ISBN: 9780062359056

Print Edition ISBN: 9780062359063

AM 10 9 8 7 6 5 4 3 2 1

CHAPTER ONE

"I got a work stoppage here," Hank Prince yelled into his cellphone as two US Army Apache helicopters buzzed overhead en route to An Nasiriyah.

"What?" Jameson yelled on the other end. "You're almost done with that branch."

"'Almost' don't mean shit in this case. One of the backhoes dug up the entrance to some goddamn tomb three hours ago."

"Tomb? Big deal. Move the stiffs and get your ass back on schedule."

Hank rubbed his forehead. "A tomb, a crypt, a buried temple. I don't know what the fuck it is exactly, but it's got the government pukes all kinds of spun up."

"Why'd you dig it up then?"

"We found it by accident, damn it. It's twenty feet below the desert and right where the T section is supposed to go. And no, ground penetrating didn't show shit. Right now, I'm losing two man-hours for every hour of standstill, Jameson, and I can't afford a standstill."

"I can't either, or did you forget who pays your salary? Who stopped you?"

"The Department of Antiquities shut us down hard."

"Why are they involved?"

"Because we're close to some place called Ur. Anywhere near an ancient site and they have to be involved."

"And there's no way around it?"

"All I can dig is one hundred feet to either side, but we're screwed if we can't get the T section in place, and the tomb is in the damn way."

Jameson yelled and Hank could almost picture his boss's jowls jiggling and spit flying. He'd seen the reaction dozens of times before. Hank tuned him out after the fifth expletive, his attention lingering instead on the growing excavation under the tall Ingersoll Rand towers pumping out eight thousand watts of light. Government officials had already come and cordoned off the pit with yellow caution tape and left, with the exception of one person. Control of the site now rested in the hands of the lead archeologist from the Department of Antiquities.

Hank shifted his gaze and chewed on the inside of his cheek. In the east, the first rays of sunlight crested the horizon. *Another hot one on the way; no doubt about it.*

"Look," Hank said, "I didn't bury the fucking thing, and I sure as hell didn't mean to find it. Just pray it's the burial place of some fifth-century nobody and not Gilgamesh's tomb, because if it is, this branch of the sewer line ain't ever getting done."

Hank hung up and swore under his breath. He hated cross-global leadership, especially when the asshole in charge was sitting in an air-conditioned office in Houston without any idea of the ground here. The whole situation was screwed up beyond his control. Dealing with pencil pushers like Jameson was the last thing he needed right now.

He slipped the cell phone into his pocket and looked at the pit. Around it stood Hank's third shift of diggers and fitters, doing nothing and getting paid for it. He took a deep breath of desert air and thought of contingency plans. All he could come up with was busy work and figured it was better than accomplishing nothing.

"Get the southern line prepped." Hank's voice rose with each word. "And get the interceptors staged. This job won't be on hold forever."

The diggers and pipe fitters started moving, but not fast enough.

"Let's go!" Hank clapped and stomped around the hole, shooing people to work. Satisfied his workers finally got the picture, Hank walked to the edge of the pit. At the bottom stood the government archeologist, next to the slab. The man who'd shut him down without a moment of hesitation.

"Well," Hank said, "how we looking, Nouri?"

Nouri al-Hasad craned his head, his dark eyes glinting with what Hank thought was pure joy. "This is amazing."

"Don't look so happy. How long?"

"Ten days, at least."

"You got to be shitting me." Hank knew Nouri from a previous dig when they'd uncovered a mass grave near Baghdad. The guy had never been anything but serious. A pure academic nerd with no sense of Western humor. If he said ten days, he meant it. "I don't have that kind of time."

Nouri smiled. "We need to be careful with this find. I have never seen anything like it before."

"It's a stone slab covering a tomb. Big deal."

Nouri climbed a ladder out of the pit. Fast. Like a monkey scaling limbs to the top of a tree. His spry frame stood next to Hank a moment later. He pointed at the slab, hand trembling. Then Hank noticed his whole body had a slight tremor moving up and down it.

"It is not stone."

"Sure as hell looks like stone to me."

"I assure you it is not."

Hank frowned. "Well then what the hell is it? Metal?"

"I do not know. And I have never seen the language carved on the surface. With its proximity to Ur, I hope for your sake more is not under there. This could be just the tip of...how do you say...the ice cube."

"Iceberg."

"Oh, yes, that is it." Nouri held a small carving the size of his palm in his latex-gloved hand. "And look at this. Remarkable."

Hank shrugged. It was the front profile of some beast's maw with long fangs. "Looks like the carving of a wolf's head."

"Not a wolf."

"Then what?"

"I do not know."

Hank shook his head. "Look, I got a deadline, Nouri. You know, to get sanitation up and running in this armpit."

Nouri chuckled. It was the first time Hank had ever heard him laugh, and it caused Hank's blood pressure to bump up.

"I see your affection for my country has not changed," Nouri said.

"I got two daughters I miss, a son who needs his ass kicked, and a wife who has earned a big old pickle tickle. I care about them and the money I get if I finish this job on time. I make it happen, and I get to go home, see them, and then get another job making more money. Your mysterious nonstone and unknown language are costing my wallet some weight and my wife some loving."

Nouri laughed even more. "Yes, but you have something truly priceless down there."

"I'm glad everything I say is suddenly funny."

"Think of the story you will tell your children."

"Oh, sure, I can see it now. My kids sitting around the fire as I describe the amazing tomb that cost them their college tuition." Hank kicked sand into the hole.

"My time is worth more than that fucking slab and whatever's underneath it."

Hank stuffed his hands in his pockets and closed his eyes. "You're sure it'll take at least ten days?"

"Absolutely."

"And there's nothing you can do for me? Can't look the other way just this once?"

Nouri shook his head.

Hank looked from the pit to Nouri and back. "Shit!"

"I am sorry, Mr. Prince."

"Yeah." Hank's voice was softer, accepting defeat. "Me, too."

The ground trembled, shifting the sand and causing his feet to sink about half an inch. Hank turned from Nouri to see a flatbed backing toward the pit. Loaded on it was the big T section for the sewer line.

"Hey," Hank yelled at the guy signaling the truck to back up. "It's not going in. Get it off-site."

As the flatbed backed, the signalman put his hands up to brake and then gestured to pull forward. When the driver shifted into drive, the rear right tires dug into the ground and spun. The driver gunned the engine, spinning the wheels faster and digging the flatbed in deeper. Sand flew in broad arcs into the pit.

The signalman yelled and waved his arms for the driver to stop. Hank took a step toward the flatbed, ready to chew some ass, when the ground around the rear wheels buckled and sank a few feet.

Before Hank could move any farther, the sunken earth collapsed another four feet and then split. Tremors knocked Hank off balance and to his knees as a crevice opened in the desert, racing like a snake from the back of the flatbed to the pit. The truck teetered for a moment before the back dropped into the new fissure. The chains holding the T section stretched taught, and one of them snapped, cracking like thunder.

A chain link the size of a man's fist screamed over Hank's head and collided with something soft and wet. Hank glanced over his shoulder. Nouri was on the ground, his body twitching and pumping blood, turning the sand crimson. The link had ripped the right side of his forehead off. Skull and brain jutted away from his smashed cranium.

Hank took two steps toward Nouri when his workers yelled to run away. He turned back in time to see the other chains snap. Hank dove onto his chest but didn't take his eyes off the pipe, even as another link sliced the air overhead. The T section rocked, tilted, and fell into the crevice, sliding toward the pit on a wave of sand. The massive weight carried it over the edge. It fell in what seemed like slow motion. The bottom of the T struck the slab covering the tomb a moment later. What sounded like concrete snapping rose up and reverberated throughout the site.

Hank pushed up and once again tried to get to Nouri, praying silently the poor bastard was still alive. As he did, his stomach cramped and his chest tightened. He dropped to his knees, attempting to breathe but failing to force air into his lungs. It was like a ton of weight pressed on him, concentrating directly on his sternum. Then his vision quit and he saw only black.

Just as quickly, the pressure on his chest eased. Hank sucked in a mouthful of air just before his muscles started twitching. Rocking over onto his side, he broke into convulsions, foam frothing out of his mouth. His insides burned.

Images of his wife and children flashed in his mind. They melted in fire and smoke. They screamed and stabbed each other with kitchen knives. The kids ripped flesh from their mother's arms and legs with their teeth.

The convulsions stopped; his muscles relaxed. The fire abated within. Hank managed shallow breaths as the grotesque images dissolved. He started to think the pain had subsided when a headache hit him so hard he screamed. His fists clenched sand and his back arched toward heaven.

Then the pain faded. The headache retreated as fast as it had attacked. His vision returned, the pale light of the moon above fighting with the light of the towers. Everything seemed still and quiet.

Until he heard the screams.

At first, Hank thought they were his own shrieks still echoing around his head. But as they persisted, he realized they were nothing like his anguished cries. These were savage and bloodthirsty and multiple. He'd heard screams like these once before on a job in Africa when he'd witnessed two silverback gorillas battle for dominance, beating one another to a bloody pulp until one had killed the other. Now he heard the same primal screams.

Hank sat up and blinked twice before he could fathom what unfolded around him.

The signalman had the driver of the flatbed on the ground, pummeling him with punch after punch, screaming in triumph. Bone crunched and flesh tore. Then the signalman took his hard hat off and beat the driver in the face with it over and over again until another worker tackled him and stabbed him in the neck with a screwdriver.

Hank's hand shook as he covered his mouth, trying to keep from puking. He couldn't form thoughts. His mouth moved, but no sound came.

Out of the corner of his eye, two pipe fitters rolled around in the sand, clawing at each other's faces, snarling like wild beasts. One gained the advantage and pushed his thumbs into the other's eyes. This time Hank couldn't stop from vomiting, bile and blood spilling down his chest.

Run, he finally managed to think. *Now. Run now.*

Hank heard what sounded like a hammer smacking a watermelon. Even with the dozens of songs of death around him, this one chilled him to his core. He shivered and turned. Behind him a worker beat another man's head in with a pipe wrench.

Run now. Hank coughed and vomited more red phlegm. *Get up and run!*

Hank pushed to his feet. His legs wobbled and his body swayed. Lightheaded, he tried to focus, his blurred vision sharpening with each blink. All around him the desert bled. Hank had forty-nine men on this shift and every one of them engaged in savage murder. They screamed, and they killed only to be killed.

Except Hank. He found the strength to move through the carnage. No one paid him any attention. It was as if he didn't exist, an invisible witness to the slaughter.

Hank shambled, shuffling forward, his body weak and his muscles aching. He wanted to run, wanted to at least walk at a brisk pace, but couldn't find any more energy. His stomach was a sack of worms, all of them wriggling, folding in on themselves. His eyes shifted left and right, expecting at any moment one of his workers would choose him and crush his skull with a hammer or wrench.

Hank made it to his company truck and climbed in. His hands shaking, he managed to pull his keys from his pocket. As he did, a pipe fitter named Julio, from the Philippines, dragged one of the locals over and smashed his head repeatedly into the truck's bumper.

Julio was a family man, like him. Working in Iraq and sending money home. All for a better life.

The hollow sound of the skull striking metal distracted Hank, and he dropped his keys. He reached down and grabbed them off the mat. When he sat back up, Julio was on the ground, a different worker destroying his face with a heavy-duty C-clamp.

Jesus Christ, he thought.

Hank coughed more blood into his hand and took one more glance at the massacre. As he slipped the key into the ignition and fired up the truck, Hank realized he didn't know where to go but feared if he didn't leave now, one of them would finally notice him and unleash their fury. Or he might contract whatever had infected them. Either way, he had to go somewhere, anywhere, far away from here.

Basra. There was a military base there, Camp Bucca. It was the only one in the south still controlled by coalition forces. Everything else had been turned over to the Iraqis.

The screams stopped. Hank surveyed the site, surprised by the sudden silence. No one moved.

He covered his mouth and suppressed a sob, listening to the quiet, hoping he'd hear someone cry out in pain or for help. No one did.

Call for help, he thought, but resisted. If it was airborne, he needed to stay ahead of it. Whatever it was, it hadn't affected him. He had a chance to escape now. Help he could call for later from the road.

Hank shifted into drive. The thought of going to An Nasiriyah crossed his mind, but he didn't trust local doctors or police. No, he wanted to find Americans. Had to find them.

Just get the fuck out of here, he thought and turned toward Basra.

CHAPTER TWO

Mike Caldwell wiped sweat from his brow and checked his watch. Sunrise had come and gone, and his target still hadn't shown up. The temperature was already eighty-five degrees, and he didn't want to be out in the open much longer. He lifted his binoculars and looked on the market four stories below him in Basra's commercial district of Ashar.

Where are you, Anwar? Mike thought as he scanned the faces of the merchants setting up shop for the day.

Anwar al-Sahd, a local rug seller and moneyman for a Shiite death squad operating in Basra, was late for work. British intel had identified him as the bridge between the death squad and Iranian intelligence operatives in the area. A banker, so to speak. The Iranians deposited, and Anwar transferred it to the people with the proper motivation. Mike hated bankers more than terrorists. Terrorists at least did their dirty work. Bankers like Anwar were slimy and ran away when the shit hit the fan. No honor in people like that, no matter what the cause.

And he was late, which pissed Mike off even more. He sat on the roof of a dilapidated Basra hotel and waited because his boss in Langley wanted him to punch Anwar's ticket for helping coordinate a suicide bomb run on a British SAS safe house for special operators. "Why can't the Brits snuff him out?" Mike had said when given his orders. "It was their people."

"Because we owe them one," Glenn Cheatum, the deputy director for operations, of Central Intelligence, had said. "And the Brits want to stay removed after putting down that IED warehouse a few weeks ago. They're not officially in-country, remember."

"Must maintain the PR even if you want revenge, huh?"

"Stow it, Mike, and do your job."

"It's bitch work."

"It's killing and it's what you're good at."

Mike let the memory go as he wiped sweat from the gaskets around the binos' lenses before scanning the market once more.

"Where are you, you little bastard?"

Probably long gone. Maybe he made the Brits surveilling him. Maybe the British intelligence was shit.

Then Mike found him. He recognized him easily from the surveillance photos he'd studied the night before. Anwar was short and round and had a wispy beard only a goat could appreciate. He rode into the market on a fire-engine red moped with flames painted on the front and a fresh pile of rugs strapped to the back. For an asshole banker, he had a sense of style. Or humor, depending how you looked at it.

Mike pushed up to a crouched position, slung the binos over his shoulder, and hotfooted it across the roof to the stairwell. Inside, he patted the dust from his clothes. He wore a pair of khaki cargo pants, black T-shirt under a tactical vest, and a pair of polarized Oakleys. Although Mike had a dark tan, he couldn't pass for an Arab. So, instead, he'd try to pass for a government contractor.

As he descended the stairwell, Glenn's words echoed around his head. "It's killing and it's what you're good at."

Mike couldn't argue that fact. Someone else would have sniped Anwar from the roof. But a rifle shot would scare the crowd in the market. A panic would follow, maybe even an angry mob, and walking out of the hotel wouldn't be easy. A silenced shot up close still would have put him in an exposed position from street-level. Guns attracted attention pretty damn fast, and Mike didn't want attention. Instead, he planned to be mobile before and after, in a position where he could hit and walk away. This required getting up close and personal to minimize attention. Not a lot of people could handle that kind of kill.

The trip down the stairwell and out onto the street took about a minute. Mike didn't rush. Anwar should still be setting up shop for the day. Plenty of time.

He would have preferred to take care of the banker at his residence, but the guy had a rotating home. The Brits quit trying to keep up with him, choosing to monitor him at Ashar. It seemed the only place he was guaranteed to be was in the market selling his damn rugs.

Once out on the street, Mike cleared the area around him with quick glances, making sure no one watched or followed him. The chances he would walk into a setup were slim, but the time he didn't act with caution would be the time they found his severed head in a gutter.

He didn't see anyone ghosting him, and no one on the street seemed interested. The windows in the surrounding buildings were clear. Nothing out of the ordinary.

Mike turned and headed into the outdoor market. As soon as he was within shouting distance, merchants barked at him, peddling their goods from their canopied booths, trying to entice him with cheap offers on everything from cigarettes to pirated movies to frankincense. Mike ignored them, pushing through the growing crowd of shoppers.

His eyes locked on Anwar, standing in his booth, flopping rugs down on tables. Mike sidestepped around an old man arguing about the price of dates. From his pocket he pulled a Spyderco Calypso knife, flipped the three-inch blade out, and held it against his thigh away from Anwar's eye line.

As Mike neared, a customer walked up to Anwar and grabbed a rug and started haggling.

Shit, Mike thought. He'd had Anwar to himself. Now he had to hope he'd get another chance before more customers showed up. If that happened, he'd probably have to back off and wait for the crowd to die down. Or risk a pistol shot. But as the crowd grew, the chances of escaping after such a hit would diminish.

Mike slowed and turned to the booth next to the rug merchant's. He feigned interest in some canteens and listened to Anwar argue for several minutes.

With a quick glance over his shoulder, he saw Anwar hand the rug to the customer, accept cash, and then the man was on his way. Mike didn't waste any time, turning and heading for the booth.

Anwar motioned for him to come closer, to see his beautiful rugs. Mike smiled as he reached the booth, three feet of table separating him and Anwar.

"You speak English?" Mike said.

"Of course, of course." Anwar slapped a rug in front of him. "Interested in a rug, are you? Something for your beautiful wife or girlfriend? Maybe you have many girlfriends, a young man like you."

Anwar laughed at his own joke and patted his gut.

Mike mimicked the jollity. "Can't tie me down with just one. But it gets expensive, you know?"

"A man can never have enough money for the amount of mistresses he requires."

Again Anwar laughed like he'd just told the funniest joke in the world. Mike only chuckled.

"A man like you, though, has much money, yes? Strong, rich contractor."

Mike looked down at his clothes and back to Anwar. "That obvious, huh?"

"I see you contractors here all the time. Blackwater, yes? Or whatever you call it these days. The clothes you all wear—so similar it is like a uniform."

Mike smiled. It was just the reaction he'd hoped for when choosing the clothes. The other merchants would remember seeing a contractor. The description they might give, though, would pretty much match anyone in the area working private security.

"So, my friend, what kind of rug would you like?"

Mike shrugged. "I really don't know anything about them. What makes a good rug?"

"Easy, my friend, easy." Anwar flipped over a red rug and pointed at the threads on the back. "Do you see how tight these stitches are?"

Mike leaned down, his nose about two inches over the rug. "I guess so."

He said it loud enough to hear but low enough to draw Anwar down toward him. He moved his knife hand up to his hip at the same time. The images of the Brits Anwar helped kill flashed through his head.

Anwar, his head about a foot away and just slightly higher than Mike's, said, "The tighter the stitchcs and the more threads there are means the rug is of top quality. This rug—"

Mike's hand flashed up, sliced the blade across the bottom of Anwar's neck, and was back at his side in under a second. Anwar's throat opened up and blood rained onto the rug.

"God save the Queen, Anwar."

Mike retracted the blade, slipped the knife in his pocket, and walked away from the booth. He glanced over his shoulder. Anwar had dropped to his knees, his head resting on the rug in his blood. No one had noticed yet.

Around the corner outside the market, the first yells of excitement and surprise caught up to him. He waited until he was a mile up the road to dump the tactical vest, Oakleys, and binos in a trash heap. Then he pulled off the black shirt, revealing a gray shirt underneath, soaked through with sweat.

Mike hailed a cab and took it to his hotel: the new Sheraton in Basra proper. It was a ten-minute trip.

Inside the hotel room, the air conditioner hummed. Chilly, like an icebox left open. It felt good. Next to the bed sat his half-full bottle of whiskey. Mike stared at it for a long moment before turning away.

In the bathroom, he washed his face and hands. The water was tepid. He tasted salt washing off his forehead and cheeks as the water passed over his lips. Then he straightened up, his back aching. His eyes lingered on his reflection as he dried his face.

"It's killing and it's what you're good at."

Mike looked away. He pulled his knife out to wash the blade when he noticed his right hand shaking.

Anwar's face flashed in his head.

Get it together, he thought and set the knife down. His eyes closed; he slowed his breathing.

Anwar's face flashed again, this time with his throat slit and blood pouring out.

Mike clenched his hand into a fist and squeezed until his nails dug into his palm. When the pain crept into his wrist, he let go. Opening his eyes, Mike peeked at his hand again.

It still shook.

Fuck it.

Mike walked out of the bathroom and sat on the bed. He poured a glass of whiskey and downed it. Poured and downed another.

He looked at his hand. The shaking had died down to a tremor. Mike drank one more glass.

The shaking stopped.

Mike set the glass down and buried his face in his hands.

"It's killing and it's what you're good at." The words rang in his head again and again. They were the same ones Glenn had said when he'd first proposed the job. They were the ones he said every time Mike started to show signs of regret for taking his current assignment.

"I want you to be the right hand of God," Glenn had said in his office in Langley, Virginia, three months before.

"And who's God?" Mike had said.

"I am as far as you're concerned."

Mike had chuckled, but Glenn only fixed him with dark brown eyes that appeared almost black. The dead eyes, as they were known around the agency.

"Well, what the hell does that mean, Glenn?"

"It's a violent world, and I hate bureaucracy. Station chiefs are necessary, but a lot of them are looking out for themselves politically. You know, they want to climb the ladder, get a job like mine. But I'm looking for results. So, I want an operator who reports to me and me only. One who performs special tasks as necessary. You up for it?"

"You mean real case work?" Mike had been a company man for over fourteen years and in the field for thirteen. Most of that time, he'd done muscle work. Never had he worked a case or real contact on his own. He'd never been a spy. "Stuff I can run to ground, cut out the red tape?"

Now Glenn chuckled. "No, Mike, you're a cleaner. And there are a lot of messes out there that need a good dose of bleach and disinfectant."

Mike focused on his shoes.

"You're a killer, Mike." Glenn held up a thick file. "Years of it. A specialist. That's what I need right now, and that's what you're good at. Take it or I'll put you behind a desk the rest of your career."

"You want me to be your hit man."

Glenn had responded with a smile. Mike didn't say any more and accepted because he knew he was good at it. And he'd forgotten how to do anything else lives ago.

He went into deep covert mode soon after. Off-the-reservation mode. The only one in the CIA who knew he was in Iraq was Glenn. Making sure he kept his identity under wraps and the station chief in Baghdad in the dark was a major concern for Mike. If his cover got blown, he'd quickly find himself with a one-way ticket out of Iraq and into a federal prison awaiting trial for being an illegally sanctioned assassin. Glenn would be right next to him, treading water in shit's creek, after his hearing before Congress.

Mike smirked. Thinking about it now, it didn't sound like such a bad fate.

He downed a bottle of water and then called Glenn over his encrypted cell phone.

"It's done," Mike said.

"Good. Any issues?"

"None. It went smoothly."

"The Brits will be pleased."

Mike eyed what remained in the bottle on the nightstand. "I'm going to lay low for a few days."

Mike lifted the bottle and started to pour.

"Not so fast."

Mike winced. *Just a day,* he thought. The mouth of the bottle hovered over the glass. He hadn't poured a drop yet.

"Yes?" Mike said.

"Something's happened at a construction site outside An Nasiriyah. A bunch of people are dead."

"Sounds like work for the military and national police."

"I want you there."

Mike rubbed his forehead. A mammoth skull splitter lit off its engines. "Why?"

"Because there are some interesting reports coming in over the military traffic, but one doesn't jibe with the next. From the way it sounds, though, could be IRG. So I want firsthand intel in case the Iranians are operating that far in-country. Since you're within driving distance, get your butt up there and take a look."

"You want me to do actual work, Glenn?" Mike set the bottle down and screwed the cap back on. "No one to kill up there? I'm shocked."

"Keep running your smart-ass mouth and I'll see what I can arrange to disappoint you."

Stupid, Mike thought and bit his tongue. *You've got a chance here; don't ruin it.*

"I'll need to be official for them to let me on-site," Mike said after a few seconds.

"Use the alias. The troops on-site won't screen the ID with Baghdad Station. Especially if you wave it around like you're important."

He'd almost forgotten about the alias Glenn had given him: a full set of papers and identification for Jeremiah Hosselkus, a fake CIA field agent. So Mike would be a CIA operative pretending to be a CIA operative. He'd thought it silly at the time. After all, why would you impersonate something you already were?

Yet here I am, being told to do exactly that, he thought. *Because I'm a rogue fucking killer.*

"I'll leave within the hour," Mike said.

CHAPTER THREE

Blood and phlegm coated the bench seat of the truck. Barely a minute would pass without Hank hacking. With the exertion and loss of fluid came the heavy toll of fatigue and dizziness, scourging his mind like a Roman centurion. He couldn't drive faster than forty kilometers an hour without losing focus completely and his surroundings blurring into one massive beige smear. He fought to keep his eyes open and barely managed anything wider than mere slits. Fragmented thoughts of pulling over and waiting until help drove by bounced around his skull.

But every time he started to brake, he remembered the tomb and what had escaped it, the devastation it had wrought, and eased his foot back onto the accelerator. Had to be a chemical weapon, some kind of nerve agent, airborne and, based on the wind, possibly blowing in the same direction he drove. No, stopping didn't feel like a good idea at all.

Calling someone, however, did. He'd tried both the company's headquarters and the local coalitional authority with the cell but failed to maintain a signal long enough. Switching to roaming hadn't worked either.

Maybe everyone else was dead. Maybe they'd all killed each other and he was the last man alive: the Omega Man sprinting at a low speed away from an invisible cloud of doom. The daydream made him chuckle until he shot another mouthful of gore onto the seat.

Just keep driving, he thought. You're not the last one on earth. Just the last poor bastard from the site. You'll get a cell signal soon. Stay ahead of the cloud.

Besides, he couldn't risk pulling over and exposing some innocent civilian. Enough had died already. The military, at the very least, would be able to quarantine him and hopefully treat him for infection. They had antidotes for fighting off chemical agents, he knew.

Get to the base, Hank thought and coughed more. Don't stop. You're lucky you're not like the others. They died fast. Whatever it is has given you time. A chance. Keep pushing.

What he couldn't figure out was why he hadn't gone crazy.

Maybe I'm immune.

Hank had taken a cocktail of vaccines, as was required by his company, before leaving for Iraq.

Maybe all those shots had worked together to ward off whatever it was driving people to kill each other. Maybe they had acted as a shield to stop it from seizing his mind, or at least slowed it enough to just poison him.

Maybe.

Up ahead something moved on the side of the road. Some things. It was just after sunrise halfway between An Nasiriyah and Basra, and all he could make out were dark smudges. As he closed the distance, he realized they were two people. Bedouin. Heading south with two loaded camels.

He didn't slow down when he passed them. Not the help he was hoping for. He even swerved into the next lane to widen the distance. Just in case. He doubted they'd catch anything since the windows were rolled up, but better to be safe than a murderer. Once past, he glanced in the rearview. Then he slammed on the brakes and stared.

The nomads who had trekked together a moment before were now locked in combat. They slashed at each other with knives until one tackled the other. The camels were even affected, whipping their necks and smacking heads. He wasn't more than ten feet away and watched as one Bedouin killed the other, the two camels, and then himself, all with a knife to the throat.

"Get moving," he said, the sound of his raw, rasping voice calming him a little. "Before anyone else shows up."

Hank's hands tightened around the steering wheel as he accelerated, the dead figures becoming shadows in the rearview. First the dig site and now here.

I'm not immune, Hank thought. *I'm a carrier. Which means no help for me.*

He swallowed bile. Whatever had caused his workers and then the two Bedouin to kill emanated from him, like a stench.

It's in me. That's what hit me like a Mack truck after the T section fell in.

Hank coughed again and spit blood and chunks of tissue onto the seat. *Can't think that way. It's not you. It's the wind carrying the agent. Need to drive fast to stay ahead of it.*

Whatever it is, he thought, *it's eating me from the inside out.*

Hank would have cried, but he'd lost so much water all he could do was blink dry eyes. His head ached and chills rippled over his skin. His vision alternated between focused and blurred as vertigo swirled through his mind. The truck swerved sharply to the right. Hank caught it and was able to straighten back up instead of running off the road.

Why don't you just lose control? Hank thought. *You're as good as dead. No one is going to help you. No one can.*

Hank shook his head. He had a family to think of. A wife. A son and two daughters. God, just the thought of them stabbed him in the chest. No, he had to push on. Had to get better.

He glanced at all of the blood and bile and tissue on the seat and dashboard. His insides. Was there a way to get better? Maybe he wasn't fighting off some nerve agent. Maybe whatever was in Hank was fighting him off, puking him out until he didn't exist anymore. Until he wasn't making it sick.

Hank wiped his mouth and wondered if it could be that simple. If there was a chemical agent inside him, feasting on his insides, killing him slowly while the others who were exposed met faster deaths.

In the distance, a bunch of blurry images headed toward him. Semis driving out of a mirage, heading away from Basra. *Probably a truck convoy,* he thought. *Need to stop them. Can't let them drive into the chemical cloud.*

But how?

Hank slowed down even more, not wanting to risk swerving into a head-on collision. He honked and flashed his lights. They showed no signs of slowing down. Then he threw up more blood, wiped his mouth, and gripped the steering wheel tight, waiting for the trucks to pass.

The lead vehicle, a Toyota Land Cruiser, raced by filled with armed contractors carrying assault rifles. Then the semis, four in all, passed, with another Land Cruiser taking up the rear guard. Hank fought the steering wheel as the wake hit him from across the median, the truck swerving right then left, and braked to keep from running off the road. He'd been going at a snail's pace and the wake hadn't been that strong and still he barely had the strength to maintain control.

Gunfire erupted behind him.

Hank glanced in the rearview and wasn't surprised. At the site, he'd been terrified. The Bedouin had shocked him. Now, though, he was impassive, watching the death dance unfold thirty feet away.

The lead Land Cruiser had swerved off the road. The contractors were out on foot and unloading their rifles. They didn't kneel or use the car as cover. Instead, they marched toward one another, rifles level, the barrels exhaling flames. The bullets shredded. Clothing and blood flew.

The first semi slammed on its brakes and managed to avoid the Land Cruiser, but the semi behind it rammed the first's trailer. Grain exploded from the sides. The sickening sound of metal crunching and folding echoed around Hank's head. The drivers from the first truck jumped out and ran toward the second only to be gunned down by the surviving contractor from the Land Cruiser.

Hank was unable to tear his gaze away from the carnage. He looked away from the rearview and over his shoulder out the back window. The third semi in the convoy had jackknifed; the fourth T-boned it. Grain flooded the highway. The contractors from the rear Land Cruiser were on foot and firing at each other and whatever survivors remained.

Hank turned away, refusing to watch anymore. He coughed again and pulled his wallet from his back pocket. Flipping through his credit cards, he found what he wanted. A picture of his wife and kids. All smiling up at him. The last sane thing in his life now.

I'm never going to see them again, he thought.

He glanced back up in the rearview. Only one man still stood: a contractor with an assault rifle. Then the victor turned the gun on himself, sticking the barrel in his mouth and pulling the trigger.

Hank closed his eyes and shook his head. *Jesus. I might as well kill myself, too.*

He'd earlier eliminated suicide as an option, but now he wondered if it were the only solution. Going anywhere with any kind of population would be disastrous, especially a city like Basra. His conscience was already heavy with the lives of over fifty people. If Hank drove to Camp Bucca or into Basra, the number would quadruple in an instant. He would not watch any more people destroy themselves.

Thank God I didn't go to An Nasiriyah.

Hank looked back down at the picture. He'd taken the job for them. Over here, he'd make double the money he could stateside. Now look what it bought him.

Another round of coughing. His lungs, what remained of them, burned like a thousand hot razors shredded his chest.

Just sit here and die, Hank thought. But then anyone who passed would meet the same fate as the convoy behind him.

No, need to drive somewhere empty. Farther away from the road. In the desert more.

Hank nodded. He would drive into the desert, away from the road. First, though, he'd call home. Say good-bye.

He pulled out his cell phone, hoping he had a signal. Instead, the battery was dead.

"Fuck!" Hank threw it into the dashboard. The battery broke free and hit him in the face. "Can't even say good-bye?"

Hank wiped his dry eyes and dropped his wallet on the seat. He took a shallow breath and exhaled slowly before shifting the truck into drive.

So this is it. No good-byes. No "I love you." Just a picture and some memories and that's it. You'll probably be dead within an hour. Just drive out into the desert and cough yourself to death.

Hank looked in the rearview. No movement. He put the truck in reverse and headed toward the nearest Land Cruiser. Once there, he got out and walked slowly, his legs shaky and unsteady, over to the contractor who'd shot himself after winning the battle royale.

A swarm of flies already coated the back of his head where the bullet had exited. They crawled over the red mass and gray matter until Hank walked up. Then they took off in a black cloud.

But they didn't leave. They hovered over the body. Then a few flies fell to the ground.

Shit, he thought. *Even the flies are fighting.* Something about them disturbed him more than any of the other deaths. He'd almost accepted that whatever he had could affect humans and complex animals. But insects?

Hank turned his attention to the ground and grabbed the rifle. Carefully, he dug through the corpse's pockets and found a cell phone. Still had half a battery left. Clutching it in his fist, Hank thanked God for giving him another chance to say good-bye to his family.

He walked back over to the truck. As he did, he turned to see if the flies had stopped fighting, hoping it was a proximity thing.

Nope. The cloud had already shrunk by half, little black bodies decorating the highway. If it was a proximity thing, he needed to get farther away.

"Well, that's that then."

He heard shouting. Hank turned, thinking one of the contractors or drivers was still alive.

No, it was in Arabic. It was someone shouting in Arabic.

Hank looked at the side of the road. Another Bedouin with a camel marched toward the convoy.

"Stop!" Hank waved his arms. "Don't come any closer."

The man shouted more words in Arabic and kept approaching the dead. He couldn't be more than fifty feet away.

"Please stop." Hank wished he could remember any Arabic. All that came to mind were words for "work" and "faster."

The old man kept coming, still shouting the same words and pointing at the bodies. Still moving closer.

Hank raised the rifle and pointed it at the man. "Don't come any closer. Please."

The man shifted his eyes from the bodies to Hank. They were old eyes. And Hank knew they had seen death before. But there was something else in them. Something unsettling. More than fear. As if the old man had found himself treading suddenly through hell itself.

He pointed at Hank and said something else in Arabic. Louder than anything he'd spoken yet. Almost hysterical.

Thirty feet away? Maybe closer.

The old man's eyes changed. The desperation that had dwelled in them faded and was replaced by rage. He screamed and for a moment Hank thought he was going to run and attack him. Instead, the old man turned on the camel, pulling his knife from his belt and drawing it quickly across the animal's throat.

The camel wailed and collapsed to its knees. The old man bellowed a primal cry and stabbed the creature repeatedly in the side and neck until it lay in an ocean of blood-mixed sand.

The old Bedouin turned to Hank, locking him with wild eyes. He breathed heavily, sucking in giant gulps of air. Drool hung from his lips and chin.

A few seconds of silence passed between them. Eyes fixed on each other. Hank knew what was about to happen but prayed it wouldn't.

The old man brought the edge of the knife to his throat and ripped it across. The arterial spray was immense, jutting six feet away from him. The man dropped to his knees, blood gushing down his robes, and collapsed next to his camel.

Hank turned away and contemplated the rifle.

Do it now, he thought. *Kill yourself before anyone else comes by.*

But what if my body remains infected even after I'm dead? Hank shook his head. *No, get somewhere in the middle of nowhere. Then do it. As long as they don't come within thirty feet, they'll be okay. But go, now, before anyone else shows up.*

Hank climbed back in the truck. He dropped the rifle in the blood on the seat, turned the wheel, and drove off the highway into the desert to die.

CHAPTER FOUR

By the time Mike found site R91, the temperature had already hit a hundred degrees. The drive from Basra was shitty thanks in large part to his Lincoln Town Car's barely functioning air-conditioning and a stereo that picked up only local music and the call to prayer. Once the sun rose higher, it beat down on the black car like the hammer of Vulcan.

Mike blasted the A/C but it didn't help. Trying to tune anything in other than tribal flare and the prayer roundup landed nothing but white noise. Hot and miserable, Mike resorted to humming Rolling Stones tunes while the constant scenery of the desert sprinkled with random palm trees and marshes along the Euphrates passed by.

Then he hit heavy traffic on the way into An Nasiriyah just north of Jalibah. Someone had raided a truck convoy on his side of the highway. The Iraqi military had the route toward An Nasiriyah completely shut down and redirected northbound traffic onto the southbound side for a few miles.

Apparently the armed contractors had resisted. The whole scene was one big fucking mess. The trucks were wrecked to hell, and grain and blood covered most of the highway. Then Mike saw the bodies of the contractors lined up neatly in a row on the median, cleared from the highway by military personnel. It didn't look like anyone had survived. Mike shook his head, sorry for the families who would soon find out the fate of their loved ones.

Once clear of that, Mike made it to An Nasiriyah only to find out site R91 was another twenty miles down the road near Ur, wherever that was. Hot, sweaty, and exhausted, Mike pulled up to a makeshift Marine checkpoint just before noon.

Four Marines stood the guard. One checked identification while the other kept an M16A4 trained on the driver. The third and fourth Marines swept the car for explosive devices. Mike had both hands up, his wallet in his left, and his window down.

"Good afternoon, sir," the Marine checking IDs said. "Can I ask your purpose in Ur?"

Mike smiled and handed his wallet out the window slowly. "Been asked to come up here and check out the damage. The agency wants to make sure a Revolutionary Guard unit out of Iran doesn't have anything to do with this."

The Marine took the wallet and then removed and examined the ID card for Jeremiah Hosselkus. "Really?

The RGs operating this far in-country? I thought they were sticking to the border and Basra."

Mike shook his head. "They're financing guerilla groups all over the country, hitting infrastructure projects like crazy. Mainly sabotage ops. Nothing spectacular. Pains in the ass, more than anything. We knew a big sewer line was going in up here and thought the RG would take a stab at it. Just figured they'd wait until the progress got closer to An Nasiriyah. They usually like to hit near populated areas. Easier to blend in with the locals. Hitting a target this remote is rare outside oil pipelines."

The Marine nodded and flipped the ID over a couple of times in his hand. "The issue is we've been cleared to allow only military investigators and Iraqi police in. No one said CIA would be coming through."

Mike smiled. "Yeah, it's a spur-of-the-moment thing. And I understand if you don't clear me. But could you do me a favor? I'd appreciate it if you ran it by your superior. No offense but it saves me a hell of a lot of time and paperwork back in Basra. Plus, the drive out here fucking sucks."

The Marine chuckled. "Sure, hold on."

He lifted a radio and dialed a number. "Major, Sergeant Haywood. Got a CIA spook down here wants to know if he can come take a look."

Mike listened as Haywood explained Mike's story while flipping the ID over and over in his hands. The Marine with the M16A4 kept it leveled on Mike and asked him to pop the hood and trunk for inspection. He did.

After a few minutes, Haywood hung up and turned back to Mike. Two of the others completed the sweep, nodding all was clear, and closed the trunk and hood. "The major said to let you on in. But he said it's got to be quick. I guess some general's coming in, and he doesn't want a territorial pissing match between DOD and CIA."

Haywood handed Mike's wallet and ID back. "The site is three klicks up the road. You'll pass an armed Humvee, but they won't bother you. They know to let you by. Once on-site, park where all the other vehicles are. Major Greengrass is waiting for you there. He'll escort you, let you take a look at the site, then probably ask you to leave after about a half an hour."

Mike nodded. "That's all the time I need. Appreciate your help, Sergeant."

"Welcome, sir." Haywood waved him by. The other Marine lowered the M16A4.

Mike passed the Humvee slowly a minute later. Mounted on top was a .50-cal machine gun, and the operator had it trained on him. Haywood had said he was expected and the Humvee would leave him alone, but Mike drove in a respectful manner, not giving the shooter any reason to open fire, especially if he was new in-country and had an itchy finger.

A couple of minutes later, Mike arrived on-site. He saw several more US and Iraqi military vehicles and a few Iraqi police SUVs. Mike parked next to them and got out. As he did, a tall man in desert camouflage, flak jacket, and helmet walked over to him.

"Mr. Hosselkus."

Mike waved. "Major Greengrass, I presume?"

Greengrass extended his hand and Mike shook it. The guy had an iron grip and squeezed just enough to let him know. Mike reciprocated but couldn't match the pressure.

"Welcome to Ur," Greengrass said and offered Mike a bottle of water.

"Thanks. I wish I had other reasons to be here."

Greengrass shrugged. "An investigation is the only reason I'd come to this godforsaken pit. It sure as hell isn't a place to visit for fun."

"I thought Ur was supposed to be a nice, archeological wonderland."

"Sure." Greengrass chuckled. "If you're a nerd or an Indiana Jones wannabe. Personally, I'll settle for watching it on the History Channel. Dead bodies and this heat—no thank you."

Mike wiped sweat off his brow. "Well, I can't blame you. It's a hot one, for sure."

"Hell, it's cool right now. You should be here in another hour."

"No thanks."

Mike made quick observations of Greengrass from behind the cover of his shades. The major looked like the kind of a guy who could share a beer with you one minute and stab you in the neck with the broken bottle the next. Mike had met guys like him before. Great and fun to be around, but flip the switch on their tempers and watch out. Which made Greengrass perfect for the Marines.

"So, all banter aside, the CIA wants to check out this slaughter to make sure the RG wasn't involved?" Greengrass said.

"That's the long and short of it."

"Hate to break it to you, Mr. Hosselkus, but the RG didn't play here."

Mike opened the bottle of water and took a sip. "Really? That didn't take long to figure out. Why'd you let me up here then?"

Greengrass scratched his chin and looked at the desert around him before settling back on Mike. "Well, sir, because I'm hoping you can shed some light on what did happen here."

Mike was confused. He didn't expect to be a consultant today. "What do you mean?"

"You see, my boss is on the way; and he's going to want answers. And I can't give him any because I haven't been able to figure it out myself. Nor has the Iraqi police."

Mike didn't like the sound of this. "It was an attack. Someone killed a bunch of contractors. It's figuring out who did it that's important, right?"

Greengrass chuckled. "No, we know who did it. It's figuring out why that's got us all confused."

"Major, what are you telling me?"

Greengrass paused a moment. "I'm telling you we've got fifty dead contractors over there and they killed each other."

Mike looked past Greengrass's shoulder toward the site. "Killed each other?"

Greengrass nodded. "I know it's not the RG, but I was hoping you'd take a look and maybe give a professional opinion because, right now, I'll take just about anything."

"Tell me how they killed each other."

"Let me show you instead."

CHAPTER FIVE

"I don't know what they'll tell you. Hell, I don't know what to tell you. What happened...Well, it's pretty unbelievable. I wish there was something else I could do. Wish I could talk to you all, tell you how much I love you. But it's not going to happen the way I want. At least I get to say good-bye. Remember, I'm doing this to protect people. I love you all."

Hank hung up the cell phone and tossed it on the floor. No one had answered but the machine. In a way, he was glad no one had. Saying good bye on voicemail left him emotionally drained. He doubted he would have been able to talk without breaking down completely if anyone had picked up.

Hank stared at the empty desert surrounding him as the sun beat down on the truck, roasting him inside. He'd managed to avoid crossing paths with other people and said a quiet thanks to God for that.

So what are you waiting for? he thought. He didn't know.

Hank had driven for a good hour away from the highway. Just wanted to make sure he placed a sizeable distance between himself and the road. Wanted to make sure he was completely alone when he put the bullet in his head and avoid any more incidents with any Bedouin or commuters.

You could have done that on the road right after that old man slit his throat. Could have done it then and there and all this would be over.

The more Hank thought, the more his head hurt. Ever since leaving the road, he'd second-guessed and doubted his decision-making abilities. His vision had failed in his left eye. His right eye saw images as if looking through a Vaseline-smeared window. He still coughed up blood and tissue and could manage only short, quick breaths with whatever remained of his lungs.

"Sad sack of shit," Hank said.

He looked at the picture in his hand of his family. The images were so blurry he could tell them apart only from memory.

"I'm sorry," he said.

Then he glanced at himself in the rearview. Hemorrhaged blood vessels had turned both eyes red. Dried phlegm, blood, and salt coated his cheeks and forehead.

"Hey, good-looking," Hank said and chuckled. Pain reverberated down his spine and across his ribcage. He didn't regret laughing, though, because it would be the last time he would.

His right eye drifted away from the rearview and settled on the assault rifle on the seat. Sitting there, waiting for him to pick it up. Waiting for him to pick it up and swallow a lead slug.

So do it, he thought.

He'd avoided it long enough. Hank nodded and reached for the rifle.

Only his hand didn't move.

Hank tried again. Still no movement.

This time with his left hand, but that arm wouldn't move, either.

Hank's heart thumped harder and faster. His short, quick breaths multiplied. He tried to kick out with his feet, to maybe rock himself over to the rifle, but his legs wouldn't even so much as twitch.

Jesus, he thought. *Fucking paralyzed!*

Only his right eye moved, swiveling around in the socket. His head throbbed as it sent panicked signals to dead nerves. No sound came even though he ordered himself to scream. Nothing responded.

Then the little bit of vision he still had in his right eye disappeared, and he plunged into darkness. He couldn't feel the heat of the cab anymore either. Or pain.

His breathing slowed and his chest tightened, constricting his airways, like a clamp slowly squeezing his torso, trying to make his breast and spinal column touch. No matter how hard he fought, he couldn't force himself to breathe faster.

Sitting in the truck in the middle of the desert, Hank stared at darkness and drew his last few breaths. He managed to flash through a few images of his family, piecing together a quick highlight reel from memory.

At…least…you're…dying…fast, he thought. *Could… have…been…worse.*

Then Hank sucked in one final breath. For a moment, he seemed to float in a black pool of calm water and thought he saw his family with him.

And then everything was gone.

CHAPTER SIX

"An Iraqi patrol helicopter found the site just after sunrise this morning," Greengrass said. "Ever since then, it's been a regular hornets' nest of activity out here."

Mike followed Greengrass, listening. The sand was loose under foot, and he had trouble walking through it, as opposed to the major, who seemed to glide with little problem.

"You from Death Valley or something?" Mike said.

"Why?"

"You seem comfortable in this climate and topography."

"This is my fourth tour in this lovely land." Greengrass smirked. "But I also grew up in Yuma, Arizona. Sure that helps."

"I bet."

"Where are you from?"

"Virginia."

"What part?"

Mike smiled. "Langley."

Greengrass shook his head. "That some spook joke?"

"Well, you know what they say, Major. Once you're CIA, everything before ceases to exist." And for Mike, it had. Both his parents were dead and his marriage had failed. And his daughter... Mike blocked the thoughts. Never thinking about her in the field was his unwritten rule. If she didn't exist to him, she couldn't exist to those who might use such information against him.

All to ensure her safety, Mike thought. He shook his head and chased the self-hate away, focused on the work.

The site had garnered quite a bit of attention. Mike noticed agents from NCIS on hand, snapping pictures. They had a forensic team with them. The Iraqi police hovered but didn't seem to be participating too much.

Then Mike saw the first of the bodies. The head had been bashed in with some kind of blunt object. Another body had a screwdriver sticking out of its chest.

"Nasty business," Mike said.

"That about sums it up," Greengrass said.

All around Mike, bodies littered the ground. From what he could tell, they had met their end by physical, close-contact means. Bloody wrenches, hammers, and other tools lay strewn about. Then he noticed the hands on one corpse, covered in dried blood. Deep lacerations crisscrossed the knuckles.

Greengrass must have noticed Mike staring because he said, "There are a couple like that. Seems some beat a few to death with their bare hands."

Mike shook his head, nothing making sense. "Why would they kill each other?"

"No idea."

"And you're sure no one else was involved here?"

"No guns, no shell casings, nothing. Not even knives or scimitars. These people turned on each other—except for two."

Greengrass pointed at one body. The stiff was on its knees, a utility knife in his right hand, both wrists slashed; the sand under both arms was black from dried blood.

"Way we figure," Greengrass said, "that guy was the last man standing. After he won, he slit his wrists."

The one time Glenn had given him a real case to work and it turned out to be a Sherlock Holmes mystery. Mike pinched the bridge of his nose between his fingers, hoping the headache starting up would subside. His flask was in the car and he longed for a small sip.

"Why would he kill himself?"

Greengrass shrugged. "Because he had no one else to kill?"

Mike had no response to that.

After a few moments of silence, Mike said, "You said there were two people who didn't kill each other. Where's the second?"

Greengrass motioned him to follow and led him to a pit a few feet away. Mike saw a flatbed whose back half had fallen into a fissure. His eyes traced the six-foot-deep crevice as it snaked away and ended at the pit. A giant section of sewer pipe lay at the bottom. Then he noticed the dead body to his right near the edge of the pit.

"This is the other one." Greengrass knelt next to the corpse. "Nouri al-Hasad. He was Iraq's top archeologist. As near we can figure, when that flatbed over there fell into the crevice, a few chains holding the sewer line snapped. One of the shackles hit Nouri, killing him on impact."

The headache hit Mike full on between the eyes. This was getting stranger and stranger. He needed a taste *now.*

"So, what was he doing here?"

Greengrass stood and pointed in the hole. "Under the pipe is a tomb or temple or something. When the pipe fell in, it broke the slab covering the entrance in half. Nouri was here to excavate whatever's down there. At least, that's what we've been able to translate from his journal so far."

Mike couldn't see any tomb under the pipe. Instead, he saw a few broken pieces of stone. "Was there an earthquake?"

"No reports of one. A sinkhole is what we were guessing."

Mike looked from the pit to Nouri's body. Then to the flatbed. And then to the bodies.

"There was a complete work stoppage, right?" Mike said. "Because of the discovery of the tomb."

Greengrass wiped sweat from his cheeks. "Yeah, standard procedure is to cease work, cordon off so many feet to either side of the find, and call in the officials to excavate."

Mike rubbed his lips and pointed at the flatbed. "That truck was carrying this section of pipe. Work was stopped, but the piece was already on-site. The ground somehow collapsed, like a sinkhole. The sudden shift of weight snapped the chains. The pipe fell in the crevice, rolled, and hit the tomb, breaking the stone doorway."

His fingers tingled as Mike put the facts together.

"Yeah," Greengrass said. "Pretty much what I just said."

"Then everyone started killing each other."

Greengrass shrugged. "Not sure when the killing started."

"Had to be after the pipe fell in."

"Why?"

Mike pointed at Nouri. "Because he died from an accident. Everyone else killed each other except the one who offed himself."

Greengrass's face slackened. "You're not saying what I think you're saying."

"There was something in that tomb. And when that piece of pipe hit the cover and broke it, whatever was down there was released." Mike shrugged. "You were looking for explanations."

"No fucking way." Greengrass placed his hands on his hips and shook his head. "No fucking way."

"This idea didn't occur to you?"

"Shit, we just put together the fact they killed each other before you showed up," Greengrass said. "And no chemical alarms went off anywhere in the area."

Mike looked around at the bodies once more. "I don't like the way it sounds either, Major. But it's the only thing that makes sense right now. Whatever was down there, whether it be some kind of nerve agent that wasn't detected or an ancient hallucinogen, caused these people to go fucking nuts."

Greengrass paced back and forth. The look on the major's face said it all. Mike could tell he was thinking hard, running through scenarios, wondering if his people were in danger.

"If that's the case, we've all been standing here breathing the same contaminated air," Greengrass said.

"Maybe. But no one else has gone crazy since arriving, right? I'd say, if some kind of agent was released, these guys took the main hit of it before the rest of it disseminated in the air."

Greengrass nodded. "True. Should still get a quarantine set up around this site. Just in case."

"I'll agree with that."

As Greengrass started to radio for a quarantine team, a short, fiery gunnery sergeant marched up and saluted. "Sir, we have all the identities of the bodies and have bounced them off the third-shift work roster on-site."

Greengrass returned the salute. "Good work, Gunny. This is Jeremiah Hosselkus. He's a CIA spook."

Gunny turned to Mike and offered his hand. "Gunnery Sergeant Lowe, sir."

Mike shook it. "Gunny."

"I'm calling in a quarantine team in case there was some kind of nerve agent down in the tomb there," Greengrass said.

Lowe looked down in the pit, nodded, and then back at the major. "I'd hate to see the agent that caused this, sir."

"You and me both."

"Sir, we've got another problem."

Greengrass lowered his radio. "What is it, Gunny?"

"There's one body missing, sir."

Mike watched Greengrass's eyes narrow and wrinkles form on his forehead. This was the angry side of the major Mike had assumed existed.

"What do you mean a body is missing?"

"Sir, we have forty-nine workers and the archeologist for a total of fifty. But there're fifty workers listed on the roster. Right now, one of those workers is unaccounted for."

"And who is that?"

"Henry Prince, sir. The site foreman."

Greengrass clenched his fists. "Fuck!"

"We've got search teams combing the area, sir."

"Find him, Gunny. If he's alive, he's the only witness who can tell us what happened here."

"Yes, sir." Lowe saluted and walked off.

"Major," Mike said, "you don't know if this guy Prince was exposed. He could have been off-site when this shit went down."

"Got to treat it like he was here and was exposed and may even be carrying whatever it is." Greengrass's face had turned bright red. "Worst case scenario. Got to plan for it."

Mike nodded. "Yeah, I guess you're right."

Greengrass kicked sand and stomped off behind Mike. "A fucking survivor. Shit."

Mike hoped if the survivor had been exposed to whatever might have been in the tomb, he hadn't carried it with him, exposing other people. Then Mike thought about it a little more and doubted Prince could be carrying it. There would have been more outbreaks of people killing each other, reports of civil violence, something. And if it was a nerve agent, it wouldn't be contagious. All he'd heard and seen so far outside R91 was the normal day-to-day cost of living in Iraq.

Mike turned back to the pit and wondered what the hell had been down there. What the hell could drive almost fifty people insane and make them savagely kill one another?

A weaponized hallucinogen, he thought. Had to be. These people caught a whiff of something, and then they saw tentacles growing out of heads and started smashing away. Nerve agents caused runny noses, blindness, and convulsions. Victims suffocated from spasms; they didn't beat each other to death. And if it was biological, these corpses would be covered in blisters or would have had flu-like symptoms. They would have taken days to die after exposure.

Mike figured Mr. Prince was one lucky son of a bitch to not have been here when the shit hit the fan.

The ache behind his eyeballs thumped. Mike pinched the bridge of his nose again and tried to figure out how he was going to report this to Glenn.

CHAPTER SEVEN

Light. Visible for the first time in thousands of years. He blinked as his new eyes adjusted to the glare of the sun's rays bouncing off the sand. After a few moments, he was able to see his surroundings clearly.

Semyaza sat in some kind of capsule. A wheel made from the skin of an animal was in front of him. Craning his head around, he saw blood and chunks of tissue from the human he now inhabited littering the seat.

Such a waste of energy and matter, he thought. But unavoidable to rid the flesh of the soul. And this particular man's soul had fought hard.

Upon entering the body, Semyaza had not known what to expect. He had never invaded a human before, and his first encounter with a soul had been both educational and violent. The desperation of the soul to hold on to the flesh had been phenomenal, and the battle had left him not only exhausted but scarred in many places. Yet Semyaza had won and cast the soul out of its host. Now he had a vessel to move about in.

"Uriel," Semyaza said with his new mouth in the Ancient Tongue. "Your prison could not hold me forever."

Semyaza lifted up his new hands and flexed the fingers, making fists. The fact that he had to reside in a human repulsed him. Yet it was the price of freedom.

"Such a crude and worthless design."

A chunk of skin fell off the palm. Semyaza didn't think anything of it at first until another piece of skin dropped on his leg. He stopped flexing and instead rubbed the tips of his fingers together. Little pieces of flesh rained down onto his lap.

So there is a higher price to freedom, Semyaza thought and wondered how long the vessel would last before falling apart completely.

"The flesh will not survive such corruption," a voice said in the Ancient Tongue. "It will dissolve and you will find yourself once again bound in darkness."

Semyaza knew the voice well. He pivoted his head, looking for the seraph, but did not see him.

"Why do you not show yourself, Uriel?"

White mist materialized around Semyaza. It twisted and swirled around him.

"You can hold the flesh for only a short time." Uriel's voice rang out from the mist. "Your prison will hold you for eternity."

"I am free of your prison and will not return." The mist burned as it passed over his vessel's skin. Semyaza tried to ignore the pain and refused to cry out.

"Yes—you will. Cling to that body as desperately as you desire, Semyaza, but know it will not last without the soul. Your grasp will fail, and your prison will pull you back as quickly as you fled it."

"Then I will find another body."

Uriel said nothing more, and the mist disappeared, along with the burning from its presence.

Semyaza wasted no more time, searching for memories and information from the body's former owner. Images of people, men and women and children of various ages, passed in quick flashes. Then he found words, odd characters, and different pronunciations from the Ancient Tongue. He located the man's language center and rapidly assimilated his knowledge. Semyaza learned a tongue named "English." He discovered the capsule he sat in was called a "truck." The vessel's name had been "Hank."

The memories of what had happened after Semyaza escaped and invaded the body were fragmented. Humans all around savagely screaming and killing each other with whatever instrument they could set their hands upon. No order to it, just chaos.

Will it be like that when I find more humans? Semyaza thought. He had no answer.

He located one of Hank's last memories, of him driving the truck down a road toward a center of great populace. Semyaza needed to find that road. He needed to go to the place where he could obtain another vessel. This one would not last much longer. If Uriel spoke the truth, he would find himself yanked back to his prison once the body failed completely. He could not take the risk and test the seraph's word.

A prison for a prison with nothing in between, he thought.

Now Semyaza delved into the memories involving the truck, teaching himself through observation how to use it. After a few minutes, he let the memory go and decided to attempt driving.

He gripped the key in the ignition and turned it, as Hank had done, feeling the engine turn over and kick and then power up. In the memory, Hank had pushed his foot down on the pedal on the floor to the left, grabbed a stick on the column, and moved it to the letter *D.* Semyaza did the same thing, pushing down on what he now learned was called a "brake" and shifted to drive. Then he eased off and felt the truck start to roll.

The road is behind you, Semyaza thought. He grabbed the wheel and turned it toward his left. The truck swung in that direction. Semyaza straightened the wheel back out as he faced the truck the opposite way. Then he pushed down on the right pedal, just as Hank had done, and the truck accelerated.

The wind whipped through the window as Semyaza pressed the pedal all the way down. The truck bounced and skidded through the sand, but he managed to maintain control. He had to reach the road. He had to find people.

Semyaza looked in the rearview and saw his reflection for the first time. Besides the dried blood and spit, he noticed flaps of skin peeling away and flying off, taken by the wind.

Not much time, he thought and rolled up the window.

He dived into Hank's memory again, looking for the name of the center of populace. Then he found it. A newly prospering city in a land named "Iraq."

"Basra," Semyaza said in English. "I must reach Basra."

CHAPTER EIGHT

Mike sucked down another bottle of water, trying to pump fluid in as fast as he sweated it out. The temperature had crested the century mark—plus ten—and it didn't seem to be stopping.

Major Greengrass had asked him to stay, at least until they tracked down the missing worker, Henry Prince. Mike didn't object. He wanted to stay close and observe and learn as much as he could. If he had information to feed to Glenn, he might be allowed to work the case longer. The longer he stayed here, the longer he went without having to kill someone.

In the command tent, Mike fanned himself with a magazine and watched Major Greengrass on the other side of site R91. The Marine stomped around, barking orders. His temper had shot up considerably since getting the word about Mr. Prince, and it hadn't subsided since.

Wish I could help, Mike thought and tossed back more water. There was nothing for him to contribute right now, other than keeping out of the way.

He glanced at his watch. Need to call Glenn. He'd tried earlier but no one answered. Might as well try again. Mike pulled out his cell phone and speed-dialed his boss.

"Deputy Cheatum."

"It's me," Mike said.

"What have you got?"

"You're not going to believe this shit."

Mike relayed everything he'd seen and thought about the massacre. Glenn didn't interrupt him once. No grunts or laughs. After Mike finished, it was almost a full minute before Glenn said anything.

"And there are no signs of further contamination now?"

"No," Mike said. "They've got a quarantine team on-site, and readings are negative. There have been no further outbreaks, if you can call it that. No one's shown any symptoms of nerve agent exposure. It's like whatever got out has faded away."

"No sign of the missing worker yet?"

"No."

Glenn was silent again for a few moments. "What do you think?"

"I think they got lucky. Whatever happened here seems to be an isolated event. They should bag the bodies, fill in the hole, and pray Henry Prince is drunk in a bar somewhere."

"Okay. Appreciate you running this to ground. The initial reports were all over the place. One gave the impression a nerve agent had been used. Another made it sound like an insurgent or Revolutionary Guard chemical attack. This allays my fears somewhat even though it bothers the shit out of me no one can figure out what happened."

Mike's grip on the cell phone tightened. "You thought the RG might have sprung some kind of chemical attack and ordered me up here without giving me a heads-up?"

"I said the reports were all over the place. I doubted the nerve agent and saw no reason to worry about sending you in. The RG concerned me more. If the Iranians had penetrated that deep in-country and attacked Americans with chemicals, I would have needed firm intel as soon as possible. Do you know what the president would have done if that had been the case? Before I let my commander in chief make any such call, I'm going to ensure he's got reliable intel. You were the closest and most reliable asset I had in the area."

"You still could have shared the reports with me."

"Get over it, Mike. It goes with the territory. I told you the reports were interesting and that there had been an attack. As far as this goes now, keep your ears open and stay close to those Marines."

"Already am." Mike hung up. "Asshole."

Glenn's actions didn't surprise him, but he hated the fact his boss had still sent him in under such conditions. All to get real-time intel.

Well, I guess you know what's more important now.

And he did deep down. After all, that's why he'd signed the contract and taken the oath. He had to be willing to die for information. But if he was going to die, he wanted a knock-down drag-out fight or to get picked off by a sniper and not see it coming. Dying like the poor bastards surrounding him was no way for someone to go. Shit, thinking about going crazy and losing control gave him the shakes. No way to go at all.

Mike let his anger at Glenn fade as Greengrass marched toward the tent. In the long run, he couldn't say he wouldn't have done the same thing. There were plenty of reasons to hate Glenn, but this wasn't one of them.

The tall major ducked as he entered and removed his helmet. "Still no sign of this guy Prince." Greengrass wiped sweat off his face with a brown rag. "Anything on your end?"

"Nothing," Mike said. "I thought your boss was coming."

"Yeah, his helo has been delayed due to some mechanical foul-up. He's en route now. Can't wait to explain the missing man to the good general."

Mike shook his head. "Wish I had something more for you."

"Me too."

"Major Greengrass!"

Both Mike and Greengrass turned to see Gunny Lowe march into the tent.

"What is it, Gunny?" Greengrass said. "Tell me you found Prince."

"No, sir."

Mike watched the hope drain from Greengrass's cheeks.

"We have another problem, sir."

"Jesus, what now, Gunny?"

"The convoy on the road to Basra, sir."

"The one that was raided earlier this morning. What about it?"

Mike remembered passing it on the way to R91 and seeing the bodies. Covered and aligned perfectly.

"It wasn't raided, sir."

Greengrass was silent for a few seconds. Mike stared at the gunnery sergeant, hoping he wouldn't say what he thought he was going to say. Lowe's jaw twitched. Shit, he was going to say it.

"What was it, Gunny?"

"They killed each other, sir. Just like here."

Greengrass walked over to a table and placed both hands on its surface, fingers spread wide, and leaned heavily on them.

"Why are we just now hearing about this?"

"The investigating unit thought they were attacked based on the amount of rounds expended by the contractors. But they haven't been able to find any shell casings other than what the contractors shot. Bullets removed from some of the victims confirm they were shooting at their own people. There were a few, too, who beat each other to death."

"And a suicide?" Mike said.

"Affirmative. One shot through the mouth and out the back."

Mike closed his eyes. It had spread. One big major fucking problem.

"Farther up the Basra highway, north of the contractor massacre, a couple of dead Bedouin and camels were found on the side of the highway," Gunny said. "One cut the other to pieces before doing himself."

Greengrass moaned.

"It gets better, sir. At the contractor massacre, another Bedouin killed his camel before slicing his own throat."

"Well, we know it's not a vapor cloud spreading it, or we'd all be fucking dead." Greengrass pushed off from the table and turned back around. "It's this Prince guy. Can't be anyone else. He was here and hauled ass when the shit hit the fan. Where he goes, they all die."

Mike nodded. "It's the only thing that makes sense."

He walked around to the table and saw a map of southeastern Iraq. Mike located site R91. Then he estimated where on the Basra highway he'd driven past the decimated convoy. The first two Bedouin had been found north of it. The next Bedouin found nearby. But nothing else beyond that. The drive from Basra had been peaceful, albeit hot, until he'd reached the highway massacre site.

"Major," Mike said, "take a look at this."

Greengrass and Gunny moved to either side of Mike and looked down at the map.

Mike pointed at R91. "We're here." He moved his finger to outside An Nasiriyah. "The Bedouin were found somewhere around here." Then he traced his finger a little more down the Basra highway. "I passed the convoy around here on my way in." Then Mike slid his finger down to Basra. "If I had to take a guess, I think Henry Prince is on his way here. There's not much in between but if he gets to Basra..."

"There should have been more outbreaks," Greengrass said. "There's traffic all over that road by midmorning, including you. Plus, he'd have been to Basra by now. We should be hearing something if he made it there."

Mike shrugged. "True. Maybe he took a different route. But so far, we're hearing everything on a delay. What people think is a normal day in Iraq with a few insurgent strikes and some random violence is showing a pattern. Do you want to assume he isn't going to Basra?"

"Jesus," Greengrass said. "What's Basra's population?"

"Over two million now." Mike took his finger off the map. "Now imagine what happened here on that scale."

Greengrass turned to Gunny. "Spread the word to Camp Bucca and Basra what we're dealing with. They need to secure all routes into Basra. Give them Prince's name and description. Fax it to them as well."

Gunny ran out of the tent without saying anything.

"Major," Mike said, "I need to leave now. I need to get to Basra in case my boss needs real-time intel."

Greengrass nodded and offered his hand. Mike shook it.

"Appreciate the help, Mr. Hosselkus," Greengrass said.

"Don't know what I really provided."

"Didn't provide. Just accelerated. But we needed the kick. We'll get this guy before he gets to Basra."

"Be sure you do."

CHAPTER NINE

Semyaza found the highway without any problems. Hank's memory had proven reliable. It was not long before he found himself on the outskirts of Basra.

Along the way, he had passed many vehicles heading both in and out of the city, but none of the drivers or passengers had resorted to savagery. Why? What had changed?

I defeated the soul, Semyaza thought. *I am spirit and the soul is spirit. Where we battle, chaos follows. When I prevail, so does order.*

As long as he had control, savagery did not reign. But as soon as he entered another body, the battle with the soul would begin again, and chaos would spread around him; that much he was sure of. Two spirits cannot occupy the same earthly flesh.

Lucky for them, he thought as more cars passed. But soon he would have to pick one and invade it. Not yet, though. He was not strong enough.

Semyaza had planned to enter the first man he had come across. He halted, though, knowing he would lose. To jump into another and commence another fight so soon would only lead to failure. No, he needed time to recover. Needed to maintain his current vessel for as long as possible. Yet he could not postpone the battle indefinitely. If he did, the body would completely disintegrate, and he would find himself yanked back into Uriel's prison.

"Timing," Semyaza said. "You must master the timing."

Semyaza looked in the rearview and saw bone. The skin on his forehead and cheekbones and mouth had completely peeled away, exposing the ligaments around his jaw and the muscles in his face. An animated cadaver.

Not much time left, he thought.

His hands, nothing more than skeletal digits, gripped the steering wheel tighter. In the distance, Basra grew closer.

"You are fighting a losing battle, Semyaza."

The words spoken in the Ancient Tongue caused him to jump slightly in his seat before realizing who had spoken them. Next to him, Uriel appeared. Not in the form of radiant light and mist as he had earlier. Instead, he assumed the appearance of a man with long black hair and clothing similar to his own. Khaki pants. A flannel shirt.

"I escaped your prison."

"You are still in prison." Uriel shook his head. "You never learn. I am surprised how much your arrogance has persisted. I thought, after you fell and were imprisoned, you would learn. Not the other Fallen but certainly you."

"Why am I special?"

"Because you were better than them. Because you know following them was unwise. You knew it then and you know it now."

"If you are hoping to hear me lament, you will be here for eternity."

"Of course. It is clear you have done nothing but plot for your own selfish gain rather than be penitent."

"Penitence brought me nothing."

"You were never sorry. And look at you now, living like a virus."

"I will do whatever I have to," Semyaza said. "I will gladly hop from human to human forever rather than return to your prison."

"This is folly. You cannot succeed. With every battle, more humans will destroy each other in your presence. Will you continue until they are all dead?"

"If I have to."

"You will not succeed." Uriel looked out the window at the passing landscape. "You have forgotten much, even your sentence."

It had been so long since he'd heard the words spoken by Uriel when the seraph had first bound him. And in the time since, Semyaza had done his best to burn them from his memory. Yet here was his jailer, reciting them to him once again.

"A shapeless mass, bound shall you be, cut off from freedom and peace and grace. All around you shall discord rule. In darkness's embrace shall you dwell."

"Thank you, Uriel. Hearing it is much more painful than remembering it. Yes, yes. Bound to your cell or bound to the flesh. And when I fight a soul, discord rears its ugly head. I have figured it out."

"The battle does not cause discord. It is you, Semyaza. Your presence free of a prison causes it. Only when you are confined, as you are now, does order return. Yet you cannot hold onto it or any other body. You are not flesh and spirit like man. You are only spirit pretending to be a man. Do you see?"

"I see you pretending to be a man."

"Materialization. A power you have long been stripped of."

Semyaza said nothing.

"What will this bring you? The soul of the next body will fight you just as the last did. Even if you are successful a few more times, you will find it harder and harder to find another vessel."

"Then I will keep going until I cannot find another and wipe out as many people as I can."

"Still the old hatred of man." Uriel rubbed his hands together. "All because they were treated differently from us."

"They were elevated over us! Mud people over beings of light! Bend the knee to them? Never. I will not serve."

"Beings of earth and light. Inferior yet superior. You hate them and yet you cling desperately to the body of a man." Uriel looked away, out the window again. "Your light, like the rest of Satan's legion, has been stripped. And you will remain that way, separated from grace and the warmth of the Firmament, until your day of final judgment."

"Then I will kill until then."

"You are not killing any souls, Semyaza, and that is what matters. These bodies, without the soul, are just flesh awaiting resurrection. And an angel, void of light, is just a demon. So who are you really punishing?"

Semyaza looked at Uriel. "It is not about punishment. These mud people do not deserve the grace I have been stripped of. They do not deserve to live while I am chained in darkness, alone and unwanted and cold."

"I can end this at any time, Semyaza."

Semyaza looked back out the windshield. "Then why have you not?"

"Because you need to be humbled. If I stop you, it will not mean anything because I have defeated you before. You will blame me. Blame God. But you will not blame yourself. Instead, you will surround yourself with the cold of your hate and plot your escape for a thousand more years. A mirror needs to be held before your vanity. And you will either shatter that mirror or accept the reflection."

"If not you, then who, Uriel? Who will stop me? One of your brethren?"

"No," Uriel said. "Man will."

Semyaza hissed. "No man will defeat me."

"Yes, he will. Maybe he will be of flesh. Maybe it will be one of the souls of a body you try to usurp. You will lose, Semyaza; and you will find yourself back in darkness, chained and alone. Maybe then you will find humility and repent at long last."

"Never." Semyaza turned to Uriel, but the seraph had disappeared. He turned back. Basra approached. "Never."

Buildings now lined the road as he entered the outlying area of the city. Semyaza slowed. He wanted to make the swap outside of Basra, where the population was still small.

A car passed him. Semyaza looked at the people inside. A young man and woman. He made his choice fast before they pulled too far ahead.

He released his temporary vessel, and his formless self flew toward the car. Fast. Any slower and he would be yanked back to Uriel's prison. As he moved, he felt its heavy grip starting to tug but managed to resist long enough to dive through the back window and plunge into the man's body.

Inside, he found the soul and, fueled by his anger toward Uriel, commenced the battle.

CHAPTER TEN

As soon as Mike reached the road to Basra, he was ordered to turn around. Glenn called with word that outbreaks were occurring in the outskirts of Basra. He didn't want Mike going anywhere near there.

"How bad is it?" Mike had said.

"Real bad." Glenn wouldn't say anything else about it.

Mike still wanted to at least progress toward the city, get closer, but Glenn would hear none of it. Instead, he wanted Mike to sit tight in An Nasiriyah, where it was safe, until the picture in Basra sharpened.

So now Mike sat in his car in an alley and thought about his next move. In reality, he didn't have one. Not yet, at least. All roads led to Basra in this case, and those roads were closed.

"Shit."

Mike lifted his flask from the passenger seat and took a sip and enjoyed the soothing touch of the slow burn. Then he closed his eyes. Tired and dehydrated, it didn't take long to drift to sleep.

"You can't kill this one, Mike."

Mike opened his eyes and looked to his right while reflexively grabbing for his gun. His hand froze over the grip when he realized Greg McDaniel sat across from him.

"You're dead," Mike managed to say.

Greg nodded, his gray hair swaying softly with the gesture. "Yes, I am."

God, he looked just like he had the last day Mike saw him. Strong, tough, yet understanding, like a knowing father. Seeing him, even though Mike knew he wasn't real, caused his chest to tighten.

"What is this?" Mike said.

Greg looked at him and smiled. "A message."

"Message?"

"You can't kill this one."

His cell phone rang. Mike opened his eyes and took a deep breath. He checked the passenger seat, expecting to see Greg. He wasn't there. Only his cell phone and flask.

Mike grabbed the phone and rubbed his eyes as he answered it. "Yeah."

"It's Glenn."

"Anything new?" *Please let them have found Prince,* he thought.

"Basra is a disaster area."

Mike leaned forward and rested his forehead on the steering wheel. "Guess the Marines didn't get the roads closed in time."

"The first report came in just as they were shutting down the highway from An Nasiriyah. The military has since closed all routes into Basra. No one in or out."

"Is the military going in?"

"Nope. They're setting up their cordon and waiting to see how bad it gets."

Mike sat back and sighed. "How bad is it now?"

"Can't really tell. Reports from the air and from the perimeter say it's pretty much confined to one section outside the main part of the city. But there's nothing but a whole hell of a lot of gore there."

"Estimates?"

"A couple of thousand. Easy."

Mike placed his hand over his eyes. "The military can't sit back and watch all those people kill each other."

"Sure they can, unless the violence stops spreading. The Iraqi police sent in a riot team as soon as the fighting started. All contact with them has been lost. The last thing the military will do is send anyone in there with firearms and watch them turn on each other."

"Is anything like this happening anywhere else in the country?"

"No. Just Basra."

Mike scratched the top of his head. "Which means our boy Prince is there for sure?"

"That's a safe assumption."

Mike thought about Henry Prince for a moment. "So this guy isn't spreading whatever he's got."

"What do you mean?"

"I mean this guy goes from place to place and people start killing each other. But after he leaves and the people wipe each other out, whatever he has doesn't linger. Like at site R91 or the convoy on the side of the highway. Once the killing is done, other people can move through and don't pick up the virus."

"Like a proximity thing?" Glenn said.

"More like a chain reaction. Prince shows up and people go crazy. Then the last guy kills himself. Prince contaminates people with whatever he's carrying."

"That's interesting. Like throwing a steak into a room of starving people and letting them kill each other for it. Then the winner eats the steak but dies because his body can't handle it."

"Sure," Mike said. Only Glenn would come up with such an analogy. It made sense to Glenn and that's all that mattered.

"So this guy is radiating whatever he has? Like heat?"

"I think that's the best way to look at it. Now we just need to figure out what he's radiating."

"He'll probably be dead before we ever find out what it is."

Mike nodded. "Any media reporting on Basra yet?"

"No, thank God. That's the last thing we need on the national news is to see Iraqis tearing each other to pieces while a bunch of Marines stand outside the city and watch."

"What other options are being discussed if it spreads to the rest of the city?"

Glenn was silent a moment. "The president is considering several courses of action, and let's leave it at that."

Air bombardment, Mike thought. Would they really destroy a city to kill one guy? Sure, if it kept it from spreading down into Kuwait and Saudi Arabia and God knew where else. Heaven help us if someone else picks up whatever Prince has and makes it out of there.

"You don't want me to stay here, do you?" Mike said.

"Correct. You're worth nothing to me dead. Lay low. If this shit calms down, I might have you go in and take a look at the aftermath."

Mike shook his head, feeling useless. "Got anything else for me?"

"No. Stay in touch, Mike."

The line went dead. Mike tossed his cell phone on the passenger seat and stared out the windshield down the alley.

He wondered if the president would actually bomb the city and risk the consequences of civilian deaths to stop the spread of something they couldn't identify or explain and probably would never understand. How would the president explain it? And did it matter if it saved millions of lives in the long run?

He drew a long breath and exhaled slowly. Mike checked his watch. Not even four o'clock yet.

Damn, he thought. *What a long, fucking miserable day.*

Mike sat there for another twenty minutes, stewing and thinking about Greg McDaniel. *"You can't kill this one." Kill what?*

He stopped trying to interpret the words of a dead man from a dream and grabbed the flask and took another swig. Jesus, he was tired but restless. He wanted to participate or sleep. But not here in an alley in An Nasiriyah like some coward waiting for a fight to end.

Part of him didn't want to go anywhere near Basra. Diving into the psychopathic fallout wasn't at the top of his list of things to do in his life. But the other part, that section of him that fed on accomplishing tasks, the same area that didn't mind executing a well-planned kill, wanted to find Henry Prince.

He looked around his car, trying to keep his mind busy. He had nothing to distract him, though. Not even a crossword puzzle. All he had were his thoughts, and all he kept thinking about was Greg McDaniel and finding Henry Prince and ending all this.

"Fuck it," Mike said.

He started the car and left An Nasiriyah. Mike knew he wouldn't find Prince, but he would be closer to the action. And that would be a hell of a lot better than hanging out like a chickenshit in an alley in An Nasiriyah.

CHAPTER ELEVEN

Semyaza sat up and looked around him. Tall walls stood on both sides of him. Underneath him was a filthy surface covered in rocks and dirt and debris. All around lay the bodies of dead people.

The soul of his new vessel had fought just as hard as Hank's had, but this time it did not last as long. Semyaza had been prepared, learning its weaknesses quickly. As a result, this vessel did not lose as much internal blood and tissue as Hank. Semyaza had minimized the damage and hoped it would delay the corrosive effects his presence would have on the body. Maybe he could hold on to this one longer than Hank. Maybe he would eventually find a way to maintain a vessel for more than a few days versus a few hours. Maybe.

Do not leap so far ahead, he thought.

Semyaza reached into the mind of the host, as he had with Hank, and learned another language. This one had spoken Arabic. Much of the other information remained the same: a family he loved, how to drive an automobile, and so on. The religious beliefs differed, though.

He glanced over at the bodies surrounding him, many piled one on top of the other. Mounds of human refuse. Some had been bludgeoned. Others stabbed. Most died clenching crude weapons. Others sharp objects. A few had resorted to using their bare hands. Blood soaked the ground of what he learned was an alley.

Semyaza stood and breathed. The air reeked of death. It held a mix of blood and excrement, folded together in an abominable stench.

The smell overpowering him, Semyaza walked out of the alley and onto a main road. There, more bodies lay.

All around you shall discord rule, he thought.

Semyaza walked down the main street, past buildings on fire and cars tipped over. More and more bodies lay strewn around him. He stepped over men and women and children, all savagely killed.

He felt nothing for them. It was because of man he was imprisoned. Bound underneath them while the little mud people danced and raped and killed, debating whether they believed in God and whether or not to worship Him. Yet they were superior to Semyaza. He was required to bend the knee.

I will not serve.

Thinking about it made him want to kill more, to employ the vessel's hands and feel the warm blood of a human as he took its life from it.

Patience, Semyaza thought. First, he had to find living people. The corpses around him served no purpose. If his vessel started to fail, he would need a breathing mud person close by.

Semyaza walked through the sea of bodies toward the other side of Basra. Toward people. Toward a collection of possible new vessels.

Yet so far, his current host seemed to stand up well to his presence. No skin flaked away. Muscles did not deteriorate. It would all dissolve sooner or later, but knowing he could extend his residence pleased him.

Progress, Semyaza thought.

CHAPTER TWELVE

Mike made it as far as the cordon outside Basra when he ran into an armed roadblock. He flashed the Jeremiah Hosselkus ID, but it didn't work. The sentries wouldn't let anyone in or out of the city no matter how important the person acted.

"Basra is secured to all personnel." The sentry had added special emphasis on the *all*, dragging it out for a good second.

Rather than beat a retreat back to An Nasiriyah, Mike pulled the car over a mile away from the roadblock, sat on the hood, and watched. Tanks, troop carriers, and Humvees swarmed the outskirts. Both armed and surveillance helicopters orbited a couple of hundred feet over Basra. Smoke rose from several places in the city, but he couldn't make out what structures burned. He wondered if one of them was his hotel.

As the sun dipped near the horizon, Mike thought about what he should do next. It didn't take long to come to a decision: nothing.

"Mr. Hosselkus," a voice said. Mike almost didn't respond until some part of his subconscious kicked him in the ass and reminded him someone had just used his alias. He twisted his torso. Gunnery Sergeant Lowe's head jutted out the passenger window of a Humvee.

"Gunny." Mike pushed off the hood and walked over to Lowe. "What are you doing out here?"

"We were the lead in the search for Henry Prince. Once Basra went ape shit, they pulled us off to help set up roadblocks. Now we're redeploying."

"Where to?"

"Back to R91." Lowe spat tobacco juice on the road. "Not much for us to do here. They got enough swinging dicks to surround the city. And I don't want to be here when the exodus starts."

"Exodus?"

Lowe nodded. "They're evacuating the city."

"What? I thought the concern was whatever Prince had might spread."

Lowe looked at him for a while. "What was the last thing you heard?"

"That people started killing each other and Basra was surrounded. No one in or out."

"Well, the situation has changed. The man-on-man violence seems to have stopped. No one is going crazy and killing each other, according to the eyes in the sky. But looting has started. Several buildings are on fire, and grain warehouses near the port are being picked clean. Now the helos are broadcasting over loudspeakers to evacuate the city."

Mike looked at Basra in the distance—more smoke rising from new fires.

"So, they're moving people out to save the city?"

"No, they're moving people out to more easily contain them. There are a couple of refugee camps outside Basra. Leftovers from the war. Get the people in the camps, isolate them, and keep an eye on them while checking for any abnormalities."

"Quarantine."

"Sure." Lowe spat again. "But it'll also give us a chance to go in, clean up, and reestablish control before letting anyone back in. Just don't have the manpower to go house to house looking for Prince while also acting as riot police. Remember, we're a visiting force now, not occupiers. Plus, we got dead bodies all over the place. In a few more hours, there are going to be some big health concerns."

Mike nodded. It would be easier to move the masses into one or two controlled locations. He crunched the numbers in his head. Over two million people lived in Basra. That's a lot of people to stuff in a few refugee camps.

"How many dead?" Mike said.

"A lot." Lowe's eyes drifted toward the road. "Close to a hundred thousand estimated, based on observations from the air. Don't know about inside buildings yet. There are whole roads covered in bodies."

Mike rubbed his chin and imagined what a hundred thousand people just lying around dead in the streets might look like. "Jesus."

"Now you see why a disease outbreak is such a concern."

"Yeah."

Mike thought about how his day had started. He'd killed Anwar early in the morning. An isolated hit. A controlled death meant to minimize panic and make sure no innocents ended up dead and only the bad guy paid the price. Now, not even twelve hours later, a good chunk of the city lay slaughtered in the streets. He knew he couldn't have done anything to prevent it but wondered what the point of order was if chaos could so easily reign.

"What are you going to do at R91?" Mike said after a few moments of silence.

Lowe shrugged. "Now that the investigators and lab techs are done with the scene, the bodies are being moved to Camp Bucca for autopsies and further arrangements. Major Greengrass plans to lift that sewer pipe out of the hole. I guess the Iraqi archeology geeks still want to excavate the tomb. First, though, we got to stamp it safe."

"Who cares? The scene is part of an investigation now. Fuck the geeks."

Lowe laughed. "Honestly, I think the major wants to go down and see what's in there for himself—see if he can make sense of all this. I doubt he'll find anything to bring closure, but, hey, if it makes him feel better. The guy's had one helluva rough day."

"I think you all have." Mike jerked his thumb toward the city. "Just be glad you didn't have to deal with whatever was in that tomb up close."

Lowe nodded and spat. "Damn skippy on that one. So what are you doing?"

Mike rubbed his hands together. "Nothing. Basra was my base of operations. I got nothing to run to ground. I'm a man without a job right now. Figured I'd just sit here and watch. It's either that or relocate somewhere else where all I'll do is sit and wait. Rather be here and see how all this turns out. Help out if I can."

"Sounds like a waste of time. If you want, you can come back to R91 with us."

Mike looked away at Basra again. He thought about how much longer it would be before he could get in. They would be evacuating for at least another day. Then there'd be the cleanup. He knew he could go in then, but what would be the point with no one there? With no intel to follow? Besides, now that he knew the scope of the damage, he wasn't sure he'd ever want to go back to Basra. He wanted to work a case, not chase a human bomb.

This case is over for you, Mike thought. *Once Glenn's done being distracted with Basra, he'll come back with more people to kill. Might as well enjoy the peace and quiet. If you can call it that.*

Either he went with Lowe or he sat back down on the hood and pondered the carnage and why he'd dreamed of Greg McDaniel while waiting for his next mope to kill.

"Sure, I'll go." Mike turned back to Lowe. "The germ and bug chasers clear the tomb?"

Lowe nodded. "No chemical or biological compounds so far. They'll make another sweep once the pipe is lifted, but if nothing is showing up now, it's pretty much safe. Other than a lot of stale air, whatever was down there didn't leave a trace."

"Think I could get a peek in that tomb?"

Lowe spat and grinned. "I think we can work something out."

CHAPTER THIRTEEN

Shipmaster Omar Yusuf looked down from the wheelhouse of the merchant vessel *al-Phirosh* at the mob looting the grain warehouse on the pier. A hundred or so people swarmed every side of the sheet-metal building. Dozens ran away with sacks of grain on their shoulders and in their arms. Others, rather than pillage, waited like jackals for the people with sacks to run by. Then they pounced, attacking the thieves and stealing the grain for themselves.

Yusuf shook his head and wondered where the police or American military were. Why had they not come and quelled this insanity? The port had the most protection of any place in southern Iraq, yet now it was left to the devices of a horde of looters. What had happened to cause Basra to turn on itself?

The mob had set fire to several buildings and automobiles in the port. Rather than extinguish them, the authorities retreated and surrounded the oil holding tanks, setting up a perimeter of last defense. That did not last long, though. After a few minutes, the authorities left the tanks to the mob, loaded in their vehicles, and fled the port like frightened rats. Thankfully, the mob did not seem to care about the oil and instead focused on the grain.

Yusuf, as soon as he had seen the first waves of the mob, had secured and lifted the amidships brow and pulled what crew he had on board inside the confines of the ship, leaving only the aft brow for foot traffic. He still had several crewmembers on shore and could only hope they were still alive unharmed and in safe shelter. If they did not have a place to hole up, he prayed they would make it back to the ship before it set sail the next morning.

"Do you really believe we need sentries?"

Yusuf turned from the looting to Alwad. He had not heard his first officer approach him and was surprised to see his grim face only a meter away. The deep scars crisscrossing his forehead and jaw seemed to have grown more cavernous over the last few hours.

"Yes, I do." Yusuf had posted two deckhands at the foot of the aft brow, armed with Kalashnikovs maintained on board in case of pirate attacks. The seas off the coast of Africa had become overrun with the scum, after all. "You do not?"

"Those idiots would have to make it over or through that fence to get to us. Why deal with razor wire when the warehouses are unprotected? The path of least resistance always wins."

"True, but I will accept being overcautious. How long have you been standing there anyway?"

"A few minutes."

Yusuf shifted back to the scene in the port. "This is bad business. Have you heard anything on the radio that might explain what is causing this?"

"No. All they say is there is rioting all over the city. Not one explanation as to why. If this continues, I do not foresee us getting underway tomorrow."

Yusuf nodded. The *al-Phirosh* had been scheduled to get underway from Basra at 1600, onload crude at the Al Basra Oil Terminal off the coast, and begin the long transit to South Africa. Those plans were canceled when port security secured all outbound and inbound traffic for the remainder of the day. He had assumed merchant traffic would resume tomorrow, knowing the economic costs to the country would grow exponentially if it did not. Listening to Alwad, though, he felt a similar doubt develop within him. Instinct told him something horrible had occurred in Basra. Second-guessing made him wish they had set sail earlier, regardless of the order.

"You are probably correct," Yusuf said. "Perhaps it will work out for the best and allow those personnel who have not yet reported to make it back to the ship."

"Perhaps."

An American military helicopter flew in low from the east and hovered over the port. Yusuf did not think anything of it at first because he had seen several helicopters flying over downtown the last few hours. He figured it was surveying and reporting on the riot so the police or military knew where to come to help.

Then someone in the helicopter broadcasted over loud speakers in Arabic:

"The national government of Iraq in cooperation with the US military has issued a mandatory evacuation of the city of Basra. This order is a precaution to ensure the health of citizens against possible exposure to chemical weapons. Do not travel through the western part of the city. Proceed south. US forces and Iraqi national police personnel are waiting to assist with food and water. All personnel who do not evacuate and remain in Basra will be subject to arrest and incarceration. This includes all merchant personnel as well. Proceed south. I repeat..."

Yusuf's mind raced, pouring through what he had just heard.

"Possible chemical weapons exposure?" Alwad said.

"It must be terrorists attempting to destroy commerce."

"No wonder people are panicking."

Yusuf paced the length of the wheelhouse. Alwad did not follow.

"Some of the crew will panic as well," Alwad said. "Others will flee."

"And the rest will demand we set sail because it is safer at sea. Most do not have any family in Basra and will not shed a tear if we left."

"Not to mention they will not receive their pay if we evacuate. No, many will insist on leaving."

Yusuf wanted to sail as well, but his motive did not rest with a desire for money. At sea, he commanded his vessel and could move it about freely. If crew members left, they could put themselves at more risk than if they remained on board and chanced being pursued by port security.

"What do you think, Alwad?"

"Set sail. There is no reason to leave the safety of this ship and join that mob, especially if chemical weapons have been used. Better to stay away from large groups of frightened people."

"Our people will be frightened as well."

Alwad shrugged. "Some, yes."

"I take it you are not."

"No. I have seen worse."

He had never heard his first officer's life story and would not shame him by asking. It was written in the many scars that covered his face and arms. One did not need to know how to read them to understand what they said.

"It will not be easy, sailing out of here," Yusuf said. "And there is no guarantee the oil terminal will let us fill our tanks."

"After dark will make it easier. And I think the terminal will pump if the price is right."

Yusuf smirked. A small stash of money, provided by the Iraq Oil Shipping Company, was kept on board in case a customs agent required a bribe or one of their crew members needed to be bailed out of a foreign prison. Alwad was correct. Bribing the terminal manager would not be difficult.

"We will wait until dark."

On the pier, the mob thinned. Many still fought over grain, but the majority plodded toward the south, arms full with what they could carry. About twenty of his fifty-man crew stood on the aft weather decks, watching and talking. He imagined what they said to one another, already knowing they discussed what to do next: stay or flee.

After a few more moments, Yusuf walked over to the port side of the wheelhouse and lifted the microphone for the vessel's main communication circuit. He keyed it, transmitting over both internal and external circuits.

"On board *al-Phirosh*, this is the shipmaster speaking." Yusuf paused and glanced at Alwad, who nodded. "All hands are to report to the galley in five minutes. I repeat, all hands are to report to the galley in five minutes."

Yusuf placed the microphone back in its cradle. He had planned to announce his decision to get underway over the circuit but thought better of it in case any in the mob heard him and tried to rush the ship in a desperate attempt to gain passage on board. Instead, he would present his decision to the crew in private.

He hoped after he told them he would still have a crew to sail with.

Semyaza stood in the eastern part of the city just before sunset. He saw water in the distance and mobs of humans running around, crazy with panic and greed. At first, he thought the chaos was brought about by his presence. Then he noticed the humans were not killing one another. Instead, they stole food and other items or destroyed buildings and automobiles for some reason he did not understand.

Such blessed creatures, he thought. Semyaza recalled the first humans in the time before he rebelled. They had fought and stolen and murdered just as they did now.

And yet we were wrong for rebelling? Semyaza thought. *Look at these animals. Take order away and they degenerate. Where is their light? Where is their devotion? The favored have proven they are nothing more than balls of mud with souls.*

Semyaza shook his head and glanced at his hands. The flesh had started to flake off. Not in large chunks as before, but he would have to find another vessel sooner rather than later.

A large flying machine hovered overhead. The sound of its wings beating the air reminded Semyaza of an insect. The machine spoke Arabic:

"The national government of Iraq in cooperation with the US military has issued a mandatory evacuation of the city of Basra. This order is a precaution to ensure the health of citizens against possible exposure to chemical weapons. Do not travel through the western part of the city. Proceed south. US forces and Iraqi national police personnel are waiting to assist with food and water. All personnel who do not evacuate and remain in Basra will be subject to arrest and incarceration. Proceed south."

So that is why everyone is heading south, Semyaza thought. He had noticed the current of humans had shifted in that direction the last couple of hours as he headed east. He had not really thought anything of it until now.

He considered turning and following the hordes, to ensure he had access to a vessel when the time arrived. But he did not like the idea of being funneled into a mass migration where the human army would have control. It would not be wise to assume the next vessel around so many humans carrying weapons. Even though they would not harm him, the devastation he caused in areas of high human concentration was counterproductive to his desire. Semyaza needed bodies. They were no good to him if they were dead before they served a purpose.

Semyaza reached into the memory of his host, searching for other avenues to follow. He found where the man had been heading. To a ship. The man had signed up as a deckhand on a ship. His wife was riding with him to drop him off at the port. It was to be his first voyage, an opportunity to gain money for his new family.

But what ship? Semyaza thought.

He dug deeper, searching for a name. He saw the applications for work, the man filling out form after form for the position, the contract of employment. A deckhand on a merchant vessel. His first voyage would be to a place called "South Africa." The cargo was oil.

There. The name. The *al-Phirosh*.

Semyaza looked at the port ahead of him. There were several ships moored to piers. Smoke billowed from a few of their stacks. He could not read any of the names.

Any of the ships provided a way out of the imprisoned and demolished city. If he did not find the *al-Phirosh*, he would stow away on one of the others. And once on board, he would have access to a small group of bodies in a more controlled environment.

Defeat the soul quickly, Semyaza thought, *and the chaos will be minimal.*

He nodded and continued walking east toward the Port of Basra.

CHAPTER FOURTEEN

By the time Mike reached R91 for the second time that day, the sun had set and the site basked in the light of several towers powered by diesel generators. He parked his car where he had earlier, pulled his cell phone off the charger, and walked with Lowe to the command tent.

Inside, Major Greengrass reclined back in a folding chair, feet propped up on a table. Eyes closed and arms crossed over his chest and hands tucked into his armpits, he snored, the air coming out in short snorts.

"Evening, Major," Lowe said. "Brought our guest back."

Greengrass's bloodshot eyes opened and focused on Mike. "Mr. Hosselkus. Welcome back to our lovely little shithole."

Mike smirked. "Thanks. Seems a bit quieter here now."

"Thank God." Greengrass dropped his feet and sat up straight. "The bodies started to get that not-so-fresh smell. Thankfully, we were allowed to bag 'em, tag 'em, and ship 'em over to Camp Bucca for processing."

Mike pulled up a seat across from Greengrass. Lowe remained standing, his hands held behind his back.

"How'd you get stuck here?" Mike said. "Figured you'd be on the front lines in Basra, running Prince to ground."

Greengrass held up his palms toward Mike. "Washed my hands clean of him when the general took control of the operation. He's personally on the ground outside Basra, overseeing the evacuation and cleanup. My little detachment here has orders to maintain security since this is ground zero."

"So this is punishment?"

Greengrass chuckled. "Nah. Just a slap for letting Prince make it to Basra. I don't think anything else will happen. It's not exactly a crime to not find somebody you never saw or had in your possession. And every effort was made to locate him. He just had too much of a head start."

"That's good. I'd hate to think someone would try to blame you."

"Well, I do blame me." Greengrass rubbed the back of his neck. "All those deaths in Basra are going to haunt me a long time."

Mike didn't say anything for a few moments. He glimpsed Lowe's head sagging, his face pointed at the ground, before looking away. Greengrass just seemed to stare into nothingness.

"So what brings you back here?" Greengrass said.

"I'm a man without a compass, so to speak." Mike scratched his chin and smiled. "All the attention is on Basra. Until it settles down, my boss will be distracted, which means I'm out of a job."

"Why not go find a hotel in An Nasiriyah—take it easy until this calms down?" Greengrass said.

Mike shook his head. "I'd rather stay close and gather information where I can." *And feel like a real intelligence officer for once.*

"A spook through and through." Greengrass grinned.

Mike chuckled. "Yeah, I guess you're right."

"Well, you're not going to learn much spying on me or my people. But I can provide something that'll take the edge off."

Greengrass reached down into a cammie bag on the ground. A second later, he set a bottle of Johnnie Walker Black Label on the table.

"Want a drink?"

Mike looked at the bottle and licked his lips. "God, yes."

"Gunny?"

Lowe pulled up a seat at the table. "Quit twisting my arm, sir."

Greengrass produced a couple of Styrofoam cups and passed them out. He filled his own before passing the bottle to Mike.

Mike sniffed the whiskey in his cup, enjoying the charred scent before taking a sip. He let it roll around his mouth a moment before swallowing. The corners of his mouth flicked up as the burn raced down his throat and warmed his stomach.

"So," Greengrass said, "how'd you become a spook?"

Mike hesitated a moment, carefully lining up in his head what he would and wouldn't say. A little info couldn't hurt but he wanted to be sure not to tell too much.

"Well, I got recruited out of college." Mike took another sip. "Grew up and went to school in the South."

"Where at?" Lowe said.

Mike wagged a finger. "'South' is the best you'll get."

"Does the CIA train you to be that paranoid?" Greengrass said.

"They train us to be that careful."

"Paranoid bastards," Greengrass said.

"Anyway, I was a Southern kid who'd never seen the world. So, when the CIA came a-knocking, I jumped at the chance. Probably like most people who join the military, the promise of exotic lands and women were too much to pass up."

"Here, here." Lowe knocked back the rest of his drink and refilled his cup. "Well, that and blowing shit up."

Mike laughed, refilled, and took another sip. He could already feel his head lightening thanks to an empty stomach.

"So I went to Langley, passed all the tests and interviews. Did well enough to get selected for field ops. Made it through Quantico." He made sure not to mention the ex-wife and daughter. "And then landed my first assignment in Ethiopia."

Mike thought back to Ethiopia and smiled. He took another sip.

"That's where I met my mentor," Mike said. "Great guy. Taught me so damn much. We did a lot of work across borders in Sudan and later Somalia."

Mike drifted off for a second as he remembered Greg, the career field agent who had taken him under his wing. Then he took a long swig, finishing off his second cup. He refilled, took another sip, and stared at the surface of the table. His vision blurred a little as he reassembled the memory of Greg sitting in his car earlier, telling him he couldn't kill this one, whatever the hell that meant.

"You were saying," Greengrass said.

Mike blinked and cleared his throat but kept his eyes on the table. "Greg McDaniel was his name. If you go to the CIA headquarters in Langley, in the lobby is the Wall of Honor. On it are these black stars carved into white marble. Each star represents a CIA agent who died in the field."

Mike knocked back the rest of his drink and stopped caring about how much he said. "One of those stars is Greg's. He was investigating the embassy bombing in Kenya when he was captured by al Qaeda. Two weeks later they dumped his head outside the US embassy in Addis Ababa. Never found the body."

"Where were you when they grabbed him?" Lowe said.

"We'd split up. He went to Nairobi and I went to Tanzania. The embassy bombings were high priorities, and all assets in the region were being assigned to them. It was Greg's idea to split up. And I got lucky as a result."

He filled his cup again and knocked the whole thing back. "So I found the guy who did the beheading. It took me almost a year to track him down. When I did, I put two in his head, one through each eye."

Mike shifted his gaze from the table and saw Greengrass and Lowe staring at him. "Sorry. I said more than I meant to."

"So that's why you do it," Greengrass said.

"Do what?" Mike said.

"Your job. You want to kill the bad guy."

Mike thought back to Anwar earlier that morning, his head down on the rug, bleeding out. Then all the others he'd killed. Not one at a time, but all at once, a surreal picture of ghosts blurring together in his head.

"Yeah. I want to kill the bad guy." But how many had been bad? He prayed all of them had been. "It's what I'm good at."

Greengrass raised his cup in a toast. "Amen, brother."

Lowe knocked back his own drink. "Ooh-rah."

Mike smirked. "Too bad there's always another bad guy to get."

"Then I guess you'll always have a job." Greengrass laughed. "We all will."

Mike didn't laugh with him. *Always will*, he thought and felt a little queasy.

"How do you do it, though?" Greengrass said.

"What do you mean?"

"Put two through the eyes. Or strangle someone. I mean, I've engaged in firefights. Probably killed a few. But never that close. Never that personal. How do you do it?"

I don't know. "You tell yourself there's a reason someone decided to punch his ticket. Ninety-nine percent of them have it coming. They've earned the bullet. So you make yourself into a tool that executes that judgment. But it isn't easy."

"They stay with you."

Mike nodded once. Silence prevailed around them for a moment or two.

Greengrass cleared his throat and grabbed the bottle, pouring out what was left into his cup. "How about we finish our drinks and then go check out that tomb? See what's down there."

Mike smirked, not wanting to think about Greg or the people he'd killed anymore. "Sounds good to me."

CHAPTER FIFTEEN

After Yusuf had expressed to the crew his desire to put to sea, all but two accepted the offer to sail with him. He let them leave, paid them what he could from the stash, and asked them not to say anything for twenty-four hours. They thanked him and agreed.

Now he stood in the wheelhouse, looking at the water around him. He had waited for sunset, knowing it would be easier to make a sprint out of port under the cover of darkness. He had experience as a smuggler when he was younger, running oil out of Iraq during the days of Saddam and the United Nations sanctions and Oil-for-Food.

"The chief engineer reports all engines are online," Alwad said.

"Very well," Yusuf said. "Any more personnel report?"

Four of nine missing crewmen had made it to the ship. All of them had decided to get underway. After seeing what they had out in town, none of them wanted to follow the mobs south to the refugee camps. Yusuf had been relieved to see them. Their stories of the horror in Basra had changed the minds of several who had considered leaving.

"No more personnel," Alwad said.

Yusuf checked his watch.

"We cannot wait much longer," Alwad said. "Those last five are not coming."

"Possibly. It will not kill us to give them a few more minutes, though. Besides, there are other ships in this port probably making the same preparations we are. I want to allow one or two of them to make their run first. Let them distract port security."

Alwad smiled. The scars on his face formed a fleshy arc. "Sometimes I forget you used to be a smuggler."

"Indeed. Rushing out right after dark would be foolish. Never be the first out of the gate and never be the last."

"Well, whenever we depart, the crew is ready."

Yusuf looked down below on the weather decks. Crewmen stood by to sever the mooring lines. He did not have a choice since line handlers on the pier were not an option. So he would put lateral thrust on the ship toward the pier, slack the mooring lines enough so that when severed they would not snap back and cut his personnel in half. Yusuf had seen what a parted line could do to a person.

"Why not just leave the lines?"

Yusuf turned to Feisal, his young second officer, standing by the gyrocompass in the center of the wheelhouse. "Mooring lines are expensive. If we cut them, we can re-splice them and use them again."

"Not to mention we have only two spares on board," Alwad said.

Yusuf approached the compass. "What would you recommend, Feisal?"

"Me?"

"If you intend to be a shipmaster in the future, you need to be able to answer these types of questions. What would you do?"

Feisal rubbed his smooth face. "Slack the lines; cut them and then pull away from the pier."

"Without putting lateral thrust on the ship?"

"If we slack the lines, we will not need lateral thrust."

"What is the speed of the current right now, Alwad?"

"Four knots pushing us away from the pier."

"You will not have time to slack them enough and sever them without lateral thrust. Do you understand, Feisal?"

Feisal nodded. "The current will push us away from the pier, and we will have taut lines no matter how fast we slack them."

Yusuf smiled. "Very good."

He did not mention putting lateral thrust on the ship would be just as dangerous. The fear was keeping the movement toward the pier for too long and hitting it. Everything had to happen quickly and timing was of the essence. Once the lines slacked, the crewmen would chop them with axes. Hopefully, the lines would sever without issue. But cutting through ten centimeters of double-braided nylon was not the easiest task, no matter how sharp the ax.

Yusuf glanced again at his watch. Just a few more minutes. He lit a Turkish cigarette and took a deep drag.

Almost time, he thought.

Semyaza made it on board the *al-Phirosh* without difficulty. Every person he approached seemed to recognize him. The sentries at the foot of the brow welcomed him aboard without challenge. One of them even slapped him on the shoulder as he passed by. He politely nodded and avoided contact and said nothing.

The skin on both hands was all but gone, and patches on his neck had also flaked off. His collar flicked up and hands tucked in his pockets, Semyaza climbed the brow and walked onto the ship and headed inside.

He reached into the memories of the host once more, learning his way around the *al-Phirosh*. From what he found, the person had a minimal familiarization with the ship other than a basic tour. He had remembered the names of the decks and the location of a few rooms. Semyaza poured through the information, searching for the best place to hide.

Then he found it.

Semyaza walked up a ladder from the main deck to the poop deck and moved through a door. He walked down a passageway, past the galley, turned left, and headed down another passageway. He stepped through another door and found what he sought on the right.

A box with a metal door. The memory told him it was called a walk-in refrigerator.

Semyaza reached out and grabbed the latching and opened the door. Cold air poured out and enveloped him.

This is what I need, Semyaza thought and walked in. He closed the door and surveyed his new surroundings. Various fruits and vegetables were stacked on shelves.

The cold, he believed, would help slow the degeneration of the flesh. He did not expect it to stop it completely and needed it to work only long enough for the ship to get underway. Semyaza wanted to ensure the *al-Phirosh* was well at sea before he assumed another host.

Well at sea and in an area of minimal people. Semyaza believed he could defeat the soul even quicker the next time. If he could minimize the number of people around, Semyaza would have a ship of bodies to pick and choose from until they reached their next port.

That was, if everything went according to plan. First, though, Semyaza would sit patiently in the cold of the refrigerator and wait.

"Is it worth it?" Uriel said in the Ancient Tongue. The white mist materialized in the refrigerator and swirled around Semyaza.

Even in the cold of the refrigerator, the heat of the Firmament radiating from Uriel burned beyond belief.

Semyaza cringed from the pain but also from how much he missed its warmth. It had been so long.

"You again?" Semyaza's words came out slow, the pain causing him to stutter slightly. "Why not appear in the form of a man once more, since you love them so much?"

"Is being outside the prison worth all this destruction? Is it worth hopping from body to body like a virus?"

"Yes," Semyaza said. "I feel the Firmament now. Even the slightest touch is worth it, no matter how much it hurts."

"Yet you know it will not last." The mist contorted and shrank before it transformed into a man, dressed in the same clothes as earlier, sitting with his legs crossed.

The burning ceased. Relief and loss flooded Semyaza simultaneously. He looked at his forearms and saw the first indication of bone showing.

"I will make it last."

"You know how to end all of this, Semyaza. The truth is there and it always has been. The touch of grace is not that far removed and can be yours again."

Semyaza shook his head. "I did nothing wrong."

"Your pride is still your undoing."

"I was not the leader. I followed. Why should I be punished in such a way and Lucifer not? Why is he given dominion over Earth, free to move about, and I am bound?"

"Lucifer has his own punishment, as do you and all the rest of your ilk. You could receive judgment if you only repented."

"But no forgiveness."

"There is no forgiveness after the fall, just as there is no forgiveness for a man after death."

"Do not compare me to a man."

"You look very much like a man to me, Semyaza. Although you are falling to pieces."

Semyaza hissed.

"Repent and accept judgment. At least all of this will be over."

"To repent is to serve."

"Yes."

"I will not serve."

"Then bound shall you stay."

Uriel transformed back into the mist and disappeared. Semyaza reached out, trying to feel the heat of the Firmament one last time, hoping it would burn him to cinders; but it had gone and again he dwelled in the cold.

Yusuf looked at his watch and nodded. Time to set sail.

"Right full rudder," Yusuf said. "Port engine ahead one-third, starboard engine back one-third. Come up to five percent on the starboard bow thruster."

The helmsman repeated what Yusuf had said, word for word, while simultaneously executing the orders.

Yusuf stood on the port bridgewing, watching the mooring lines. They were not taut but had enough strain on them that snapback still posed a danger. It took only a second or two for the ship to start moving. The stern shifted toward the pier. Normally, the bow would kick away; but ordering five percent on the forward thruster compensated for twist, putting lateral movement on the hull.

Yusuf lifted a handheld radio and keyed it. "Slack all lines."

"Slack all lines, aye," said the personnel at the mooring stations.

The gap between the ship and the pier closed to only a few feet. Yusuf watched the lines slack. He wanted to see a good dip in them before giving the orders to sever.

The pier grew closer. Fenders between the hull and cement pylons started to compress. Almost there.

Satisfied all the mooring lines had enough slack, Yusuf gave the order. "Sever all lines."

Crewmen on the weather decks repeated the order. Those holding axes commenced hacking.

As soon as the first ax made contact, Yusuf turned to the helmsman and said, "Shift your rudder. Starboard engine ahead one-third, port engine back one-third. Indicate zero percent on the starboard bow thruster. Indicate five percent on the port bow thruster."

The helmsman repeated back the order and did as ordered. Yusuf turned back to the weather decks. The stern line was separated. As were several of the athwartship lines.

The lateral movement toward the pier halted. For a moment, the *al-Phirosh* was completely motionless. Then the recent engine and rudder orders took effect and the ship slid sideways from the pier.

The midship line parted. Yusuf counted. All mooring lines were free with the exception of the bow. The crewman wielding the ax up forward chopped at it like a madman but to no avail. He kept hitting the line in different areas, his aim off as the ship moved.

"Indicate zero percent on the port bow thruster." The bow's movement away from the pier slowed. The stern began to twist. "Rudder amidships."

Several men with axes from amidships sprinted to the bow and started hacking. The slack in the line started to disappear. If they did not sever it in another second or two, Yusuf would have to either put forward movement on the ship back toward the pier or evacuate the bow and let the line part under heavy strain.

Before Yusuf made the call, one of the axmen succeeded in severing the line. It recoiled slightly, hitting the side of the ship but not snapping through the bullnose chock.

"That was close," Alwad said behind him.

Yusuf turned and smirked but said nothing. Instead, he focused on navigating safely out of Basra and avoiding port security.

Semyaza sighed as the bulkhead vibrated against his back. The ship was moving. It lurched to one side for a few moments and then shifted in the opposite direction. Minutes later, the ship accelerated and the sideways movement stopped.

Finally.

He looked at his hands, now only bone. The skin had peeled off up to the elbows but no farther. The blood did not pour out as it had before. Instead, it turned to powder. The red dust saturated his clothes and the floor. The muscles of his biceps had crumbled in chunks. He had slowed the rapid disintegration he had experienced with Henry Prince, though. The cold of the refrigerator seemed to help. Progress.

Now that the ship was underway, he did not have to work so hard to maintain the flesh. He would find a new host soon. Until then, he would rest and prepare and let this body disintegrate.

CHAPTER SIXTEEN

A large crane had already removed the infamous section of sewer pipe from the pit. The broken pieces of slab remained down there, though, glimmering under the generator lights. Mike wondered what those pieces were made of. They had a dullness to them, like once-polished stones left in a garden too long. But the way the light danced across the surface reminded him of metal flake paint. Weird.

The ancient writing carved into the fragments bothered him more. Mike read and spoke Arabic and Hebrew. This language resembled neither. Nor did it look anything like cuneiform. For this region, it was extremely out of place.

The entrance to the tomb was a black rectangle in a sea of sand. He couldn't make out anything beyond the surface. Like gazing into the mouth of a bottomless pit. A mouth with perfectly squared corners. After a few seconds, he looked away, his half-drunk mind losing to a bout of dizziness.

"Ready to go down?" Greengrass said.

"Lead the way."

Greengrass climbed down the ladder into the pit, followed by Lowe and then Mike. At the bottom, the fragments appeared less like metal than they had from above. They also lost their stone resemblance. Mike had never seen anything like it. Maybe the whiskey skewed his vision because, for a moment, he thought the surface of a piece rippled, like a calm pool of water that a pebble's been dropped into. As he moved by it, though, the effect ceased.

"We found a journal on the dead archeologist," Greengrass said.

Mike turned and found Greengrass staring at the same fragment he had been hypnotized by. "What'd it say?"

"He noted the slab seemed to be made of a material neither metal nor stone. He wrote the surface looked both static and kinetic at the same time. Like water moving under ice."

"You saw it, too?"

"Yep. Freaky."

Mike nodded. *Good, I didn't imagine it.*

"Did the archeologist say what writing this is, sir?" Lowe said.

"He couldn't identify the language."

Mike rubbed the back of his neck. "This keeps getting better and better. Can't wait to see what's down there. Maybe a unicorn."

Lowe snorted.

Greengrass walked over to the side of the tomb and shined a flashlight down. Mike followed and looked over the major's shoulder.

Below, the light illuminated a wall constructed of the same material. The surface seemed to dance as the beam passed over it. A flowing solid, if such a thing existed.

As Greengrass swept the light back and forth, Lowe brought down a halogen lamp from above and set it up. He flicked the switch and the entirety of the tomb came into focus.

Mike saw four walls and a floor, all constructed of the mysterious substance. The tomb, he estimated, was probably ten feet by ten feet by ten feet. Every square inch had the unknown language carved into it. *It's a box,* Mike thought. A box that had been built and buried.

"Want to go down?" Greengrass said.

Mike hesitated, but his curiosity got the better of him and he eventually nodded. Lowe brought over the ladder they'd climbed down into the pit with and lowered it into the tomb.

Greengrass motioned his hand down in a sweeping gesture. "Be my guest."

Mike smirked and stepped on the ladder and took the first couple rungs down. Cold air tickled his legs as he descended. As his waist and torso entered the tomb, the cold grew more intense. By the time he reached the bottom, Mike had to hug his chest, shivering uncontrollably.

"Holy shit, it's cold down here," Greengrass said as he stepped off the ladder onto the floor of the tomb.

Mike's teeth chattered. "I didn't feel the cold when we were looking down in here."

Greengrass shook his head. "Neither did I."

Lowe climbed down and shivered as well. "Jesus, it's like the cold exists only in here."

It did feel like the cold couldn't escape the tomb even with the cover gone, as if it existed in the tomb and nowhere else.

Impossible, Mike thought. Hot air rose and cold air descended, but this was ridiculous. It sure as hell wasn't cold on the surface, so Mike couldn't even begin to imagine how it got like this.

"Maybe an underground spring runs beneath here," Greengrass said. "Keeps this place naturally cold."

"That would have to be one cold damn spring," Mike said, his breath rising in clouds.

"Look at this," Lowe said.

Mike pivoted and almost slipped.

"Careful," Greengrass said. "This stuff is like ice."

Mike nodded and shuffled to Lowe. Gunny ran his hand over the wall. At first Mike thought he was tracing some of the letters with his hand. But as he got closer, he realized it wasn't writing but a picture.

"What is that?" Greengrass said.

Mike didn't know. A two-dimensional head turned on its side. But it wasn't human. The eyes, narrow slits, had no pupils or irises. No nose, either. The mouth opened in a permanent scream. What looked like a foot without toes stamped its heel down on top of it.

"Got me," Lowe said. "But it doesn't look happy."

Mike's eyes drifted off the weird creature and gazed at the other walls, searching for any other pictures that might shed some light on the mystery. He didn't find anything other than letter after carved letter of the unknown language.

"No dead bodies," Mike said. "You'd think there'd be a skeleton or something in a tomb."

"Not if they already turned to dust," Greengrass said.

Mike shook his head, his whole body shivering. "Doesn't make sense. Walls made out of some material that looks like its flowing water in different lights. A language an archeologist couldn't identify. A picture of some kind of creature getting its head crushed by a foot with no toes. And whatever was in here escaped and sent everyone nearby into a killing rage. I'd like some damn answers instead of more questions."

"Well," Greengrass said, "whatever was down here is gone, and I doubt anyone will ever be able to shed light on what this place was built for."

Mike sighed and walked over to the ladder. "I'm tired and cold."

"Fuckin' A," Lowe said.

They climbed out of the tomb, one after the other, with Mike in the lead. Then they climbed to the surface. It didn't take long for Mike to warm up. Once he did, his thoughts soon turned back to the box in the desert floor.

Something had been down there, Mike thought. *It took a lot of time and energy to build that tomb just to bury it without a purpose or function. So what's the reason?*

"Maybe we're looking at this all wrong," Mike said after a few minutes.

Greengrass stood at the edge of the pit. "How so?"

"Well, we keep calling it a tomb and expected to find a mummy in it. But that place was spotless, like a cleaning crew polished it before we went down there. Even if the bones turned to dust, there should have been dust."

"Not if it was never used," Lowe said.

Greengrass nodded. "Maybe it was supposed to be part of a bigger complex that never got built beyond a certain point. The tomb could have been abandoned after construction stopped."

Mike bit his thumbnail and rolled the idea around his head. It sounded plausible, but there was something there he didn't buy.

"Well, how did the hallucinogen get in there?" Mike said. "Whether it was gas or something else, it had to get in there after it was sealed."

"Right," Greengrass said. "Over time, some kind of gas seeped in through the walls. When the pipe broke the cover, thousands of years of mystery gas escaped."

"That actually sounds pretty reasonable," Lowe said.

Mike, though, only shook his head.

"What?" Greengrass said.

"I don't know," Mike said. "It just doesn't feel right. Every inch of that tomb is meticulously intricate. I don't think anything could get in or out with that cover on. I think it was perfectly sealed."

Greengrass put a hand on Mike's shoulder. "You could wrack your brain for a year trying to figure it out, but the simple solution is usually the right one. Something got in, built up over thousands of years, and then was released when the lid broke."

"What about Henry Prince?" Mike said. "How did he transmit it if it was a gas?"

Greengrass shrugged. "Maybe he had something wrong with his lungs that allowed his body to hold on to traces of the unknown agent. So, when he exhaled, he exposed anyone around him."

Mike rubbed his temples. "That would mean Prince would have to be genetically capable of carrying the substance and immune to its effects. What are the chances of that happening?"

"What are the chances of any of this happening?" Greengrass said.

"No way he was exhaling it. The people up close could be infected that way. But the truck convoy? No fucking way."

"It's a freak occurrence." Greengrass's voice rose a few notches. "Look, I know you want to find the answer; but in this case there isn't one. Got to accept that."

"Yeah." Mike stopped rubbing his temples. "I guess you're right."

"Why don't you go back to the tent and relax. Gunny, see if you can scrounge up a cot for Mr. Hosselkus to rack out on."

"Yes, sir." Lowe walked off toward the other side of site R91.

"Thanks," Mike said.

"No problem. It'll do you some good to get some rest and peace and quiet."

Machine-gun fire echoed in the night. Mike turned toward the familiar sound of an AK-47 discharge. Muzzle flashes lit up the night a couple miles in the distance. The return fire of several M16A4s followed.

Greengrass lifted his radio. "Chief of the Guard, Company Commander, report."

A voice crackled back. "Under fire. Looks like insurgents moving toward the site—"

Down the road, the guard post exploded. A ball of fire shot skyward, illuminating the darkness in shades of orange and yellow. In the brief moment of light, Mike saw dozens of armed insurgents advancing on foot toward them.

"Enemy sighted," Lowe said, a pair of binos pressed to his eyes. "Estimate two dozen on foot, all carrying AKs advancing up the road."

Mike dropped down to one knee and unholstered his Beretta nine millimeter. Around him Marines swarmed, taking up defensive positions. Lowe directed them, setting up firing lines.

Greengrass took position in the center of the site. "Mr. Hosselkus, hang tight." He lifted the radio and barked another command Mike couldn't make out.

A few minutes later, the Humvee pulled up to the site in reverse at full speed, its .50 cal pointing down the road toward the advancing insurgents. The driver slammed on the brakes and sent sand flying all over Mike.

"Stand by to open fire," Greengrass said to the gunner. He turned to Mike. "Get in the car."

"I can take care of myself."

Greengrass smirked. "Yeah, I know. But this won't take long and you don't have body armor. When that .50 cal opens up, these ragheads will run for the hills. Just in case, though, I want you safe."

Mike started to protest when the sound of several shrill whistles filled the night air. He recognized it immediately and jumped to the ground.

"Mortars incoming!" someone shouted.

"Take cover!" Greengrass yelled.

CHAPTER SEVENTEEN

The fully loaded *al-Phirosh* sliced through the waters of the Shatt al-Arab toward the northern Arabian Gulf, the Al Basra Oil Terminal well behind them now. Alwad had been right: a little money to the right person and the oil was pumping in no time. The crew could relax now, knowing it was free of Basra and heading toward South Africa and a paycheck.

Yusuf breathed easy and smiled in the darkened wheelhouse. The Furuno marine radar showed a clear channel ahead with little traffic. Hopefully, it would remain that way.

Port security had not proved a problem. One ship had been detained, and all the others that had set sail had been able to depart without hassle. Yusuf thought maybe port security had been told after the first detainee to let the rest of the traffic go, knowing the cargo on the merchants still represented income for

Iraq. But then the *al-Phirosh* passed port security's base. All their boats sat moored and abandoned.

"They ran away," Yusuf had said at the time.

"Cowards always do," Alwad had said, "no matter the uniform they wear."

Thinking about it now, knowing even the authorities had panicked and abandoned their posts struck at Yusuf's national pride. Although he was glad the *al-Phirosh* had not faced a challenge upon departure, it would have been more comforting to maintain the belief the civil authorities still worked to protect the people rather than fleeing with them in the face of a crisis.

How are we ever going to govern our country if we run away every time there is a problem? Yusuf thought and shook his head.

After dwelling on it a moment longer, Yusuf chased the thoughts and disappointment away and focused on the task at hand. He had to keep a speed of fifteen knots until they entered the gulf. Then they would come up to twenty knots and head for the Strait of Hormuz. It would take a little over a day to clear the Arabian Gulf, and then they would turn southwest for a ten-day transit to South Africa.

Yusuf rubbed his eyes and yawned as he considered the voyage ahead and the long day he had experienced. He would stay in the wheelhouse until they reached the gulf. Then he would turn the watch over to Alwad and try to sleep.

"We need figs," the ship's cook said.

"How many?" Sayid said.

"Just bring a whole box."

Sayid washed his hands, dried them, and walked out of the galley. As he moved through the steam emanating from the scullery to his left, he fanned it away from his face.

"We need figs," Sayid said. "Fetch them."

He had taken the position as cook's assistant because, like everyone on the crew, he needed the money. Unlike everyone else, though, Sayid had a tough time swallowing his pride. A former member of the Republican Guard, Sayid had sunk from a life of authority to one of desperation. He had tried to land a position in the new Iraqi army but had been rejected by the Shiite majority. They said it was because of his ties to the old regime, but Sayid knew it was because he was Sunni. When he applied for the national police, the same thing happened.

"We need rice, Sayid." He walked the length of a passageway and through a door. "Be a good dog and bring a sack up."

Sayid had held several jobs on oil wells and pipelines only to lose them and see the work contracted to foreigners from Russia and China. Those he did not lose to competition, he lost to fear. Once they learned of his past, he was let go. They had to take precautions in case he might be tied to an insurgent group. Cowards, all of them.

Outside the refrigerator, Sayid clenched his fists as thoughts of pummeling the cook raced around his head. Then thoughts of his wife and children took their place. His anger abated. His temper calmed. His fists relaxed.

"You must endure this humiliation," Sayid said. "For them."

Sayid reached out and grabbed the handle and opened the refrigerator. The door swung open and cold air hit his bare arms and face, raising goose-flesh. The contrast to the heat of the kitchen was refreshing.

He stepped in and started looking across the shelves for figs. His eyes passed over an assortment of fruits and vegetables. Milk. Soft drinks and juices.

The figs resided in a small crate under the bottom shelf. Sayid lifted it and turned to leave when he heard what sounded like a marble hit the floor behind him. Then he heard several more, as if a bag of dry beans had spilled from one of the shelves.

Sayid turned and took two quick steps backward. The crate fell from his hands. The figs scattered across the floor.

A corpse sat on the floor, its back against the far wall. The skin and muscle had peeled off the arms and hands and neck. Most of its face was skeletal except the muscles around the cheekbones. The ears had fallen off. Its eyes had dissolved. The teeth dropped from its mouth. He realized the noise he had heard was teeth hitting the floor.

Sayid was transfixed by the sight; he was frozen in place. He knew he had to report it but could not tear his gaze away. It was not the first dead body he had seen, yet he had never seen one in such an alarming state of decomposition.

What happened to this man? Sayid thought. *And how did he end up in here?*

It was then, while he tried to find the ability to break his stare, the body moved. It happened fast, and Sayid had not the time to react. It raised its arms toward him, its skeletal fingers outstretched. Its head turned, and the vacant sockets locked on him.

He tried to scream and run, but something stabbed him. It hit him in the back and ripped up his spine. Sayid collapsed. His brain folded on itself. Every one of his muscles convulsed.

His vision failed and the world went dark. He tried to pray but could not form words.

Then his breathing ceased, and Sayid's grip on his life failed.

On the deck above the refrigerator unit, two stewards swabbing a berthing compartment attacked each other, beating each other with their mops. One cracked the handle across the head of the other and then ran the broken and jagged end into the chest, right of the sternum.

The survivor watched the other man twitch on the ground, blood spreading out below him. He looked around for another to kill, but the compartment was empty.

He gripped the mop handle and yanked it from the corpse's chest. He turned the splintered end toward his face, opened his mouth, and drove it through the back of his head.

On the deck below the refrigerator unit, an engineer dropped his clipboard with tank readings on it and sprinted across the deck plates toward another man taking similar readings. He prepared to launch himself toward the man when his mind suddenly cleared, as if a mysterious dense fog had lifted.

The engineer froze and looked around him, not sure what had happened or where he was. He rubbed his head.

"What just happened?" the other man said, rubbing his head much the same way.

"I do not know."

"Captain."

Yusuf turned from the gyrocompass he had been reading to his second officer. "Yes, Feisal."

"We just received a call from the ship's cook."

"Let me guess: he forgot to order cumin before departing."

Feisal leaned in closer and whispered, "We have a fatality."

Yusuf's back straightened, and he immediately wondered if whatever had broken out in Basra had made it on board. "Where?"

"Refrigerator unit number one. It...it...I do not know how to describe it. What he said is ridiculous."

"What did he say?"

"That there is a human skeleton in the refrigerator."

Yusuf tried to make sense of what he had just heard. "A skeleton?"

"Yes, Captain. The cook has secured the refrigerator and is not letting anyone enter in case it is the same substance that caused the riots in Basra."

"Feisal, you have the deck. I will go down and see this for myself."

"Captain, what if it is contaminated?"

Yusuf shook his head. "I did not hear any reports of people turning to skeletons in Basra. We will take all necessary precautions, but I want to hear the cook's report firsthand."

CHAPTER EIGHTEEN

The first mortar hit the Humvee, turning the armored car into an inferno. The sound of the explosion ruptured Mike's left tympanic membrane, causing temporary deafness. The concussion that followed immediately brought on rapid disorientation and a loss of oxygen. Metal chunks shredded the air over his head. The heat of the flames singed him even though he lay twenty feet away.

The screams of Marines burning alive sounded far away and underwater. Mike ignored them and forced large gulps of smoke-filled air into his lungs. He coughed and puked bile and whiskey.

It took a few seconds for him to regain his bearings. Breathing normally took a little longer. His eyes adjusted to the flame-filled night. He couldn't hear anything with his left ear, and everything coming to the right sounded muffled. What he heard was a firefight.

Mike rolled onto his hip and saw Marines unleashing solid bursts of fire into the night. Lowe walked up and down the firing lines, yelling out orders. The insurgents returned fire. Site R91 was a battlefield.

He yanked his knife from his pocket, flipped the blade, and sliced a small strip from his shirt and then cut it in half. After he wadded the sections, Mike stuffed them as far as he could into his ears and then put the knife away.

Mike held his Beretta close to his chest. To his right he heard dampened screams through breaks in the gunfire. He looked. Greengrass lay on his back, his hands clutching at his stomach. A corpsman knelt beside him, treating the injury.

Another series of mortars exploded all around them, sending sand and shrapnel flying in all directions. More screams cut the night air. Mike's ears rang and the shouts of pain sounded far away.

He pushed up to a crouched position and moved toward the nearest firing line. As he did, he caught movement out of the corner of his eye. He pivoted and dropped to one knee, Beretta extended and both hands ready to fire. Two insurgents moved in fast, sprinting toward the site, trying to outflank the left firing line.

Mike aimed and fired. The nearest one's head rocked back and his body hit the ground. Mike shifted his aim, sighted the second man still running at full speed, and squeezed the trigger. Another head shot.

A mortar exploded close by. The ground shook and Mike fell forward. His left hand braced him, keeping him from hitting the ground. As he did, he saw another insurgent running at full speed, AK-47 firing on full automatic. Mike dropped all the way to the ground, pivoted to a sitting position, and squeezed off three shots in rapid succession. All three shots hit the man in the torso: one in the chest and two in the stomach.

Mike didn't see any more insurgents advancing on the left flank. He turned his attention toward the front line. All the Marines, probably forty in all, unloaded their M16s on what remained of the attackers.

The mortars stopped falling. Mike moved to a kneeling position, the Beretta pointing forward, and waited, scanning from side to side for any more insurgents.

The firefight moved from full-on battle to intermittent firing to silence. The smell of cordite and blood and shit blended together like a quilt that blanketed the desert. Screams and cries and even whimpers saturated the air.

Around him Mike counted several Marines on the ground, dead. Others jerked and yelled as corpsmen treated their wounds. Greengrass lay to one side, his stomach covered in battle dressing.

Mike walked over to Greengrass and knelt beside him. The major was alive but unconscious. An M had been written on his forehead in black marker. He'd been given morphine to kill the pain.

"He's got shrapnel in his stomach," a corpsman said.

Mike turned to him and pulled the wads of shirt from his ears. "Is he going to make it?"

"Should. We've got air evac en route."

"How many dead?"

"Of us? Looks like ten, counting the sentries. Seven more injured. You're bleeding, by the way."

The corpsman pointed at Mike's side. He looked down. Blood seeped through his shirt and ran down his right thigh. He didn't feel any pain until he touched underneath his ribcage and found the wound. He winced.

"You need to get that looked at," the corpsman said.

Mike looked from him to the firing line where Lowe had been commanding the defense.

"Shit," Mike said.

"I said you need treatment."

"Not now, Doc."

"Fine. I got other people to tend to. Excuse me." The corpsman walked off.

Mike stood and walked over to Lowe's body. The gunnery sergeant had a hole through his throat and another wound to his chest. Blood dotted his face. His eyes were closed.

Rubbing his mouth, Mike cursed. He'd just been talking to the guy. Now he was dead, the victim of some random attack.

Mike rose and looked around him. *Some random attack,* he thought.

He heard screaming in Arabic. Mike walked to the noise and found two Marines pointing their rifles at an insurgent squirming on the ground. Blood poured from wounds to the bastard's shoulder, stomach, and leg. A different corpsman stood to the side, ready to treat the injuries; but the Marines held him at bay.

"I need to look to those wounds, or he's going to die," the corpsman said.

"You can fix him when we get some fucking answers," the Marine on the right said.

"Who the fuck are you, Haji?" the Marine on the left said, the barrel of his M16 pressed against the insurgent's forehead.

The guy responded in vowels and cries of pain.

Mike walked to the closest Marine. "Let me talk to him."

"Who the fuck are you?"

"CIA," Mike said. "I can ask him questions you can't."

"Like what?"

Mike pulled out his Spyderco knife and flipped the blade open and looked directly at the insurgent. "All kinds of stuff not subject to the Uniform Code of Military Justice."

The Marine looked at Mike, his knife, and then the insurgent. "Uh, sure. We'll just back up some." He smacked his comrade pressing the barrel against the survivor's head. "Back off, man. This guy's CIA."

The other Marine did as told.

"He's going to die unless I treat him," the corpsman said.

"With that amount of blood loss," Mike said, "I'd say he's going to die even if you do treat him."

The corpsman held up his hands. "I want no part of this."

"Then leave."

The corpsman left. Mike moved forward and squatted in front of the insurgent.

"Who are you?" Mike said in Arabic.

The man didn't speak and refused to make eye contact with Mike.

Mike moved the knife toward him, the blade a few inches from his face. "Who are you?"

"I am no one," the man said.

"You're about to be a dead no one. Why are you here?"

No answer.

Mike took the knife and dug it into the wound in the man's leg. He screamed and wretched.

"Why are you here?"

The insurgent took deep breaths. "To stop you."

"Stop what?"

Again no answer.

Mike pushed the blade deeper into his thigh. "Stop what?"

The man screamed until Mike pulled the blade out. Between rapid breaths the man said, "The prison. We came to stop you from opening the prison."

"The thing in the ground?"

He nodded.

"It's a tomb," Mike said.

"No, it is a prison."

"How did you know this prison had been found?"

"We had a man on the crew of diggers. He reported the progress of the sewer line to us. He was not sure if it would get close to the prison. When he did not report this afternoon, we knew we had to come here in force. The prison cannot be opened."

"Why? What's in the prison you don't want out?"

The insurgent did not answer.

Mike decided to use the truth instead of the knife. "Well, you're too late."

"What?"

"This prison of yours was opened this morning."

The man's eye widened. "Then it is free."

"What is free?"

The man shuddered. "I know not its name, but it is evil, imprisoned in the days before man."

"Imprisoned evil?"

"Yes."

"Bullshit."

"It is true."

"And how do you know this?"

"The knowledge has been passed down from generation to generation." He lifted his shirt, wincing as he did. Tattooed all over his stomach was the same cryptic language carved into the surfaces of the tomb. "I am a Guardian of the Prison. And I have failed. Kill me, please."

"What language is that?"

"It is the language of the Jinn," the man said. "It was written on me as a child as a reminder of my responsibility. Now it is a testament of my failure. Will you kill me?"

Mike looked over his shoulder at the pit and then back to the survivor. "You're telling me that was a prison for a genie?"

The man nodded. "A great demon."

Mike shook his head. *This is ridiculous,* he thought and rose.

As he did, the blood rushed from his head. The world seemed to spin around him. He closed his eyes until the dizziness abated.

The whimpers of the insurgent brought him back to the present. Mike looked the wounds over and then at the amount of blood the guy had lost. He wouldn't last much longer no matter how much treatment he received.

Mike lifted the Beretta and fired two rounds through the insurgent's head, giving him the death he'd requested.

The Marines ran up. One said, "What the fuck? Why'd you do that?"

"Because you couldn't," Mike said.

He turned and tried to walk away. He took a few steps, stumbled, and collapsed in the sand. The world around him blurred before he passed out.

CHAPTER NINETEEN

Jibril, the ship's cook, stood outside the refrigerator, waiting for Yusuf. The large round man paced back and forth, rubbing his hands together. Yusuf wanted to order him to stop but noticed the gooseflesh covering the cook's forearms and bit his tongue. Better to calm him down first.

"Jibril," Yusuf said, "how are you holding up?"

Jibril stopped rubbing his hands together and looked at Yusuf. He smiled but it appeared halfhearted. Then Jibril held up his hands. They shook.

"It is just a skeleton, yes?" Yusuf said.

Jibril nodded. "I am more concerned with what I may now have."

Yusuf nodded. "I see. Well, how do you feel?"

"Dizzy. Short of breath. Nervous."

"Do you feel like all of your skin and muscles are about to fall off?"

Jibril shook his head.

"And has any of your skin or muscles fallen off?"

Jibril shook his head.

"Then I think you will be just fine."

"But what if it takes a while for the symptoms to occur? What if there is an incubation period?"

Yusuf smirked. "You read too many books, Jibril. Besides, if there is the threat of transmission, we all would be in trouble."

"Why? I am the only one who encountered the skeleton."

"Yes, but someone had to put the body in the refrigerator, correct? Which means it was exposed to our spaces and air?"

Jibril shivered and said a prayer.

Yusuf chuckled. "Jibril, have you considered the possibility that there is a rational explanation for this?"

"It is a skeleton, Captain. Someone died and was put in the refrigerator so we would not smell it. What happened in Basra is now happening here."

"Were there reports of people turning to skeletons in Basra?"

Jibril shrugged. "I only heard of the chemical weapons. But there are chemical weapons that can do that to a man."

"Are there? What are they called?"

Jibril looked at the wall as if he would find the answer there. "I do not know. But I am sure there are."

"Ah," Yusuf said and patted Jibril on the shoulder. "Let us examine the facts before we panic. If we panic first, then the crew will panic. And then we will have problems like we saw in Basra."

Jibril nodded.

"So, why did you come down here?" Yusuf asked.

"I sent my assistant Sayid to fetch some figs. When he had not returned after twenty minutes, I decided to look for him so I could kick the shit out of him. When I walked into the refrigerator, I found the crate of figs all over the floor. Then I saw the skeleton."

"And where is Sayid?"

Jibril shrugged. "I have not found him yet. I have people looking, though."

"Shall we go in, then?"

"Captain, it is in there and it is not bothering anyone. Maybe we should just assume it is unsafe. Why not just keep the refrigerator closed? We have other refrigerators to draw food from."

"We need to know who it is," Yusuf said. "If it is a crew member, then we know we have a problem. If it is just a skeleton someone brought on board, then we can relax."

"Relax?"

"Yes, if someone brought it on board, we can breathe easier. I said there is probably a rational explanation."

"That does not sound rational. Why would they do such a thing? And where would they get one?"

"Iraq is full of skeletons. And why people collect grotesque things only Allah knows. Perhaps they thought they could sell it."

Yusuf reached out and gripped the handle and opened the refrigerator. The cold air hit him, and he walked in without hesitation.

Jibril stayed in the passageway.

The first things Yusuf saw were the figs. They dotted the floor everywhere. The crate that had held them had broken upon impact. Then his vision settled on the skeleton, crumpled on the floor, its arms stretched out in front of it. The lower part of the jaw had separated from the rest of the skull and lay to one side. Teeth were strewn about. All around the skeleton was dust of varying shades of brown and red.

This is not a joke, Yusuf thought. The clothes, nothing more than a shroud now, looked familiar. Yusuf squatted and reached toward the pockets of the deceased. Then he hesitated, his hand halfway there.

What if it is infected? he thought. *Well, then you are already doomed.*

Yusuf reached into the pocket and found a wallet. He removed and opened it and found the identification of the corpse. He recognized it as belonging to one of his crew.

"Now we have a problem," Yusuf said.

Semyaza had found an empty fan room to hole up in and rest. The body he now possessed, the one that had belonged to Sayid, was strong, but the soul it had held was not. Semyaza had overpowered it easily and thus would not require much time to recover.

Hopefully, the flesh would hold up longer this time as a result.

As Semyaza studied the memories of the man, he learned why the fight had not lasted long. Sayid had wanted to die. All of it was there, his whole sad life. His struggles, his failures, his total contempt for all those around him. Except for his family. The one thing that had kept him going, even at the end, could not motivate him to fight even a little. Sayid had been broken and Semyaza was better off for it.

In his search for an isolated place to rest, Semyaza had not seen any other dead bodies. He had not heard the sounds of violence. He had not felt the chaos his battle with the soul brought.

I was right, he thought. *The shorter the battle, the less damage to those around me.*

He would hold on to this vessel even longer than the last. And those around him would not kill each other, providing him with an ample supply of bodies until the ship reached its destination.

Yusuf walked out of the refrigerator and closed the door behind him.

"Well?" Jibril said.

"He was a crew member."

Jibril put both hands over his mouth. "Allah, be merciful."

Yusuf started to reassure his cook when an announcement came over the ship's communication circuit.

"Shipmaster, please contact the wheelhouse."

Yusuf put a hand on Jibril's shoulder. "Stay calm. Please."

Jibril nodded.

Satisfied the cook would remain in control of his faculties, Yusuf walked over to the bulkhead across from him and picked up a ship's telephone and dialed the number for the wheelhouse.

"Wheelhouse," a voice said after the third ring.

"This is the captain."

"Please wait, sir, the second officer wants to speak to you."

A moment later, Feisal was on the line. "Captain?"

"Yes, what is it?"

"We have completed our transit of the Shatt al-Arab and entered the northern Arabian Gulf. We have increased our speed to twenty knots per your orders."

"Thank you very much for the report, Feisal. Is there anything else?"

"Yes, Captain." Feisal was silent a moment. "We have found two more bodies."

Yusuf closed his eyes. "Where?"

"Right above refrigerator unit number one, in a crew berthing."

"Skeletons?" Yusuf said.

"No, Captain. They are…whole. They killed each other, according to those who found them."

Yusuf's chest felt tight and his stomach contracted. Was this how it had started in Basra?

"Very well. I will go up and see them. Tell those who found them to remain there."

"Yes, Captain."

Yusuf hung up the phone and turned back to Jibril. "Two more deaths."

Jibril was sweating now. He wiped his forehead and mumbled prayers. Yusuf wanted to do the same, to pray for mercy and beg that what had happened in Basra was not now happening on the *al-Phirosh*. But he could not. As the captain, he had to exude calm and confidence, no matter how scared he was.

"Jibril, I want you to turn over your duties to your steward cook and report to medical."

"I can still perform my duties."

"I know you can. But I want you to get checked out. Just in case. I will as well, once I examine this latest scene above us."

Jibril nodded. "I will turn over my duties. If I show no symptoms, may I return to work?"

"I expect you to."

"Thank you."

Jibril started to walk away when Yusuf reached out and grabbed him by the bicep.

"Do not mention any of this to anyone, understand?"

"They will find out. There will already be rumors."

Yusuf nodded. "Let them speculate for the time being. But if one of the crew confirms anything before I do, we will have panic throughout the ship."

Jibril was quiet for a moment and then said, "I will stay quiet."

"Thank you, Jibril."

Yusuf watched to make sure the cook walked down the passageway and turned a corner toward medical. Then the captain found the nearest ladder and made his way up to the crew berthing with the two dead bodies. As he did, Yusuf managed to squeeze in a short prayer, asking his crew be spared the brutality witnessed in Basra.

CHAPTER TWENTY

Mike stood in the middle of the highway, facing Basra. Greg McDaniel was to his right, hands in his pockets, looking in the same direction. He appeared just as he had when Mike had seen him in the car.

Black smoke rose from the city and turned the sky the color of pitch. Dead bodies lined both sides of the highway leading into Basra. Surrounding them, instead of desert or marshes, was a vast ocean. Now the road seemed more like a bridge to Mike, leading to a mystical island of death.

"You can't kill this one, Mike," Greg said.

"You told me that already."

In the ocean, heads bobbed. Their white eyes, the color of milk, stared at Mike. Their hands rose from beneath the surface and stretched out toward him, but he was far from their reach. Did they want him to help them out of the water or to pull him in?

"I just want you to know what you're going to face." Greg pointed at the Beretta in Mike's shoulder holster. "That won't help you."

"And what am I going to face?" Mike turned from the bobbing heads. "Some obscure chemical weapon? An airborne hallucinogen?"

"A demon." The voice came from Mike's left. He pivoted and found the insurgent he'd killed facing him, two round holes in his forehead. No blood, though. No brains either. Mike saw the ocean through his head.

"Right," Mike said. "A demon. Or was it a genie? And that wasn't really a prison but a bottle, correct? Will he grant me three wishes when I meet him?"

The insurgent smiled. For some reason, it made Mike's heart beat a little faster. There was knowledge in that smile, and it bothered the hell out of him.

"It will kill you." The smile broadened. "And there will be no mercy in it."

Mike looked away, unable to take any more of the smile. "Nonsense."

"Mike," Greg said, "you can't kill this one."

"But it's what I'm good at."

"Don't succumb to vanity."

"It's not something I'm proud of."

"Yet you never fail to embrace it."

Mike said nothing.

"And get a handle on the self-hatred, too. When you face this, you need to control both."

"Stop relying on my skills, and stop thinking about myself. Got it."

"Don't be a smart-ass."

"Anything else, Greg? What about you, Mr. Dead Insurgent?"

"Time to stop feeling guilty, Mike. You can't judge yourself. But you will be judged." The voice of the insurgent had changed. Mike's head snapped to the left. The smiling dead man had been replaced by Gunny Lowe, standing in his cammies, hole through his throat gone.

"You are what you are," Lowe said. "There's a reason for that. Accept responsibility."

Mike shook his head. "You sound like my damn boss."

Lowe jerked his right thumb over his shoulder at the sea of bodies. "All those are yours, Mike. Some you've killed already. Some you're going to kill real soon."

Mike looked past Lowe's shoulder at the water. So many. Impossible.

No way could he kill that number. Then he shifted and looked at the sea on his right. Even more white eyes, all staring at him, hands reaching out.

Don't kill me, those eyes said. Please. The hands didn't want to grab him. They were up, palm out. Stop. They wanted him to stop what he would do to them. What he had done to him.

"You can't listen to them," Lowe said. "Marines kill the enemy to achieve victory. That's what you do, Mike. You kill the bad guys. Accept it because there are many more to come. Take responsibility. There's a difference between just and selfish."

"Accept it, Mike," Greg said. "Because if you can't, you won't survive when you face it."

"You're a killer, Mike," Lowe said. "But you're still a good guy. Remember that. It's how you'll win."

Light shone in Mike's right eye. Then his left. Then he saw blue dots and he blinked and sat up. He found himself in a bed of white linen. Around him were similar beds arranged in several short rows. In them, there were soldiers and Marines with various wounds treated.

"Good morning."

To Mike's left stood a short balding man with a stethoscope hanging around his neck.

"Morning." Mike cleared his throat, trying to forget the dream. "Were you just shining light in my eyes or did I dream that, too?"

The doctor held up a pen light and smiled and then slipped it in his breast pocket. "Just checking your pupils. You're not in shock or anything."

Mike shifted and pain from his side rocketed up his spine. He gritted his teeth and breathed hard.

"Easy there, Mr. Hosselkus. You had to have surgery to remove shrapnel. It's going to smart for a while."

That damn alias. "How bad was it?"

"You got lucky. Other than blood loss, you had no problems. Should be able to move around well enough in a couple of weeks."

"Where am I?"

"Medical Ward at Camp Bucca."

"Where's my stuff?"

"The gun is in the armory. Your clothes were ruined." The doc reached into his pocket and pulled out a cell phone. "But you can have this now."

"Thanks." Mike took the phone. "How long before I can be discharged?"

"Not anytime soon."

"Best case? I need numbers, Doc, or my boss will throw a shit fit."

"Three days. But even then, you should stay in a bed most of the time for ten days, minimum."

Mike shook his head. "I got work to do."

The doc chuckled. "Sure. But how are you going to do it if you can barely move?"

"I guess I'll find out."

The doc motioned to the injured servicemen around them. "I hear similar tough talk like that every day. Don't think you're so special."

Mike shrugged. "Okay."

The doc walked away and Mike turned on the cell phone. There wasn't much of a charge left but enough so he could give Glenn an update. A few moments later, he had his boss on the phone.

"About time you checked in," Glenn said.

"I had a bit of an accident."

"Yeah, I know. Heard all about the firefight at R91."

"How did you find out?"

"I am the eye that never blinks."

Mike chuckled. "Fine. I'll leave it alone."

"How are you feeling?"

"Fucked up." Mike lifted his gown and looked at his injury. The skin on his right side was bruised and swollen, colored purple and blue and pink. A long line of sutures curved from his love handle up to his ribcage. Blood had congealed between the stitches. "I'll be okay to get back on this case in a few days."

"Don't worry about it."

"What?"

"I want you to take it easy and recover."

"What about figuring out what caused all this?"

"It's done. There's nothing for you to do."

"But—"

"Mike, relax. Basra is still under an evacuation order. The military is cleaning it up. The citizens are in refugee camps. The press finally got wind of the situation and are broadcasting from outside Basra twenty-four seven. Showing long-distance shots of piles of bodies. Real family stuff."

"Other outbreaks?"

"None."

Mike flexed his free hand into a fist. "What about the attack at R91?"

"Isolated incident. No survivors among the attackers. But I know you have information."

Mike gritted his teeth. "What do you mean?"

"I heard a report filed by a couple of Marines that some CIA agent tortured and killed one of the insurgents."

Fuck, Mike thought.

"Want to tell me what happened?"

Mike hesitated, thinking about the insurgent, both at R91 and in his dream. "It was crazy talk. The guy said they were attacking to prevent anyone from opening the tomb. They didn't know it had been opened earlier that day. Called themselves 'Guardians of the Prison.'"

"Prison?"

"That's what he said. Said it was a prison that contained unspeakable evil. So, I guess they were supposed to make sure whatever got out and drove everyone crazy stayed inside."

Glenn was quiet on the other end for a moment. "So, did they think there was some kind of evil spirit down there or something?"

"Yeah," Mike said. "Something like that."

"Well, that's just stupid."

"I said it was crazy." Mike remembered how cold the prison had been. The unusual material it had been constructed from. The mysterious writing on its walls and tattooed on the insurgent's body. The dream with Greg and the insurgent and Lowe. The sea of bodies. "The whole thing is crazy."

"What do you mean?"

Mike told him about going down in the prison and all the strange stuff inside it. Glenn didn't interrupt him while he spoke.

After Mike was done, Glenn said, "Well, they believed something was down there and they were right. Whether it was a spirit or a hallucinogenic gas doesn't matter much now. It made it to Basra and hasn't appeared anywhere else. It appears our boy Henry Prince managed to carry it for a short amount of time before it ate him up."

Mike's eyebrows narrowed. "Ate him up?"

"Once they went into Basra to clean up, they found his remains in a truck just outside the city. Coincidentally, it was the exact place the first riot started. All they found was a skeleton."

"Jesus."

"No shit. Whatever it was gobbled him up while it fucked with the heads of anyone around him."

"Wait a minute," Mike said. "They found him on the outskirts of the city, right?"

"Yeah."

"But the murder rampage spread toward the middle of the city."

"Yes, but the deaths stopped there and didn't spread to the rest of Basra."

Mike rubbed his head. "Why did they stop?"

"I guess the stuff wore off. Probably weakened and died after Henry did."

"Yeah, but that doesn't fit the pattern."

"What do you mean?"

"Well, were there any deaths like at R91 between the convoy massacre and the outskirts of Basra?"

Mike heard papers shuffling on the other end.

"No," Glenn said.

"But there are plenty of people between the two?"

"Sure. Lots of car traffic at least."

"So why didn't anyone else between the convoy and the outskirts of Basra go crazy and kill each other?"

Glenn was silent.

"Why did they start killing each other again in Basra only to stop?" Mike said. "At all the other sites of death, every single person was killed and the last man standing killed himself. But in Basra, that didn't happen. They never made it to the last man. Something broke the chain reaction."

"And what was that?"

Mike pinched the bridge of his nose as his head started to ache. There was an answer, an explanation for all this, he just couldn't find it. Or make sense of it. And it sure as hell wasn't a demon.

"I have no idea."

"Well then, I guess there is no answer."

"There is. I know there is."

"Perhaps. But we'll probably never know and need to accept that. If we do find it, it'll be a logical one. And it'll probably be figured out in a lab somewhere far away from Iraq."

Mike's head throbbed. He wanted to know now, but Glenn was right. It would take months, maybe a year or two of investigations, before any scientific answer would be reached.

Unless it was a demon, Mike thought. The supernatural answer was a lot closer and easier to latch on to, if he believed in that kind of shit. But he didn't, so he just smiled and rubbed his temples and blocked out memories of the dream.

"Yeah, you're right," Mike said.

"Of course I am. Now, for what I want you to do…"

"Recover, I got it."

"Yes, and I want you out of Iraq."

Mike leaned his head back and stared at the ceiling, thankful his killing days were done. "Back to Langley?"

"No."

Mike's chest tightened. "If you're not bringing me home, leave me here. At least I know the ground here."

"You're compromised, Mike. I want you out."

"I used the Hosselkus alias. No one knows who I am or what I'm doing here."

"You've interacted with a lot of people, ended up in a battle, got yourself injured. They may not know your name and why you're there, but they know what you look like and that you are there. You're not dwelling in the shadows anymore. So, I want you out."

"This is horseshit, Glenn. Don't move me somewhere else just to be your muscle boy again. Bring me home or let me work this case."

"This isn't open to discussion. When you're healthy enough to travel, I want you on a plane to the military base in Djibouti. There's work for you in the Horn of Africa. Iraq is closed for you now."

The low-battery warning beeped. "Goddamn it, Glenn."

"Love you, too."

The cell phone went dead. Mike looked at it for a moment and then clenched it in his fist.

"Fuck."

CHAPTER TWENTY-ONE

Yusuf smoked the last cigarette in his second pack of the day and stared out the windows of the wheelhouse at a fog-blanketed sea. His hand shook as he took a drag. Then he sipped coffee.

The images of the two dead men in the berthing haunted him. The first man, with the puncture in his chest, had disturbed him; but the second man had shaken him to his core. How had he driven a broken mop handle through the back of his own head? What could impel someone to do something so abominable?

Even now, thinking of it, Yusuf found chills running up and down his back. He shivered and sipped more coffee.

The doctor had only added to the horror of the scene. He had told Yusuf that the force it took to drive the mop handle through a skull in such a short distance was impossible for a man to do to himself. Yet there were his cold dead fingers wrapped around the handle.

"You need sleep, Omar," Alwad said.

Yusuf took another drag off the cigarette. "I tried. I could not shake those images from my head."

"They were just bodies."

"You did not see them." Yusuf's tone cut sharp. He checked it, not wanting to alarm any of the crew in the wheelhouse. "It is not an easy thing to forget."

Alwad held up his hands. "Very well. It still does not change the fact that you need sleep."

"I would rather be here in my chair than alone with my memories."

"I will not argue with you."

"Good. Instead, help me figure a way to tell the crew without causing uproar."

Alwad stood silent. A few moments passed before he said, "The bodies are all in refrigerator unit number one. The men who found them are restricted to medical, along with Jibril. Keeping them isolated has at least stemmed the tidal wave of rumors for now."

"What is your point, Alwad?"

"Maybe we should not say anything at all."

"Say nothing?"

"For now, yes."

Yusuf shook his head. "I have already overheard whispers among the crew up here, wondering why those people are in medical. I even heard one mention a dead body being found."

"Let them talk. They will anyway; even if nothing happened, there would be rumors."

"Yes, rumors about machinery problems or not making our port. This though—"

"Is too fantastic to believe as it is." Alwad lit his own cigarette. "Let them banter about. We will work them hard, keep them so busy that all they will want to do is eat, sleep, and complain. What they will not want to do is push the matter further."

"And why won't they?"

"Because we are continuing on course for our destination. If there were a real problem, we would put into port. If we maintain our voyage plan, the talking will persist, but it will not grow to panic."

Could it be that simple? Yusuf thought. He had his doubts but also did not have a better idea.

"Maybe you are right," Yusuf said.

He had considered pulling into a port. But since the incident in the berthing, no one else had turned up dead. For those who had stuck it out with him in getting underway from Basra, pulling into a port now, well short of their destination and their paycheck, could lead to a riot of outrage.

So Yusuf had decided to stay at sea, to push for the Indian Ocean and hope nothing else happened. And nothing else had happened.

Alwad exhaled slowly. "Do you accept my recommendation?"

"Yes." Yusuf finished his cigarette. "In the meantime, we will keep Feisal searching the ship."

"Very well." Alwad walked over to his chair and lifted a radio to call Feisal.

Shortly after finding the bodies in the berthing, Yusuf had ordered his second officer and two deckhands to search the ship for the cook's assistant named Sayid. He wanted him found and isolated with the others in medical. So far, the search had turned up nothing. Until they found him, Yusuf could only assume he, too, had met some kind of end. Why else would he have not checked back into the kitchen?

Perhaps he saw something, Yusuf thought. *Maybe something else happened in the refrigerator. Something that could make a man drive a stake through his own mouth.*

Yusuf shook his head as if all the paranoia and fear would fall out.

You are worrying too much, Yusuf thought. *Just isolated incidents, nothing more. It has not spread. The surprise of finding a skeleton in the refrigerator scared Sayid into hiding is all. He probably comes from a superstitious sect who thinks the dead can walk. Besides, the crew is still performing its duties. Get to South Africa and be thankful.*

No matter how much he tried to encourage himself, though, Yusuf found he could not avoid glancing at the clock, expecting something new and horrible to occur at any moment. He did not know if he could make it to South Africa. He did not even know if he could make it out of the gulf, and that was only half a day away.

Stop it, he thought. *You must remain calm. The crew needs to see you acting rationally. If anything else happens, we will pull into port. But until then, you must remain in control.*

Yusuf sat up straight in his chair and sipped more coffee. He reached for his logbook and a pen. He had avoided committing the events to permanent history. If he was going to behave normally, he would have to perform his duties. This meant maintaining an accurate log.

After another sip of coffee, Yusuf began his first log entry in regards to the deaths that had occurred on board the *al-Phirosh.*

Semyaza sat in the darkness of the fan room with his legs crossed and his eyes closed. He devoted all his focus and energy to maintaining the vessel. Thus far, the corruption of the flesh had been minimal. Only a few flakes of skin had fallen from his hands. Everything else appeared intact.

"The more things change, the more things stay the same."

Semyaza opened his eyes to find Uriel sitting across from him. He appeared in human form again versus the white mist. His legs were crossed, too, and his hands rested on his knees. Semyaza closed his eyes again, ignoring the seraph.

"This room is small and confined," Uriel said. "Remind you of someplace?"

Semyaza said nothing.

"Do you not see the pattern, Semyaza? Look at you, stuck in a human jail and hiding in a small room, dwelling in darkness, surrounded by the cold of your anger, biding your time."

"I am free." Semyaza opened his eyes.

"Free from what?"

"From your confinement."

"Only for a short time."

"I am mastering this flesh. Soon I will not have to swap bodies."

Uriel shook his head and pointed at the floor. Semyaza looked. More skin had fallen from his hands.

"You can slow the degradation," Uriel said. "But you will never stop it."

"We shall see."

"I already know."

Semyaza closed his eyes again and tried to regain his concentration.

"I thought you hated man," Uriel said. "Hated the so-called privilege given him over us. Yet here you are, a parasite latching on to a man. Do you think this will bring you closer to the Firmament?"

"Man is loved and spoiled—"

"Man fell, Semyaza. Just like you and your comrades. He acted selfishly and fell and is now separated from God, just like you. So perhaps this prison is more appropriate."

"Man is not bound in a prison under the sand for eternity."

"Yes," Uriel said. "You are bound, separated from the Firmament, living under the feet of the species you detest. Yet you still have knowledge of its existence.

Man is separated through his lack of knowledge. He has the choice of whether to believe. And his world is a cold and cruel place as a result. The light is there, but it is surrounded by darkness."

"It is not the same."

"It is."

"You do not understand!" Semyaza's eyes bulged and his hands clenched. "You do not know how it feels! To be unwanted! To be abandoned! How does that feel, Uriel? Tell me. How does it feel to lose everything? To lose the warmth of love and be cast into a pit of indifference? To lose your light?"

"You rejected that love." Uriel opened his hands, palms down toward Semyaza. "But you have the power to change all of that."

Semyaza took a deep breath and closed his eyes. "I am trying."

"Not this way. This is unnecessary. It always has been."

Semyaza said nothing.

"Why are you punished?" Uriel said.

Semyaza did not open his eyes. "Because I took a stand."

"Because you are selfish. Your vanity has led you here."

"I did what I needed to. I do what I must now."

"Then you will remain lost, Semyaza."

Semyaza opened his eyes and found Uriel gone. He looked at his hands and saw more skin had flaked off.

CHAPTER TWENTY-TWO

Mike managed to wrangle up a wheelchair. He talked one of the nurses into bringing him one. Then he had to bribe a few more to help lower him into it. It cost him a few sodas.

His right side ached like a bastard, and it hurt to do everything from laugh to swallow, which made eating dinner while watching old episodes of *The Simpsons* on armed forces television interesting. Fatigue dogged him. He wanted to sleep, but the bed was uncomfortable. Thoughts of the dream and the prison and the battle and the interrogation kept dancing around his head, weaving in and out of each other. Never separate or in chronological order but blended like a putrid soup.

Rather than lie in bed and stare at the ceiling and fail to chase these thoughts away, Mike wheeled around the ward, talking to vets, listening to stories. Anything to pass the time.

In another day he would leave. Even if he had to rest up in a hotel somewhere else, he wanted out of the hospital and away from its stark whiteness and its smell of shit and blood and disinfectant. He hated feeling vulnerable and helpless, and right now he felt both.

"Glad to see you made it out alive."

Mike stopped the wheelchair and twisted to his left. Major Greengrass sat up slightly in bed. He had an IV stuck in his right arm. A bandage covered most of his forehead. Mike couldn't see his stomach under the sheets but assumed they were bandaged, too.

"I'm hanging in there," Mike said. "How about you?"

"Can't complain. What's your damage?"

"Shrapnel in the side. Some blood loss. Nothing to brag about."

"Better than shrapnel in the gut. They had to remove almost a foot of intestine."

Mike shook his head. "At least it wasn't your balls."

Greengrass laughed and then moaned and rubbed his stomach. "Fuck."

"I got that same problem."

"Well, be thankful you don't have to shit in a bag."

"I wish I could shit," Mike said. "I've had gas since waking up and haven't even been able to pinch out a nugget."

Greengrass laughed and moaned again. "Stop that, man."

Mike chuckled but stopped as soon as he felt the stab in his side. "Okay, okay."

Greengrass breathed deeply, like a woman in labor. "God, this sucks."

"What about your forehead?"

"Just a fucking scratch." Greengrass picked at the bandage. "Did you hear about Gunny Lowe?"

Mike nodded. "Yeah, I saw him."

Greengrass nodded. "Fucking savages. What was that attack about?"

Mike thought to tell him what the insurgent had said but decided against it. "Just taking advantage of the situation. They saw the military was distracted with Basra and figured they could wreak havoc on your company."

"So it wasn't the RG?"

"Nope. Just insurgents. Probably thought the RG would reward them, though, for taking the initiative."

"Doesn't make any sense."

You're telling me, Mike thought. "I know."

"Why would they attack a fortified position? These guys are hit-and-run types. They don't go for the straight-up fight."

Mike shrugged.

"And you didn't get anything out of that guy you tortured?" Greengrass said.

Mike rubbed his mouth. "Heard about that, huh?" The image of Lowe from Mike's dream popped up in his head. *"But you're still a good guy, Mike. Remember that. It's how you'll win."*

"So, why'd you kill him? For Lowe?"

Mike blinked and Lowe's image disappeared.

Because he asked me. "For everything. The guy deserved to die."

Greengrass nodded. "Fuckin' A."

Mike looked away for a moment, unable to take Greengrass's gaze of appreciation. "So how long you in here for?"

"Couple of days. They're flying me to Germany. I'll probably stay there another few days for observation before heading back stateside. What about you?"

"Another day then I'm off."

"On your own?"

"Yep."

"Where to?"

Mike lifted his hands and shrugged. "Who's to say?"

Greengrass grinned. "Fucking spooks."

"I'm afraid I have to break this meeting up."

Mike turned and saw a nurse standing with his arms crossed. "Why?

"The major needs rest. Sorry, not my policy."

Mike nodded and turned back to Greengrass. He extended his hand. Greengrass took it in his monster grip.

"Good luck, Major."

"You too." Greengrass shook it. "And thank you for what you did."

Mike squeezed his hand. *It's what I'm good at.* "No problem."

"I hope you find those bad guys."

Images of the dead in the sea, white-eyed and hands extended, flashed in his mind. "I'll always have a job, right?"

"Damn straight."

Mike let go of the hand and backed the wheelchair up. He pivoted it and nodded one more time to Greengrass. Then he pushed away and headed back toward his bed.

CHAPTER TWENTY-THREE

"We have entered the Arabian Sea," Alwad said.

"Praise Allah," Yusuf said.

The *al-Phirosh* had completed its transit of the Arabian Gulf, through the congested waters of the Strait of Hormuz and the Gulf of Oman, ahead of schedule. Though time seemed to drag minute by anxious minute, Yusuf had pushed the tanker hard. Thankfully, the strait had more commercial traffic than military; and so things flowed smoothly.

Now the *al-Phirosh* departed the calm waters of the Gulf of Oman and plowed into the buckling waves of the Arabian Sea. The ship tossed and rocked. The movement brought a smile to Yusuf's face. The rolling seas and steady wind were therapeutic. He felt like a mariner again, having to focus on navigating the ship rather than a manhunt.

"Right fifteen degrees rudder," Yusuf said. "Steady on course two-three-five."

The helmsman turned the bow into the seas. The rocking eased and the ship settled into a gentle pitch-and-yaw motion.

"Feel better?" Alwad said.

Yusuf nodded. "I will be even more relieved once we can see South Africa."

"Patience."

"I think I have shown remarkable patience. Even slept a little."

"But not enough."

The night before had come and gone without further incidents. Yusuf finally relaxed enough to manage a few hours' sleep. Alwad kept the crew actively employed and the rumors remained just that, rumors.

Yusuf lit a cigarette. "If we find Sayid, I might make it a whole night."

"He probably jumped overboard. Jibril informed me the man had emotional problems. If that is true, the discovery of the skeleton may have driven him over the edge."

For some reason, Yusuf took comfort in that thought and hated himself for it. A great fear for sailors is losing a man to the sea. What made it worse was that he'd never thought to search the waters. Instead, he had maintained course and assumed the man had hidden within the skin of the ship. And now, relief flooded him because the idea Sayid had jumped overboard meant he would not have to further worry about the man being a danger to his crew.

"It is possible," Yusuf said, smoke riding his words. "Keep up the search nevertheless."

"For how long?"

Until my guilt subsides. "Not much longer."

"And how long shall we keep the personnel in medical confined?"

Yusuf's confidence had grown with each passing hour of routine operations not interrupted by chaos. Yet his reluctance to free the personnel he kept isolated in medical had not disappeared. He still feared they might cause rumors to blossom into panic. "Not much longer."

"Captain?"

Yusuf turned his attention from the whitecaps on the ocean and the gray sky on the horizon to his left. Feisal now stood next to Alwad, hands at his sides.

"Any luck?" Yusuf said.

"No, Captain. This Sayid is nowhere to be found."

"Very well. Go get some sleep."

"What about the search?"

"I will have Alwad continue it. If Sayid is not found in the next few hours, I will assume he leapt overboard in the Arabian Gulf."

"I have the next watch," Alwad said.

"I will take it."

Alwad shook his head. "Captain, you need sleep."

"We all need sleep. But Feisal needs it more than I. Besides, I love sailing in this kind of weather. So go—sleep."

"Yes, Captain." Feisal turned and left the wheelhouse.

"Are you sure you wish to take my watch?" Alwad said. "I can have the bosun take over the search."

"The bosun needs to keep his people busy. It will not kill me to spend a few more hours up here."

"Very well. I will continue the search." Alwad walked away.

Yusuf watched him leave and then turned back to the horizon. The cobalt sea rose higher and the gray sky grew darker in the distance. He considered sailing around the storm but decided not to. The more direct course through the inclement weather was a better option than avoiding it and adding more time to the voyage.

Besides, according to the radar, it was a small storm. The seas would be more of a problem than the wind and rain. The *al-Phirosh* had a full load of oil. As a result, it sailed squat and heavy and would not roll as it would if empty.

Yusuf would plow through the storm. It brought a smile to his face.

The flesh had completely fallen from Semyaza's fingers. He had stunted the decomposition as much as he could, but like Uriel had predicted, he could not find a way stop it. The skin on his arms and neck had also flaked away, and now the muscle tissue crumbled in small chunks.

He did not quit, however. Semyaza sat cross-legged, his eyes closed, his mind focused on slowing the decay of his vessel. He was convinced he could eventually master the flesh enough to maintain it longer than a few days. Beyond that, he accepted he might never control it completely.

This is no way to exist, he thought. Yet it was still better than living in a box under the desert. At least here he could maintain his freedom even though he had to constantly change vessels. It was a better existence than the cold loneliness of his prison.

"Except I am in a prison," Semyaza said and looked at the bones of his hands. Then he glanced around at the dark, box-like fan room. "Just a different form."

Uriel's words haunted him and Semyaza's anger stirred. None of this was fair. None of it was just.

Semyaza shifted from his sitting position to his knees and bowed his head. "Please end this. I beg you to judge me, to rid me of this curse and let me return to your grace or toss me in the wasteland of Sheol. Give me the Firmament or the Abyss. Whatever your judgment, I will accept it. Just let this futile existence end."

Nothing happened.

"Please, I beg you. End me."

Nothing.

"I do not deserve this suffering!" Semyaza clenched boney fists. "Judge me now!"

Nothing.

Semyaza rocked back and arched his spine and lifted his head toward the ceiling and roared.

Alwad led the three other members of his search party down a ladder onto the upper deck just above the portside engineering spaces. This part of the ship had already been searched once by Feisal earlier, but Alwad wanted to investigate the fan rooms again. There were many small places to hide in them, especially around motor controllers and pumps. If someone had not shone a light in the right place, Sayid could have been easily missed.

As they walked down the port passageway toward the aft of the ship, Alwad heard what sounded like a cocooned lion roar. He froze, as did the other three.

"Did you hear that?" Alwad looked at all of their faces. Their eyes were focused down the passageway, where the sound had originated. They nodded but did not say anything. Alwad watched as thin beads of sweat broke out on their foreheads.

Alwad felt his own forehead and found sweat there as well. His hands trembled. He had not felt fear in years, yet something in that sound shook him. *What could have made such a noise?* he thought.

The roar came again and, this time, louder and closer.

"We should call the captain," one of the men said.

"We should run," said another.

Alwad kept his eyes trained down the passageway. His fingers rubbed together as he thought of what to do next.

Then a door opened twenty feet away and someone stepped out. In the dull light of the passageway, Alwad could not make out who it was. The face was cast in shadow. The body, skinny and gaunt.

The man looked their way and turned, walking toward them.

"Who goes there?" Alwad said, his voice steady even as his stomach rolled over.

The person did not answer and kept walking. The thud of his boots echoed off the metal bulkheads.

Alwad heard the others backing away. His heart hammered and his nerves told him to flee, that something was wrong here. Before he could, the person walked directly under a light and Alwad received a full view of the man's face.

If the horror before him could even be called a man. Alwad saw a skull with hair marching toward them. Pieces of skin hung loosely, flapping back and forth as it walked. The eyes, gone. An ear dangled by a single strand of cartilage.

One of the men screamed. Another ran. Alwad tried to turn and run himself, but as he did, his stomach cramped. His chest tightened. Every muscle fell into spasm. He collapsed on the deck and the world went black. Before he lost hold, he heard feral screams.

Semyaza made quick work of the soul in his new vessel, attacking as he never had before. Though the new vessel's soul had been stronger than the last, it shrunk and fled before his burgeoning power, leaving a trail of fear in its wake. Now he looked through his new eyes.

Two dead men lay at his feet. He stood in blood pouring from head wounds. One of their skulls had been smashed and flattened. The other had both eyeballs ripped out.

His gaze drifted up the dimly lit passageway and found another man on his knees. The man's hands pressed against the wall as if he held it up. His head reared back as though he was prepared to beat it against the steel.

Then the man stopped. He looked around him as if lost. His face slackened and his eyes widened. Blood soaked his hands and dripped from his fingers. He breathed slow and deep.

This was the first time Semyaza had witnessed a survivor of the chaos. They had always been dead if they were within a certain distance. Not this time, though.

The last one kills himself, Semyaza thought. *Except this time. I won too fast.*

And now the man lived, not understanding what had happened or realizing what he had done.

"Alwad?" the man said.

Semyaza reached into the vessel's memory. *Yes,* he thought. *My name is Alwad now.* The first officer on board the *al-Phirosh.*

"Is that you?"

"Yes," Semyaza said, his voice flat.

"What happened?" The man cried and wheezed. He fell to a sitting position and hugged his knees. "What happened?"

So weak, Semyaza thought.

"You killed them," Semyaza said. "Murdered them with your bare hands."

The man shook his head. "No."

"Yes." Semyaza walked toward him. "You did."

"Allah, be merciful." The man bawled into his blood-soaked hands. "I do not remember."

"Mercy? Why should God show you mercy? He does not show me any."

The man looked up at Semyaza who now stood over him. The blood from the man's hands covered his cheeks, giving him the appearance he wept blood. His lips trembled.

"What?"

Semyaza squatted next to him. "We have fallen. God has no time for us. No time to grant mercy or damnation. No time to judge. We are not worthy of it."

"I am crazy."

Semyaza ran his hand through the man's hair. As he did, he thought of Uriel. He thought of his own pleading to God to end his existence and the total disregard he'd received in return. The anger stirred again within. The rage festered.

The man screamed as Semyaza clenched a fistful of hair.

"So I will judge you," Semyaza said.

He grabbed the man's chin with his other hand and bashed his head into the steel wall. Over and over he rammed until he heard the skull crack. The man's body twitched underneath him. Brain matter and blood oozed from several openings where the cranium had split.

Semyaza let the dead man slump over to the deck. He rose and took in his work. The anger did not subside. He glanced at his hands. Around the blood he saw skin already flaking away, falling and drifting to the floor in small amounts.

He did not care.

"Judge me!" Semyaza shouted.

He waved his right hand over the bodies. "Do you want more of this?" Semyaza swept his hand back. "Do you?"

As he swept his hand back and forth, the bodies jerked and moved. Semyaza noticed this and stopped, his arm still extended.

No movement.

He moved it left and right.

The bodies twitched.

What is this? He extended both hands. Nothing happened.

Move, he thought.

Nothing.

He waved his hands back and forth, skin flying off as he did. "Move."

Nothing.

Semyaza closed his eyes. He thought about the bodies. He imagined them standing, moving, walking under his control.

He opened his eyes.

The bodies of the dead men stood in front of him. The heads lolled to one side or the other. Their arms hung limp.

Semyaza could not believe what he saw. What he now knew. *I can control the dead.*

His concentration broken, the bodies fell back to the deck.

"This will take some practice," Semyaza said.

CHAPTER TWENTY-FOUR

"One Beretta M9A1 handgun."

Mike reached through the cage and grabbed his gun from the Marine corporal. "Where's my ammo?"

The corporal passed two fifteen-round clips through the cage. Mike took the first and slipped it into its holster on his belt. The second mag he picked up and walked over to a large red barrel with a narrow mouth, which sat on the other side of the room. It was filled with sand. He pointed the pistol into the mouth and slid the second mag of nine-millimeter rounds into the bottom of the grip and released the slide, chambering the first round. He set the safety and holstered the gun.

Having his gun helped him feel normal again. The hospital had not wanted to discharge him, but Mike hadn't given them a choice. Once the sun rose, Mike had insisted on his release. The doc was good enough to give him a new set of clothes, though: a pair of desert camouflage pants with a black T-shirt.

"This is all you've got?" Mike had asked. He hated the fact he looked like a Blackwater guy again.

"You can always wear the hospital gown," the doctor had said. Then he made Mike sign a stack of forms.

Mike figured he could pick up some better duds in Baghdad. In the meantime, there were more important things to worry about, like getting his stuff back.

"My knife," Mike said as he walked back to the cage.

The corporal passed the Spyderco through the cage in a plastic bag. "I won't ask where the blood stains came from."

"Good."

Mike took the knife from the bag and slipped it into his pocket. He pushed the empty plastic back to the corporal.

"My flask."

The corporal slid it through. "Don't worry; no one drank any."

"That's right, because it was empty last time I checked." Mike slid it into one of the cargo pockets in his pants. "Where's the airfield from here?"

The corporal gave him a rough set of directions. The airstrip was on the other side of Camp Bucca, but within walking distance. Mike had already arranged, with the help of some wounded pilots with connections, a ride on a CH-53 Super Stallion helicopter heading to Baghdad. Once there, he would pick up an air force MAC flight to Djibouti. And then he would eventually get new tasking from Glenn.

"Thanks," Mike said and left the armory.

The walk across Camp Bucca felt longer than it took. The sun was bright and harsh. It still hurt to breathe. His side ached and the pain pills did little to stop the brief but sharp stabs that shot up from his side every time he took a step with his right foot.

Mike limited his breaths to slow deep ones. The dry hot air didn't help. The inside of his mouth tasted like cardboard.

At the airstrip, he saw several stretchers loaded into helicopters, their rotors already spinning. As Mike checked in for his flight, he noticed the manifest for the helo lifting off the ground. Major Greengrass was on it, heading to Baghdad and then Bamberg.

Must have caught an early ticket to Germany, Mike thought. Then he smiled when he read Greengrass's first name. He hadn't realized until that moment that he'd never caught the major's given name. It wasn't really surprising, either. From Mike's experience, most people in the military went either by positional title or surname. What surprised Mike was the actual name: Francis.

"If I ever meet you again, I am going to bust your balls hard."

Mike chuckled, but then a sense of failure overtook him. Greengrass left a wounded warrior, a man who'd done his job and suffered a casualty as a result. There's no shame in that. Mike, however, left Iraq having accomplished nothing other than killing a bunch of people.

That's why I was sent here, Mike thought. *It's what I'm good at.*

He remembered the sea of dead bodies, their white eyes boring into him, pleading for him not to kill them.

"But you're still a good guy. Remember that."

Lowe's words from his dream echoed in his head like a bad song. Mike wished he had a full flask.

He tried to distract himself with other thoughts and ended up reliving the events at R91. The mystery of the tomb or prison or whatever it was. Whatever the hell had escaped it and left a string of death from An Nasiriyah to Basra. The battle. The insurgent.

He had found himself knee-deep in the craziness and had nothing to show for it other than surviving while a bunch of good men died or went home maimed. That and torturing and killing a mad Arab babbling about an escaped demon.

Mike sighed and shook his head and wished he could have a drink. As he reflected on his Iraq experience, he couldn't help but feel, well, low.

"You can't kill this one, Mike."

Mike smirked, remembering Greg's words. *Not from Djibouti I can't,* Mike thought. *But I'm sure I'll be able to kill a few warlords in Somalia for Glenn.*

It's the only reason Glenn would send him to Djibouti. Warlords. Maybe a few al Qaeda operatives based in Somalia or Sudan. Maybe pirates. Can't use

Mike in Iraq, move him to a place where his skill can still be put to work.

"Time to stop feeling guilty, Mike. You can't judge yourself. But you will be judged." Lowe's words, again from the dream. *"You are what you are. There's a reason for that. Accept responsibility."*

Rubbing his forehead, Mike hummed the Rolling Stone's song "Paint It Black." He hoped it would block out the voices. It didn't help.

CHAPTER TWENTY-FIVE

Yusuf sat in his chair, enjoying the seas as the ship cut through the storm. He smoked and sipped coffee and actually relaxed a little. Rain pelted the windows faster than the wipers could clear them. It brought a smile to his face.

On the other side of the wheelhouse, the phone over the messenger's table rang. Yusuf, hoping it was Alwad reporting he had found Sayid, heard the messenger answer it.

"I cannot understand you—slow down," the messenger said.

Yusuf's eyebrows narrowed. He turned in his seat and saw the messenger had his finger in one ear and the phone pressed hard to the other.

"Screams?" the messenger said. "Did you say 'screams'?"

Yusuf jumped out of his chair and walked over. "Who is that?"

The messenger shrugged. "Some engineer. I can barely understand him. He is having trouble breathing or something."

"What was that about 'screams'?"

"He said he heard screams on the port side, aft. That is all I could make out."

Yusuf snatched the phone away. "This is the captain. Who is this?"

"Inhuman screams," the engineer said through desperate gasps for air, not bothering to identify himself.

"Inhuman?" Yusuf said. "Did they sound like an animal?"

"They sounded like nothing I have ever heard before."

The line went dead.

Yusuf hung it up. The phone rang immediately. He reached out and grabbed the messenger's wrist before he could answer it.

"I will take the call. Go and wake the second officer and get him up here right away."

"Yes, sir." The messenger left.

Yusuf answered the phone. "Wheelhouse."

"There is blood everywhere!" a panicked voice yelled.

Yusuf had trouble holding the phone. "Who is this? Where is the blood? Are there bodies?"

"No bodies, just blood. Upper deck aft, port side."

The messenger entered the wheelhouse with Feisal in tow.

"Captain?"

Yusuf held up a finger to give him a minute. He hung up the phone and grabbed a radio. "Ship's bosun, Captain."

The radio crackled. "Bosun, sir."

"Form a security detail. Arm them and meet me on the upper deck, port side forward."

"Sir?"

"Just do it, Bosun. I will explain later."

Yusuf set the radio down and turned to Feisal. "You have the deck. Maintain course and speed and stand by for further orders from me via radio."

"What is happening, Captain?"

"I do not know." Yusuf hesitated a moment, running through scenarios in his head. "Have medical prepare for multiple casualties."

"Casualties?"

Yusuf saw the nervousness in Feisal's eyes. He reached out and grabbed his right bicep. "Keep it steady. This is all a precaution."

"This is not like Basra, is it?"

"I do not know yet."

Feisal mumbled a prayer.

"You have the deck, Feisal. Are you able to handle it?"

Feisal nodded. "Yes, Captain."

"Very good."

Yusuf turned to the messenger. "Sound the general alarm."

"Yes, sir."

The messenger passed the word throughout the ship and sounded the alarm, signaling the crew to report to their emergency stations.

As Yusuf grabbed his radio and headed for the door, Feisal said, "What about Alwad?"

Yusuf halted. "I do not know where he is. He has not reported."

"I will radio you when he does."

Yusuf nodded and left.

He descended ladder after ladder on the port side as fast as he could without falling. The *al-Phirosh* weathered the storm well, but the seas still tossed the ship enough to make running down ladders and passageways difficult. Normally, Yusuf would not condone such recklessness; but this was not a normal time.

Throughout the ship, crewmen ran to their damage control stations: manning up firefighting and dewatering equipment, preparing wooden and metal shoring for any hull damage, and breaking out pipe patches and welding equipment. Yusuf did not know what he was dealing with but wanted his crew prepared and alert. The general alarm was the quickest way to achieve both.

Yusuf jumped the last couple of steps to the deck. The metal surface had zero give and sent shocks of pain vibrating up his shins, through his knees, and into his thighs. Yusuf cursed and, pushing the discomfort aside, swam through several crewmen sprinting to their stations.

Over the ship's intercom rang the alarm in loud monotone bursts that reverberated off the steel bulkheads. The noise, along with the shouting of personnel, pierced his ears.

Everything happened fast, not in a blur but like a movie where frames have been removed, skipping a few seconds ahead over and over. Flashes of people in mad rushes. Images of equipment moving from hands to hands. Broken words spoken over each other. It was like this until Yusuf reached the upper deck port side.

Then time returned to normal and Yusuf caught up with himself. It was quiet. Nothing moved. There were no damage control stations on this deck. He had tuned out the general alarm and the pounding of feet above and listened and tried to make anything out in the dull light of the passageway beyond.

A few minutes later, Yusuf heard feet hammering down the ladder behind him. He turned and saw the ship's bosun and his makeshift security detachment of four personnel. Two carried the Kalashnikovs, and the others held Glock 22 pistols.

"Captain," the bosun, a large man named Mahmoud, said, "what is going on?"

Yusuf still breathed fast from his hurried race down from the wheelhouse. "I do not know."

Mahmoud stepped forward, away from the other men, and whispered, "Then why are we here? Why is the whole ship at their emergency stations?"

"There was a report of…violence at the aft end of this passageway."

"Violence?"

Yusuf did not know how to explain the fear in the voices of those who had called the wheelhouse and made the reports. "I believe it may be something similar to what happened in Basra."

"Why would you say that? Do you have proof?"

Yusuf wanted to avoid any mention of the other incidents. "I am just being cautious. If it is something similar, the crew will be better able to respond if they are at their stations."

Mahmoud held up his Glock. "And these? What are the men at their stations going to do if they need one, too?"

Yusuf looked away. "I do not think we will need those. But having an armed security detachment is prudent in case of a riot." He looked back to Mahmoud. "It is all just precautionary."

Mahmoud took a deep breath and looked at the bulkhead. He seemed to be thinking, probably deciding if he should follow his captain. And Yusuf could not blame him. After all, the whole ship had been sent to their stations without any reason given. Usually by now, Yusuf would have gotten on the ship's intercom and given an explanation, whether it be fire, flooding, or just a drill. In this case, though, there was nothing to give other than the truth. Well, the truth as far as Yusuf knew it. But that would be more hazardous than what might lay at the end of the passageway. If he told anyone else what might really be happening, the control and discipline would break down into panic.

"All right, Captain," Mahmoud said, "let us go down there and see what this violence is. But if it is anything like Basra, I would recommend leaving quickly and securing this part of the ship to all traffic."

Yusuf nodded. It was a good idea. "Very well."

"Anyone have a flashlight?" Mahmoud said to everyone. No one answered. "Wonderful."

Mahmoud gestured for the two men with the Kalashnikovs to take position in front and lead the way. Yusuf walked behind them with Mahmoud. The other two men with Glocks took up the rear.

They moved slowly. The dim lighting did not reveal much, and they saw no more than a few feet in front of them at any given time. The general alarm had been silenced. The ship was dead quiet except for the creaking of the hull as it pitched and yawed in the stormy seas.

The sounds of footsteps on the decks above had ceased. Everyone had reached their stations except the security detail. Their footfalls down the passageway were light but still echoed off the rusted steel. Yusuf heard his heart beating.

A minute passed before they saw the first traces of blood. The two men in front halted and they spoke in loud, fearful voices. Mahmoud moved to them and exchanged words, ordering them to stay calm. Then he walked back to Yusuf.

"Blood," Mahmoud said. "Droplets on the deck. Smears on the bulkheads. Not much but enough to scare the men."

Yusuf wiped his mouth. Sweat had broken out all over his face. His lips were dry.

"Bodies?" Yusuf said as quietly as he could.

Mahmoud shook his head.

"Then we must press forward."

"Captain?"

"What if someone is injured? We cannot just turn and leave because blood is on the walls. If someone is injured, we must investigate."

Mahmoud nodded. "Of course."

The party resumed its movement, careful not to step in the blood. Yusuf observed the droplets on the deck. The smears on the bulkhead looked like they'd come from a hand.

Perhaps the man is injured and holding his wound, Yusuf thought. *He probably needed to place his hand on the bulkhead for balance, to keep from falling over in the rough seas.*

They had advanced only a few more feet when one of the men in front screamed. This time Mahmoud ran forward, his Glock ready. Yusuf did not wait for him to walk back and report. Instead, he rushed ahead, too, and slipped and fell.

Yusuf's back and buttocks hit the deck at the same time. His head thunked a split second later. His teeth snapped together from the force of the impact. Green specks of light filled his vision. The wind in his lungs escaped and was hard to replace.

More screams echoed around him. Yusuf blinked away the green specks and sat up, his whole spinal column feeling as if it had been hit with a sledgehammer. In front of him, he saw Mahmoud squatting over a lake of blood and chunks of tissue. One of the men with the Kalashnikovs leaned against the bulkhead, crying. The other tried to calm him down. The two men with Glocks still stood behind him, unwilling to move forward.

Yusuf pushed up to his feet and walked forward to Mahmoud.

"We need to leave here and secure this deck," Mahmoud said.

Yusuf's eyes moved over the gore around them. Blood and brain tissue covered the deck and bulkheads. "My God, what happened here?"

"I do not know and do not want to stay here and find out."

"Where are the bodies?"

Before Mahmoud could respond, a scraping sound drifted up the passageway.

"What is that?" Mahmoud said, his Glock pointing down the passageway into the darkness.

Yusuf squinted, hoping it would help him see better in the dim light. It did. He saw something down there. Moving. Not one person, but a group. It looked like they took up the whole width of the passageway. The scraping sound grew louder as it approached.

Mahmoud stepped backward. Yusuf looked at him and then back to the mass coming toward them. Now, though, he could distinguish more. Arms and legs and torsos of three individuals walking shoulder to shoulder.

Yusuf felt the first waves of relief until the three passed under a florescent light. Blood covered their faces like masks. Their heads had been cracked open in places and flattened in others. Pieces of brain oozed out of the crevices.

He wanted to say something. His voice made noises. His throat contracted and narrowed. His lips formed the shape needed to utter a series of syllables. Yet the only thing that escaped Yusuf's mouth were a bunch of phonemes in no discernable order.

Gunfire erupted next to him and made Yusuf temporarily deaf in his left ear. Both of his hands shot up to cover his ears as he watched Mahmoud fire three rounds into the body farthest to the left. All three rounds hit the man, tearing through his chest. Pieces of skin and bone puffed out in a debris cloud. The man kept coming.

Now Yusuf took a step back. The man with the Kalashnikov who had been trying to calm his comrade down stepped forward and opened fire.

The thunder of gunfire was amplified by the steel passageway. The dull light was overtaken by the bright burst of flames erupting from barrels. The men with Glocks stepped forward and fired. Even with his hands covering his ears, Yusuf could barely take the noise.

The three men kept walking toward them, even as parts of their bodies were severed by bullets. Arms fell to the deck. Pieces of skull and torso disappeared in clouds of flesh. Legs got shot out from under two.

They hit the ground but clawed forward, their hands pulling them through the lake of blood.

"We need to leave here now!" Mahmoud yelled.

Yusuf barely heard him but made out enough to understand what he said. He could not agree more.

"Yes," Yusuf yelled over the continuous gunfire. "Run!"

The man who had been crying was already gone. Yusuf watched the two men with Glocks flee as well. The man with the Kalashnikov stayed steady, reloading and opening fire once again. Yusuf checked the status of the three bodies. All of them were on their bellies crawling toward them like snakes.

"Allah, be merciful," Yusuf said.

Down the passageway beyond the crawlers, Yusuf saw another man, this one standing and walking toward them. He could not make out a face, but its arms were stretched out in front of it.

As it grew closer, Yusuf could make out more. He still could not discern a face, but looking at the clothing and stature of the person, he knew who it was.

"Alwad," Yusuf said. Which meant the three dead men crawling toward them had been his search party.

Alwad stepped underneath a light and Yusuf received a clear view of his face: the nose was gone; the eye sockets were empty black voids; what skin remained around his cheeks hung in flaps. Then he noticed the smile. The lips had fallen off, revealing a permanent toothy grin.

Mahmoud fired down into the bodies, only a few feet away now. The action broke Yusuf's fixation on Alwad. He turned and ran, not looking behind him once.

At the top of the ladder on the deck above, Yusuf slammed the watertight door shut as the last man ran through. He latched it closed and posted a watch on it until chains could be wrapped around it and locked.

Mahmoud breathed heavily. "What in God's name just happened?"

Yusuf shook his head. "I have no idea."

"That was Alwad!"

"*Was* Alwad," Yusuf said. "We cannot consider it him any longer."

"Then what do we consider it?"

Yusuf, still able to hear only out of his right ear, ran both hands through his sweat-soaked hair. "The living dead."

Mahmoud spat to avert evil. "The hell you say."

"You saw what I saw, Mahmoud. How many bullets were put into those three? And yet they kept coming, as if nothing would stop them."

Mahmoud closed his eyes. "We are doomed."

"No, we are not."

"We cannot tell the crew. They will tear each other to pieces to get off the ship."

Yusuf nodded. "And we cannot pull into port. It could spread back to the shore."

"Just like Basra."

"Just like Basra." Yusuf reached into his pocket and fished out a cigarette and lit it. He took a long, slow drag. "We may have to abandon ship."

"And what happens to the ship that discovers the *al-Phirosh* and decides to board her? Do we leave a possibly infected vessel for them to enter?"

Yusuf shook his head. "We have no idea what we are dealing with but know we cannot allow this to go any further. Whatever happened in Basra is now happening here. How would it look if we perpetuated it by exposing others?"

"Then what do we do?"

Yusuf closed his eyes. He knew but could not believe it was the only option. He also knew the longer he waited, the more crew members would be killed. Whatever had crept aboard the *al-Phirosh* had led to the deaths of at least eight crew members since setting sail. What had happened to Alwad had probably happened to Sayid. And probably the poor man found in the refrigerator.

The refrigerator. Was that ground zero for all of this? It had to be. Yusuf looked at his own hand as if skin would fall off at any moment.

The skeleton, the member of his crew who had somehow decomposed in a few short hours. It could all be traced to him. Sayid's disappearance. The two men dead in the berthing above. And now this. It had spread slowly, allowing Yusuf to fool himself into thinking it was just an isolated event.

You idiot, Yusuf thought. *You have signed the death sentence of your crew. All because of greed.*

Then I must save as many as I can. And not let this spread any further.

"Mahmoud," Yusuf said, "take your team and finish securing the passageway. I need to go back to the wheelhouse and start making preparations."

"Preparations for what?"

Yusuf dropped the cigarette on the deck and crushed it with the toe of his boot, exhaling smoke. "To scuttle the ship."

CHAPTER TWENTY-SIX

Mike sat in a bar in Baghdad's old coalition-protected Green Zone, nursing his fifth glass of Johnnie Walker while he waited for his MAC flight. He still had a couple of hours to kill.

He hadn't headed straight for the bar. First, Mike stopped and bought a decent pair of pants, a couple of shirts, and a windbreaker. He also bought a small travel bag and loaded up on socks and underwear. Then he headed for the bar.

"You look like a man who has a lot on his mind," the bartender said in English with a thick Iraqi accent.

Mike smirked. "You could say that."

"As a bartender I have discovered I must also be a part-time therapist. Especially in this part of the city."

"I don't doubt it." Mike polished off the rest of his glass and signaled for another. The bartender dutifully filled it. "How is it Muslims can be bartenders? I thought you couldn't touch alcohol."

"Simple really. What I serve I do not drink, and what I get on my hands I wash off."

Mike nodded and sipped from the fresh glass. "Makes sense."

"So, do you need someone to talk to?"

"Can't. Not allowed."

The bartender nodded. "I see. Perhaps you should talk to a priest."

"You need to be sorry to receive absolution, not guilty."

"So you are stuck keeping it all inside?"

Mike nodded and held up his glass. "Johnnie helps, though."

"Of course."

Mike's cell phone rang. "Excuse me."

The bartender bowed his head and moved on to another customer.

"Hello?" Mike said.

"It's Glenn."

"Hey."

"You out of Iraq yet?"

"No. I'm in Baghdad waiting for my flight."

"How's the injury?"

Hurts. "Better. Still smarts."

"Are you drinking?"

Mike's hand holding the glass froze halfway to his mouth. "Yeah."

"Don't fall into a shame spiral on me, Mike."

"Have I ever before?"

"There's a first time for everything."

Mike took a sip and set the glass down. "It's a switch, Glenn. Always has been. I can flip it on or off anytime I want."

Glenn didn't say anything for a few seconds. "All I'm saying is you've dealt with a lot of strange shit lately and haven't had anything to show for it. Don't let it get the better of you."

"I won't." *Because I'm still a good guy,* he thought.

"Good. I need you frosty. I've got lots of work for you to do in the Horn."

Translation: I've got lots of people for you to kill. "Got it."

"Call me when you get to Djibouti."

The line went dead. Mike slid the cell phone back in his pocket. Then he stared at his glass of whiskey and wondered if he should leave it.

Just walk away, Mike thought. *You've had enough.*

Then Mike thought about Greg McDaniel blown to bits by a suicide bomb. He thought about Lowe, mowed down by crazies in the desert. He thought of Major Greengrass, heading home, shitting out of a hole in his side into a plastic bag. And he thought about all the dead in Basra. Mike shook his head and grabbed the glass and knocked back what was left.

The drinks had managed to keep the thoughts at bay since getting to Baghdad. Now, though, they flooded in like a damn tsunami. The images of dreams rode with them. The bodies in the sea. The smiling insurgent with the two holes in his head. The lone highway leading to Basra. Leading to death.

Mike pinched the bridge of his nose. A skull splitter was brewing. He could already feel it fermenting behind his eyeballs.

"I'm still a good guy," Mike said, barely whispering. "It's how I'll win. I am what I am. Accept it. There's a difference between just and selfish."

"Did you say something?"

Mike released his nose. The bartender stood across from him again, smiling.

"One more for the road." Mike reached into his jacket and pulled out his empty flask. "And fill this for me."

CHAPTER TWENTY-SEVEN

Semyaza needed a new body immediately. Controlling the dead had forced him to relinquish his focus on preserving his vessel. As a result, the deterioration of it had actually multiplied compared to the first one, Henry Prince. In less than an hour, all the skin and muscle had eroded up to the shoulders. He couldn't see his face but knew the eyes had dissolved and ears had fallen off, as had the nose.

Not much time, Semyaza thought. He stepped over the bodies and walked toward a closed door. Controlling them had been fascinating but not worth it. The men with guns had all escaped and had left him with a near worthless vessel. In addition, moving the dead required Semyaza to extend part of himself into each body, to branch out. The experience left him exhausted, as if he had been stretched over an infinite distance.

The door would not budge under his grasp. He moved farther down the passageway to another. Again, it would not move.

Semyaza walked up a ladder to yet another door. Like the previous two, the handle would not pivot.

They have locked me in. They are not as dumb as they look.

For the first time since escaping the prison, Semyaza felt the initial inkling of desperation. If he did not indwell in another body soon…

He heard something move on the other side of the door. A rattle of some kind. It was brief, but Semyaza had no problems discerning it. He leaned forward and sniffed.

Man. He smelled a man separated from him by a few inches of steel.

A vessel.

But can I penetrate this steel and possess him fast enough?

Then he noticed more skin and muscle falling from underneath his pants legs to the deck.

I do not have a choice, he thought.

Yusuf had kept the crew of the *al-Phirosh* at their emergency stations, explaining over the ship's main communication circuit there had been reports of pirates operating off the Omani coast. It was not the best lie but one that would afford him some time. Then he assembled his senior ranking officers in the wheelhouse.

He looked over their concerned faces, taking quick drags of his cigarette as he did. *How do I tell them?* he thought.

"Captain," Jibril said, "where is Alwad? Will he be here for this?"

Yusuf had not seen Jibril since confining him to medical. Now, he thanked him internally for providing a way to start.

"No, Jibril, he will not." Yusuf stubbed out the cigarette in an ashtray by his chair. "It is why I have asked you all here."

He told his crew everything, from the skeleton in the refrigerator to the dead men in the berthing to the demise of Alwad and his search party. Eyes widened and heads shook and hands fidgeted as he informed the leadership of what he considered their only option remaining. The only people who nodded in agreement were Mahmoud and Jibril.

Yusuf had decided to allow those confined in medical free to return to their duties. He did not see the point anymore with what had happened to Alwad. Plus, having Jibril and Mahmoud, two witnesses to the horrors, up there to corroborate his story helped Yusuf's confidence. For his crew to execute what he asked of them, Yusuf needed the leadership behind him. He needed to sell them on what he recommended. And having two senior leaders in his corner, right from the beginning, was a major advantage.

After Yusuf finished, silence greeted him.

"Does anyone have anything to say?" Yusuf said after a few more moments of silence.

"Captain," the chief engineer said. "This is insanity."

"You have not seen what we have seen," Mahmoud said. "The captain is being truthful."

"But sink the ship," the chief engineer said. "There must be a better solution. That is a last resort you are speaking of."

"Exactly," Yusuf said. "Even if we successfully lock it down in the lower decks, it will have to be dealt with sooner or later. Would you risk releasing it in another populated area like Basra?"

"I do not even know what *it* is, Captain," the chief engineer said. "What it sounds like is something causing people to hallucinate."

"So Mahmoud, myself, and the others down there imagined all this? We all saw the exact same hallucination?"

The chief engineer started to say something else, but Yusuf cut him off, his anger rising. "Perhaps a hallucination is responsible for the death of Alwad and his search party. Tell me how a dream can smash in a person's skull."

The chief engineer lowered his eyes toward the deck.

"We saw three dead men walking toward us," Mahmoud said. "We saw Alwad moving freely, most of his face gone, his hands mere bone. Jibril found the skeleton of a man who had decomposed within a few hours of setting sail. There is something greater going on here than any one of us can imagine."

"I tried to treat this whole situation logically," Yusuf said. "Ever since leaving Basra, I have rationalized everything that has happened. But those dead men walking toward us betrayed all logic. And I will not let this go any further. We fled Basra. I will not be responsible for starting another one."

"How will we explain this?" the chief engineer said. "Millions of dollars of oil and property sunk because of, what, something supernatural?"

Yusuf nodded. "Sure."

"They will arrest us."

"They will arrest me," Yusuf said. "The captain takes full responsibility. It will be logged. And you know what? It is a small price to pay considering the alternative."

Everyone was silent. Yusuf looked every individual over. They were all visibly nervous. So was he.

"Very well," Yusuf said. "You know my plan as I see it. Will it work?"

The chief engineer nodded. "Yes, it will. It will take some time, but it will sink the ship."

"Then let us get to work."

Fahad sat up to the sounds of gunfire and death. The pain that had torn at his insides ceased. The tightness of his chest eased. And the vision he had lost returned. He did not know what had happened. One moment, he had guarded the locked door as the ship's bosun had ordered. The next, everything had gone dark and the pain had attacked. He had dropped to the deck, every muscle twitching; and for a few seconds, Fahad had prayed for death.

Now, as he took in his surroundings, he began to pray again. Three dead bodies dotted the passageway around him. Blood covered the floor and bulkheads. Around a corner echoed screams followed by the unmistakable sound of an automatic weapon. He looked to his sides for his gun. Gone. Someone had picked up the Kalashnikov.

And that someone was using it.

Fahad pushed up to his feet. His head spun and he braced against the bulkhead to prevent himself from falling down. Then his stomach turned over and he leaned forward and vomited blood and tissue all over the side of the wall.

More screams and gunfire.

Fahad looked from his vomit to the end of the passageway, where the screams originated. He wiped his mouth with his wrist and backed away, not wanting to know or see what happened around the corner.

As he took a few steps in the opposite direction, primal yells from the other end of the passageway assaulted his ears. Fahad froze and listened as the yells became cries and shrieks. Then he heard thumping, like a rubber mallet striking a hollow well.

Fahad wretched and vomited again. More blood and tissue. His throat burned and his breaths came harder. He was surrounded by a symphony of death and he did not know what to do.

His hands shook and his knees buckled. The dizziness combined with fatigue sapped what strength he had left. Kneeling, his hands moved from the bulkhead to the deck as more blood and tissue forced its way out from within.

Through his heaves, Fahad heard footsteps. He looked up and saw two men with their arms wrapped around each other, backpedaling into the passageway. Their mouths snapped at each other. One bit the other's neck and tore. Blood gushed from the wound.

Fahad stared in disgust as he watched the one man sink his teeth back into the neck wound and tear and tear and tear. Then Fahad scrambled to his feet as fast as he could and tried to run away.

Yet everywhere he went, there was blood. Around the corner, one man stomped the head of another into the deck. Further down, he found an engineer slamming a door on the face of a now unidentifiable comrade. Up a ladder, his friend Nazir beat a crewman with a fire extinguisher.

"Nazir," Fahad said, his voice trembling. "Nazir, stop."

But Nazir paid no attention to him, as if he could not hear him, as if Fahad did not even exist.

Then Fahad saw his friend's eyes. They were wide and glassed over, completely locked on the destruction of the man below him.

Fahad hurried away, not able to watch anymore. But every corner he turned, every door he passed through, and every passageway he looked down, a fresh scene of murder greeted him. He could not move more than a few feet now without stepping through blood. And the vomiting grew worse. Every minute or so, he had to stop and heave.

"What is happening?" he said and ran down another passageway. He did not know where to go or what was happening. He just had to get away from all the death. Unfortunately, everywhere he went, death waited.

Yusuf was finalizing the plans with his leadership when the report came.

"Gunfire, port side aft near engineering."

His heart sank and his stomach contracted. He had failed to stay ahead of whatever it was. Before he could lament further, more reports came in. Not just gunfire. Reports of screams, lots of screams on multiple decks. All aft at first. But then moving up a deck. Then forward. Then up another deck.

It's spreading, Yusuf thought.

"I need to get to my engineering plant," the chief engineer said.

"No," Yusuf said. "Radio down to the machinery spaces to secure to all outside personnel. But you will stay here."

"What?"

"If this is spreading, you may get stuck while trying to reach your spaces," Yusuf said. "All of you will remain here. No one moves." Yusuf turned to Mahmoud. "Contact spaces above, below, and around the last areas of reported violence within a few frames. We will track its movement via sound."

"We need a visual report," the chief engineer said.

"No," Yusuf said. "Proximity is the key. Wherever this thing goes, violence follows."

"How do you know?"

"Because the incidents are always isolated to a specific area. Whatever happened in the refrigerator the first time affected two men in the berthing directly above. If it did not relate to proximity, the whole ship, including us, would be experiencing...the sickness, so to speak. A visual report puts a person too close to it."

"Just like Basra," Mahmoud said.

"What?" Jibril said.

"Basra did not erupt. The riots spread from one location to another. It created a very specific path of destruction. Then it just stopped."

"How do you know these details?"

Mahmoud shrugged. "I listened to the port security radio band. They were broadcasting on public frequencies until they switched over to their secure ones."

"So the Americans lied," the chief engineer said. "They told us it was a chemical attack."

Yusuf held up a calming hand. "I do not think they knew what they were dealing with. They probably still do not. We know it was not a chemical attack only because of what we saw down there. And now it is spreading. But if it is like Basra, hopefully it will stop soon."

"And then what?"

"And then we take advantage of what little time we are granted and sink this ship."

As more blood and tissue and bile rose from his gullet, Fahad's vision failed again; and he was tossed back into darkness. He collapsed to the deck but felt no pain. Everything seemed to drift, like a small boat on the sea. He could not hear anything anymore. All the screams and other sounds of death faded away. The stench of blood and vomit dissipated.

Fahad's grip on life and the earthly realm lessened and lessened. The more he released, the better everything felt. And then he surrendered completely and found peace.

The people they could reach in spaces about five frames from the most recent report of screams and gunfire and other violence said they no longer heard anything. It had once sounded like all-out war, but then it just stopped. And they had not heard even a rat move since.

Yusuf wanted to allow another twenty minutes or so to pass before he would permit anyone to move from their stations. He needed to avoid sending his people into the heart of a possible reflash. Yet he also knew he could not wait forever. Time was against them. If they were to sink the ship, they had to start now in case violence did break out again. And all indications said it would. It was just a matter of when.

Twenty minutes came and went. Yusuf smoked three cigarettes as he watched the clock. Then, when his deadline passed, he stubbed his cigarette out and turned to his senior leadership.

"It is time," Yusuf said. "Mahmoud, take your people and investigate the locations in the reports. Do not get too close. Then secure those areas as you clear them. Once done, prepare for the order to abandon ship. Everyone else, proceed as planned."

They all nodded and left the wheelhouse with determined eyes. Yusuf knew his people did not like this solution, but once it had been decided, they would execute the task like the professionals they were.

Before the chief engineer left the wheelhouse, he turned to Yusuf. "Once the water intrudes the engines and generators, there will be no restarting them."

Yusuf nodded. "Understood."

The chief engineer left to commence his tasking. Yusuf watched him and prayed the remainder of his crew would escape safely.

Semyaza had no idea what it felt like to die but imagined it was very close to what he experienced now. Every part of his being felt as if it had been set on fire and extinguished with acid. The battle with the soul had almost destroyed him. Now he had wounds to heal.

He did not bother to dive into the memories of his new vessel or take in his surroundings. He located a door, opened it, and discovered a small space full of cleaning equipment on the other side. He crawled in and shut the door and focused on recovering his strength and slowing the decomposition.

CHAPTER TWENTY-EIGHT

Mike stepped off the plane at Camp Lemonier and was welcomed by the blistering heat of Djibouti. After grabbing his bag, he found a ground crewman and asked for directions to the officers' quarters building.

Twenty minutes later, he had a room. It was small, but the bed was soft and the shower inviting. He took a quick cold one to rinse off the sweat and grime that came with flying in the back of a military C-130. Then he pulled on a pair of khaki pants and a green polo shirt. He slid his shoulder holster on and eased into his windbreaker and headed out.

At the check-in desk, Mike said, "Is there an officers' club on this base?"

The quarterdeck watch, an army sergeant, nodded. "Here's a map."

He pulled out a photocopied map of the base and circled where they were. Then he drew another circle around the O-Club.

"About a five-minute walk."

"Thanks." Mike took the map and headed out.

He found the officers' club without problem. It, like the officers' quarters, was one of many new structures built on the old French Foreign Legion base. When the US Marines and Navy had moved in back in 2002, they'd found a base that had not been used since the legion had left years before. The concrete buildings had been hollowed out. The pool had been used as a trash dump. The infrastructure had been crumbling.

Now, though, the base thrived as the central headquarters for the DOD's young Africa Command. New buildings had risen, new had been streets paved; and other modern Western amenities had been imported, including enlisted and officers' clubs. All thanks to the navy's Construction Battalion and a bunch of civilian contractors.

At the club, Mike flashed the identification card for Jeremiah Hosselkus to a civilian sentry outside. The man barely glanced at it and waved him in. Mike nodded and thanked him.

A narrow room designed to resemble a British pub in North Africa circa 1937 greeted him inside. The walls were painted the color of sand. Pith helmets and aviator goggles and other old military garments covered almost every square inch of vertical space. An old wooden airplane propeller hung mounted on the other side. The bar, made of dark wood and polished to a high gloss, stretched most of the length of the room. Two other men, both wearing camouflage uniforms, sat there conversing.

He walked over and pulled up a seat a few stools down from them. His eyes passed over a row of tap handles, all American brews with the exception of Heineken and Stella Artois. Then he looked at the shelves of liquor.

The bartender, a tall dark-skinned African who looked Kenyan, walked over. "Would you like something to drink, sir?"

Mike nodded. The guy's English was better than his own. "Johnnie Walker Black Label, neat."

The bartender bowed his head and made Mike's drink and pushed the glass to him on a napkin. "Will there be anything else?"

"Ask me again once I'm done with this drink."

The bartender bowed his head again and moved to check on his other customers. Mike picked up the drink and sniffed it, taking in the sweet scent of oak before he took a small sip. The mellow taste of smoke rested on his tongue a moment before he swallowed. He enjoyed the burn down his throat and how it warmed his belly.

Mike smiled. It had been a long flight, and the flask had lasted only so long.

He pulled his cell phone from his jacket and dialed Glenn.

"You in Djibouti?" Glenn said after picking up on the second ring.

"Yes."

"Good. I've got a job for you. Call you back in two days."

Glenn hung up.

Mike looked at the phone, thankful for such a brief conversation. He slid it back into his jacket and motioned for a refill.

Eight glasses and a few hours later, Mike stumbled out the front door and made his way back toward the officers' quarters.

"Do you need a ride to your quarters?" the sentry said.

Mike turned. It was a different guy from earlier. "No. Thank you."

It took him a lot longer to walk back than it had earlier to find the club. He made a wrong turn at one point and had to retrace his steps. Then, finally, he found the officers' quarters and flashed his ID as he staggered in.

The quarterdeck watch, a lance corporal this time, nodded and waved him in. Mike walked past him toward the elevators, when he heard the slow beat of a blues song. Over his right shoulder, he saw what he'd thought was a café earlier when he'd left but now appeared to be a small lounge. Curious and not ready for bed yet, Mike walked into the lounge to check it out.

The room was dimly lit by track lighting. There were several overstuffed chairs and a sofa. A couple of tables. Mike realized why he'd thought it was a café earlier: it looked like the inside of a Starbucks. With one exception. In the back there was a coffee bar with two pots and an espresso machine. But it also had two tap handles and a small shelf of liquor behind it. If Mike had noticed the alcohol earlier, he would not have left the building.

The lounge was empty with the exception of two older men in civilian clothes seated at one of the tables. They drank beer. Mike overheard them discussing contracts.

The only other person in the room was a woman. She sat in one of the overstuffed chairs, a glass of wine in her hand. Her dark hair reached her shoulders. Her eyes focused on the pages of a book.

Mike didn't notice anything remarkable about her. Athletic frame. Plain face. She looked to be in her late thirties.

"Are you going to stand there and stare or sit down?" she said without looking up from her book.

"Busted," Mike said. He walked over and sat across from her. "Hi."

Now she looked up and seemed to take Mike in the same way he had her. "Hi."

"You're not military," Mike said.

"What gave it away?"

Mike pointed at her shoes. "Gucci."

She smiled. "I'm impressed. You're not military, either."

Mike nodded. "What gave it away?"

She pointed at his windbreaker. Mike looked down and saw the butt of his pistol stuck out from underneath.

"Either you're a contractor," she said, "or something else."

Mike grinned. "Something else."

"A spook."

Mike shrugged. "I'm guessing you're a contractor."

"Contractors can't afford Gucci. I'm corporate legal."

"Oh, you review the contracts."

"Something like that." She sipped her wine and offered her hand. "My name's Katherine."

"Mike." He accepted her hand. Her skin was soft but her grip firm. She was used to shaking men's hands.

Katherine sipped more wine. "So, what brings you to Djibouti?"

"Orders."

"Wow, you're good at ducking questions."

"I'm not lying. I was told to come here and I'm awaiting further orders. What about you? Your company just land a big gig?"

"Yeah. So, would you like a drink?"

Mike held up his hands. "I've had enough already."

"But you just walked in."

"I've spent the last few hours at the officers' club. Didn't know this place"—Mike jabbed his finger into the padded arm of the chair—"existed until I got back a few minutes ago. Should have hung out here and saved myself the walk."

Katherine smiled. "I lucked out. Guy on the plane told me about this place. With the time and weather change, a little wine and a good book is just what the doctor ordered."

"Those were my thoughts exactly. Only sub whiskey for wine and forget the book."

"You don't sound like you've been drinking."

"Why? Because I'm not slurring words?"

Katherine laughed. "And you can form sentences."

"You haven't seen me walk yet."

Both laughed. Mike liked her. Liked her laugh. Liked the way she traced the rim of her glass with her finger.

"I've sobered up a little since walking back over here."

"Not too much I hope." Katherine finished off her wine. Her legs uncrossed and then crossed in reverse. She smiled at him. "Think I might have another."

Mike nodded. "I think you should. Wouldn't want you to sober up."

"No, definitely not. Wouldn't be as fun. Plus, I'd lose the courage then."

"Courage for what?"

Katherine shrugged. "To relax."

"It was a long flight."

"Yes, it was."

"Relaxing sounds nice."

"I couldn't think of a better way to recover."

Mike leaned forward and rested his elbows on his thighs. He really liked her now. "And what relaxes you?"

"Wine." Katherine laughed again. "But wine in bed is more relaxing than in a lounge."

Mike smiled. "So why don't you have some wine in bed?"

"Do you think they'd let me buy a bottle here?"

"Can't hurt to ask."

"So what relaxes you?"

"Wine in bed."

Katherine nibbled on her bottom lip and gazed at Mike. Mike returned the look with an unblinking stare.

"Would you like to join me for some wine?" Katherine said.

"Yes," Mike said. "Yes, I would."

CHAPTER TWENTY-NINE

Yusuf lit another cigarette and took a deep drag, looking out into the night. The storm had passed. The wind had died. The ocean had calmed to small ripples reflecting a full moon on its glassy surface.

So beautiful, he thought. He could not ask for better conditions to abandon ship.

"All departments report preparations are complete," Feisal said.

Yusuf turned from the sea. "Thank you."

Feisal nodded and walked away.

Everything was ready. The senior leadership had told their people what to prepare for. No one had protested or resisted. All Yusuf had to do now was give the order.

He looked down at his log, reviewing the entry regarding what they had found after the recent outbreak. The visual report from Mahmoud had not been pleasant. He had not counted the dead, refusing to allow any of his men into the spaces soaked in carnage. His word was good enough for Yusuf. If anyone was alive, they were not in those spaces; and it was not worth the risk of exposing those still lucky to breathe. The time for identifying the dead would come after they abandoned ship. Then they could finally ascertain an accurate picture of who'd made it off the *al-Phirosh*.

For now, he calculated at least fifteen dead based on departmental musters. Added to the earlier fatalities, Yusuf had lost over half his crew.

Yusuf closed the log. Time enough for depression later. Now he had to focus on saving those who remained.

It is time. He picked up his radio. "Chief Engineer, this is the captain."

"Chief Engineer," the voice crackled with static.

"Commence opening sea strainers, port and starboard side."

"Aye, Captain."

It had been the chief engineer's idea. All the main spaces housing the engines, generators, and associated auxiliary equipment lay below the waterline. Seawater suction pumps had strainers on the inlet side that prevented marine life and other debris from being sucked in and fouling the pumps' impellers. Normally, to change or clean a strainer, the pump had to be secured and then the strainer isolated by valves to prevent flooding. Now, as Yusuf finished his cigarette, personnel opened the strainers and allowed the seawater to flood the main spaces at five hundred liters a minute.

The watertight hatches to the main spaces would be left open. Once the water flooded the main spaces, it would spread to the lower decks. At first the flood would be slow, but as each space filled, the *al-Phirosh* would sink deeper and deeper. Hours would pass before enough could flood the ship and take it down to the salty deep. If their calculations were correct, though, by sunrise the oiler and whatever was aboard it would be at the bottom of the ocean.

"Captain, Chief Engineer. All sea strainers open."

"Very well. Secure all engines."

"Aye."

Yusuf decided to let the ship go dead in the water. They had been in a busy shipping lane, but he had changed course out of it, heading south. Once the ship lost power, it would lose all of its navigational and operational lighting. Yusuf did not want to present an obstacle to any possible traffic in the middle of the night. He also did not want to venture too far away from the lane, knowing his crew would still need to be rescued.

The generators would run until the saltwater breached the sets, which would require only a few feet of water in the space, and then they would have to operate with portable lanterns and flashlights in the dark. Yusuf figured they had an hour.

"Captain, main engines secured."

"Very well. Evacuate your spaces."

"Aye, Captain."

Yusuf walked over to the ship's communication circuit and picked up the microphone and ensured he was broadcasting both internally and externally. "On board the *al-Phirosh*, this is the captain. All hands, abandon ship. I repeat: all hands, abandon ship."

He set down the microphone and looked out the window. On the main weather deck, crewmen were already scrambling to break out the lifeboats. Mahmoud stomped around, barking orders and maintaining discipline.

Yusuf nodded and walked back to the table next to his chair. He opened his log and made what would be his last entry. Once the crew was safely off, he would debark with Feisal, now his first officer, and Mahmoud and a few others. Before that, he would make one last transmission, a distress call, and hope someone close by would be able to save his people from the sea.

Semyaza heard the announcement to abandon ship, ripping his concentration away from healing. He opened his eyes and saw all of the skin and tissue had fallen off his hands.

No, he thought. He had been unsuccessful in both recuperating and stemming the decomposition. And now the personnel on board were abandoning their ship.

Why would they abandon ship? They could pull into a port, save their people without losing their merchandise.

And then it dawned on Semyaza. They were leaving because of him. The chaos had scared them into fleeing. And if they were fleeing, he would soon be alone without another body to leap into.

"They are not just fleeing," Uriel said. He did not appear in any form. Just his voice echoed around Semyaza. "Did you think they would stand by and let you slaughter them?"

Sinking. They are sinking the ship.

"Soon, you will be back in your true prison."

Semyaza stood. He had to find a body and get off the ship. He opened the door and stepped into the passageway filled with carcasses and gore. He moved forward, not caring if he stepped in blood or guts, searching for another vessel before it was too late.

All he found, though, were the victims of his presence. He tried to open a door into another passageway, but it would not budge. He moved on to another door only to meet the same results. And this time, unlike before, there was no human standing on the other side.

They have trapped me. They have locked me in and are sinking me to the bottom of the sea. And when I lose grip on this body, I will be yanked back to my prison.

"Yes," Uriel said. "Your fun playing with the dead has cost you dearly."

Semyaza ignored Uriel and tried to think of a way out. No humans were close, so he could not leap. He had little enough strength left to maintain his current vessel. Knocking down a door would be impossible. The body would break before the steel of the door would give.

Still determined to find an escape route, Semyaza moved farther down the passageway. Every door he came across was steel, watertight, latched down, and locked. Some doors had one quick-acting latch. Others had six latches: one at the top two corners, one halfway down on each side, and one at the bottom two corners. The hatches he found above and below him were also locked.

Then he found a door much like the one that led to the gear locker he'd hidden in. This one, though, had a small round window at eye level he could see through. Instead of a locker on the other side, he saw another passageway.

The door did not have latches but a knob. Semyaza grabbed it and turned only to find it, too, was locked. He felt the metal. Not thick and dense like the other doors. He wrapped it with his knuckle. Hollow and thin sounding.

Semyaza considered trying to knock it down with his feet or hands but doubted his vessel could even dent this flimsier door. The skin and tissue all the way up to his elbows had fallen away. He could only imagine what his face now looked like.

Then he focused on the bodies around him. He did not have much strength but perhaps enough…

Semyaza extended his hand and spread his skeletal fingers and reached into one of the bodies on the deck.

It was a large man, and he had trouble lifting him but eventually got him to his feet. Then he backed him up across from the door. In one fluid movement, Semyaza swung his arm and the body ran and crashed into the door.

The collision did not knock the door open, but it did dent it severely. Semyaza backed the man up again and swung, harder this time, putting more of his strength into him. And more of his skin and tissue fell off as a result.

The dead body slammed into the door, busting the top hinge.

Semyaza moved the body back across the passageway once more. His grip was slipping on his vessel, increasing its rate of failure the longer he controlled the dead man. He could attempt this only once more before releasing the corpse and focusing his will on preserving what remained of this vessel.

The body slammed into the door one last time; the girth of its torso hit the center of the door square and broke the middle hinge.

Semyaza released the body and it fell to the deck. He approached the door and grabbed it and pushed it, widening the opening as much as he could muster. Then he wedged through. The fit was tight and his chest scraped across jagged pieces of metal, tearing through his shirt and what flesh remained on his breast. He paid no attention, forcing himself through to the other side.

Once there, he wasted no time, hurrying down the passageway, looking and listening for anyone.

He heard nothing. He found no one.

Semyaza raced up a ladder and down another passageway.

Again, nothing.

He ran up another ladder. Listened. Then another. Then another. Every level he found the same as before and accepted the fact he was probably the last thing still on board.

Then the lights went out and he plunged into darkness.

Semyaza dropped to his knees and leaned against the bulkhead. There was no one left on board and his hold on his vessel was almost finished. He prepared himself to lose control and be ripped back into the cold embrace of his prison.

"Is there someone down there?"

Semyaza twisted his head to see a man standing in the doorway, a lantern silhouetting his frame. Semyaza did not hesitate, jumping to his feet and racing toward the man, closing the distance as fast as he could.

"Who's there?" the man said.

Semyaza was a few meters away when the man saw what ran toward him. He screamed and turned and tried to flee, but Semyaza had closed the distance enough to leap.

And leap he did, releasing his vessel and plunging into the man with furious desperation.

Yusuf heard a scream from the weather decks. He turned from his log, his pen hovering over the page. Then another scream. Then gunshots.

He darted over to the starboard side of the wheelhouse and looked out the windows. Below near amidships, crewmen were tearing at each other like wild animals.

"My God," he said. In the water, the first of the lifeboats had lit their green chemical lights and drifted far enough away as not to appear to be affected by whatever had taken over the men on the ship. Then he checked the boat that had just entered the water. And there, like on the ship, men attacked each other, turning the sea around them into a thrashing nightmare.

Yusuf backed away from the window, his whole body shivering. He thought he had beaten it, able to evacuate his crew safely. And now, below him, the stinging sound of failure met him in the screams of crewmen ripping each other to pieces.

And this meant it had escaped and was close to the weather decks. Which means it could have infected any of those men down there. Could he allow them to leave now? If any of them survived? Or would he have to execute them?

No, he thought. *I cannot execute them.* And he needed to get those men in the other lifeboat, the ones who had made it clear of the madness, rescued.

Yusuf ran over to the bridge-to-bridge radio and picked up the handset.

"Mayday, mayday, mayday," he said in English. "This is the merchant vessel *al-Phirosh*. We are sinking and abandoning ship. Request immediate assistance. I repeat: mayday, mayday, mayday. This is the merchant vessel *al-Phirosh*. We are sinking and abandoning ship. Request immediate assistance. Something is killing my crew."

CHAPTER THIRTY

Mike stood on the end of a wooden pier surrounded by ocean. The water, black as oil, lapped gently around the pylons. A solid gray sky hung overhead. A foul wind blew from the sea, carrying with it the scent of decay.

He glanced over his shoulder. The pier stretched on forever and he saw no land. Just more gray sky and black water.

Mike leaned on the rail in front of him. He dug into an old barnacle with his thumbnail, chipping it away from the rotting wood. The wind caught it when it broke free and blew it away.

"You need to pull yourself together, Mike." Greg leaned on the rail next to him. "It's almost time."

"No, it isn't." Mike dug his thumb into the wood, pulling up chunks and flicking them into the water.

"I'm in the Horn of Africa, waiting for word on who to kill next."

Greg shook his head. "You really are a sad piece of shit, you know that?"

"I am what I am, right?"

Greg pushed off the rail and straightened up. "You'll learn who you are real soon. I hope you figure it out before it's too late."

"I can't kill this one, right? So, what does it matter? Sounds like I lose either way." Mike went to say something else, but Greg was gone. Instead, he went back to picking at the pier.

"I am what I am," he said.

"And you need to accept that." Lowe stood on his left side, still in his cammies.

Mike smirked. "Yep, sure do. Because I'm still a good guy. I'm a good killer and a good guy. It's how I'll win, right? Can't kill it, so maybe I defeat it by being nice to it? Whatever *it* is?"

"Cut the smart-ass shit, Mike."

"Tell me what the hell is going on and maybe I will."

"That's not important right now."

"And what is?"

"Answering your phone."

The ringer on Mike's cell phone sounded twice as loud as it normally did. It echoed around his head like an amplified burst. He blinked hard, his vision blurry, and winced as it rang again.

Where the hell am I? Mike thought, expecting to still be on the pier, looking out at the black ocean. It took him a moment to realize he was in bed.

He sat up and his brain seemed to slosh back and forth in his skull like a small boat on a rough sea. A small sliver of light filtered through the drawn curtains of the room. He squinted, trying to find his phone. It wasn't on the bedside table.

"Will you get that already?" a female voice said.

Mike looked to his left and saw Katherine curled up under the covers next to him, her eyes closed and the sheet pulled over her ears.

"Trying to," Mike said, his mouth dry as sandpaper. "Do you know where it is?"

"Check your pants."

Mike turned and looked on the side of the bed. On the floor were a couple of empty wine bottles. Then his shirt. Farther away, his boxers. His gun lay a few feet away from there. And his knife. He finally located his pants near the edge of the bed in a coiled mess.

He pushed off the bed, almost tripped over a wine bottle, and stumbled for his pants. He lifted them, rifled through his pockets, and found his phone.

"Hello." Mike walked back over to the bed and sat down and took a deep breath.

"Drinking again, huh?" Glenn said.

"How'd you know?"

"It only took you about three minutes to answer your damn phone."

Mike rubbed his eyes. "Right."

"I need you to get your head straight quick."

"I thought I had two days."

"Plans change."

"What's up?"

"It looks like whatever happened in Basra might have spread."

Mike stopped rubbing his eyes. "What?"

"A merchant ship, an oiler, in the northern Indian Ocean sent a distress call last night. The captain said his ship was sinking. Before he gave the coordinates, he said something on board was killing his men."

"How do you know it's the same thing?"

"The ship, the *al-Phirosh*, set sail from Basra the night of the riots."

Mike sighed and pinched the bridge of his nose. "Jesus."

"You could say that."

"Well, it sank, right? So maybe whatever it is sank with it."

"A US Navy warship is in the process of rescuing what crew made it off."

"Shit." Mike stood and walked into the bathroom and shut the door. "And how do I come into this?"

"The president does not want this thing, whatever it is, to spread to a ship full of America's bravest."

"So tell them to call off the rescue."

"Someone else will rescue them then. And then it will make it to another city. Not to mention the black eye the navy would get if anyone found out they left mariners in distress on the sea. Plus, the navy isn't part of my jurisdiction."

Mike flipped on the cold water in the sink and ran his hand under it and splashed his face. "You just said the president didn't want it to make it onto one of his ships. I think the navy's in his jurisdiction."

"The president needs to stay away from this."

"Why?"

"Like I said, it can't appear the US turned its back on humanitarian assistance."

"What do you want me for then?"

Glenn was silent a moment. "I need you to make sure those remaining merchants never make it off that ship alive."

Mike turned off the water and closed his eyes. "This isn't funny."

"I'm not joking."

"You want me to kill a bunch of people just in case they might be carrying this…thing? How are you going to explain that?"

"The same way we're explaining Basra."

"And that is?"

"Biological attack. The biologic is highly communicable but survives for only a short period of time when airborne due to its inability to survive in solar radiation. But in confined places where lots of people are gathered, it can spread and kill in alarming numbers. Someone who had been contaminated with a small dose made it onto the ship. But unfortunately, said person eventually succumbed to the illness, and it became communicable again once the incubation period ended."

"That sounds like a big load of horseshit."

"Regardless, it's the story. The *al-Phirosh* left Basra with an infected person. It later spread with alarming speed once they were at sea. What crew did make if off the *al-Phirosh* later died in quarantine on board a navy ship. All possible treatment was rendered."

"This is insane." Mike walked over to the toilet, flipped the lid down, and sat. "There's no way you'll keep the crew who made it off quiet on this one."

"The crew will be debriefed once they're in port again and sworn to secrecy."

Mike chuckled. "And if they violate their oath?"

"Do I really need to answer that?"

Mike shook his head. "What if it spreads to the navy crew later, after the others are disposed of?"

"The ship will be kept at sea for thirty days, isolated with all noncritical communication secure. If they make it through the quarantine without incident, they will pull into Bahrain and receive their debriefing."

Mike rocked back on the toilet, his bare back leaning against the cool porcelain. "What if it spreads to the navy crew before I get there?"

"We'll address that if it comes to that."

Mike didn't say anything for a minute or two. Instead, his mind drifted to thoughts of killing innocent people. All as a precaution.

"Mike?"

"Yeah."

"I know it's ugly. But it has to be done. And it needs to be handled by someone who'll ensure it gets done without error. This isn't a job for a couple of guys with machine guns."

"It's a job for a professional killer."

"That's correct. And you're the best one I got."

Mike's stomach hurt. He leaned forward and clutched it.

"I need you sober, Mike," Glenn said. "You can deal with the demons afterward."

"Right."

"And I need you on a helicopter in one hour."

Mike stood and turned the shower on. "An hour?"

"A CH-53 will shuttle you from Djibouti to the USS *Rushmore*. Once the ship recovers the survivors, it's going to turn west and close the distance. Shouldn't take you more than a few hours to get there."

"What's my cover?"

"The *Rushmore*'s captain has been told a team of investigators is being flown out to determine whether the survivors are infected with any communicable disease. The survivors should already be quarantined by the time you arrive."

"And once he realizes I'm a team of one?"

"Once you're on-site, get the CO in private and call me. I'll inform him of why you're there and tell him to provide all assistance as necessary."

Mike felt the hot water on his hand and inhaled steam. "Well, I better get going then."

"Call me once you're on the ship."

Ten minutes later, Mike had toweled off; he walked around the bedroom, picking up his clothes and getting dressed.

"Leaving me already?" Katherine said.

"Afraid so." Mike pulled his pants on. "Got to go save the world."

Katherine smirked. "Sure. I know a one-night stand when I see one."

Mike pulled his shoes on. "Not the deal here."

"So you're coming back."

"I don't know where I'm going after this."

Katherine sat up in bed, the sheet pulled up over her chest. "Look, you don't have to try and make me feel better. I knew what I was doing last night. It was fun."

Mike pulled on his shirt and smiled as he tucked it in, ignoring the pain in his side. "It was, even if I didn't do much of the work."

"Couldn't have you ripping your stitches, could we?"

"Nope. And I wasn't trying to make you feel better. I'm just saying last night wasn't a one-night stand."

Katherine shrugged. "Sure."

Mike moved up the bed until he was beside her. He looked her in the eyes and smiled. "I'm saying, if I weren't leaving, I'd want to see you again tonight. And tomorrow night. And every night you're here until you head back home. But I am leaving and, believe me, I wish to God I wasn't. So, don't cheapen last night as if it was a passing fancy. I sure as hell don't want to feel like I was used."

Katherine giggled.

"Don't laugh," Mike said. "After where I've been, what I've seen, and where I'm going, I needed last night."

Katherine's face sharpened and Mike could tell she was suddenly serious.

"What are you going to do, Mike?"

Mike smiled. He'd forgotten he'd told her his real name. And he didn't regret it for a moment.

"I can't say," he said.

Mike stood and lifted his gun and holster off the ground and slid it over his shoulders and secured it. Then he found his knife and put it in his pocket.

"Wait." Katherine pushed out of the bed and walked over to the dresser. Mike admired her naked body as it seemed to glide across the room. She reached into her purse and dug out a business card. Then she scribbled something on the back with a pen and walked over to him.

Mike looked from her body to her eyes as she extended the business card.

"Take this," she said.

Mike did and read her title and business phone and e-mail on the front. He flipped it to the back and saw her personal phone number in black ballpoint.

"If you're ever back in the States, give me a call." Katherine smiled.

Mike nodded, slipped the card in his pocket, and leaned in to kiss her softly. "I will."

Then Mike turned and walked out of the room.

A few minutes later he was in his room, packing his bag. Before heading out, he pulled the card from his pocket. He smiled again as he looked at her poor handwriting. Then he dropped it in the trashcan on the way out the door.

He checked out of the hotel and walked toward the airfield. He already regretted throwing Katherine's card away, but he didn't have a choice. In his world, he had sworn off attachments. He'd already lowered his guard and allowed himself to get too close to someone in just a passing night. Now, though, he had to steel his heart and prepare himself for what was required of him.

"I am what I am," he said. He had no room in his life for women like Katherine. He barely had room in it for himself.

CHAPTER THIRTY-ONE

Mike glanced at his watch, the numbers bouncing with the movement of the helicopter. If he stared too long, he got dizzy. Almost noon. He lowered his wrist.

The engines of the CH-53 were loud, but the cranial helmet with earmuffs he wore blocked the noise enough to make it bearable. He had tried sleeping but failed. Instead, he read up on the specifications of the navy ship he flew toward. Glenn had e-mailed the document to him an hour ago.

The print on his cell phone screen was small and bounced with the helo as well, no matter how much he attempted to steady his arm. Every so often, Mike looked away to regain his focus.

From what he'd managed to read so far, the *Rushmore* was an amphibious ship, type LSD (landing ship dock), hull number 47. Mike remembered the Marines in Iraq had arrived there on similar ships, off-loading in

Basra. They called them "Marine Ferries" and "Gator Freighters."

The Marines on the *Rushmore,* though, had not gone to Iraq. Instead, they had debarked in Djibouti for several weeks of training and possible operations against al Qaeda in North Africa.

Which meant only the ship's crew was on board, along with one platoon of Marines used for vessel boarding and anti-piracy operations. Mike took some comfort in that. The crew size approached four hundred. Keeping that many people silent would be hard. Throw in another four hundred Marines and silence became impossible.

Mike looked at some of the other specs. The ship had four diesel engines with a top speed of twenty-two knots. Slow boat.

It had no offensive weapons other than a few mounts for .50 cals and M60s. The bulk of the ship consisted of a huge well deck for carrying high-speed Landing Craft, Air Cushions (or LCACs) and other Marine amphibious assault platforms. The LCACs had also remained in Africa for training. So cross one way of evacuating the crew off the list.

The *Rushmore* could ballast down to a point where eight feet of water filled the well deck. Mike shook his head as he realized why the Marines referred to it as a "ferry." The damn thing was nothing but a slow truck on the water.

It also had a flight deck capable of supporting two helicopters, but none were permanently stationed because the ship did not have a hangar in which maintenance could be performed. Mike frowned. His helo would drop him off, refuel, and then leave. With the Marines' toys on the beach and the helo not sticking around, ways to evacuate personnel in bulk looked slim. The *Rushmore* carried a couple of small boats but nothing four hundred people could leave on. Other than life rafts, they were hurting if they had to flee the ship.

The letters bounced in his hand and Mike looked away. He'd read enough anyway. He slipped the cell phone in his pocket and closed his eyes.

Not much longer, he thought.

The CH-53 touched down on the flight deck, bounced, and then hit the deck again. Mike looked out the window next to him and saw several flight deck personnel wearing blue life vests running toward the helicopter, carrying landing gear chocks and chains.

Mike turned away as the back of the helicopter lowered, sunlight flooding the fuselage. He squinted until his eyes adjusted. Then he stood, grabbed his bag, and walked toward the exit. An escort wearing a cranial helmet, goggles, and a khaki uniform met him there, shook his hand without saying anything, and then motioned him to follow.

On the deck, Mike saw other people in colored vests and jerseys. People in purple hooked up fuel hoses to the CH-53, its rotors still spinning. A guy in yellow held paddles for directing the aircraft. A couple of others wore red and stood near fire hoses lying on the deck. Finally, he saw two people in suits that looked like they had been made from aluminum foil. Firefighters in hot suits.

Mike followed the escort down a ramp to another deck, a few feet below the flight deck but still outside the skin of the ship. On his right was a large crane. On his left was a hole. He looked over the railing and below saw into the well deck.

"We'll wait here a minute," the guy yelled over the whine of the engines. "The captain is on her way down."

Mike nodded. He turned and saw the CH-53 lifting off the deck. It rose to about ten feet, lowered its nose, and flew off to the left of the ship, climbing higher as it did.

Everything quieted as the sounds of the engines and the rotors faded. His escort removed the cranial helmet and muffs and handed them to one of the guys wearing red. Mike did the same, as well as removing his life jacket. He heard the voices of the flight deck crew gabbing about what was for lunch. He heard the diesel engines of the ship and saw the smoke of their exhaust rising from a stack near the crane. He heard the sound of the sea lapping the sides of the hull.

Mike had never been on a navy ship and had not been to sea on anything in years. His legs wobbled as the ship rocked gently to the right and then the left. His escort next to him flexed and adjusted naturally with the movement.

"Need your sea legs," he said.

Mike nodded. "I guess so."

"Lieutenant Schiffer, ship's operations officer." Schiffer extended a thin hand. "Call me Bob."

Mike shook it and realized he didn't know what name to use for a moment: his real one or the alias. Then he decided it really didn't matter.

"Mike Caldwell."

"Welcome aboard the *Rushmore*, Mike. Wish you could have come under better circumstances."

"Me, too."

Bob walked over to the starboard side, spat into the ocean, and walked back. "Do you dip?"

"No."

Bob pushed his hands into his pockets. "Captain should be down soon."

"Any reason why you're keeping me out here?"

Bob smiled. "No. But the captain wanted to meet you down here and show you around. If I take you in, she'll come a different way and we'll miss her and then I'll get my ass chewed."

"Ah," Mike said. "Don't want that."

"Definitely not."

Mike looked at a serene blue sky. The little puffs of white cloud seemed to move back and forth above them. He smelled exhaust and salt and fuel.

Feeling suddenly lightheaded, Mike turned his attention back to the hole above the well deck. He leaned on the gray-painted rail. The sides of the well deck and bottom were lined in wood.

"Why wood?" Mike said.

"What?"

Mike pointed down into the hole. "Why are the sides of the well deck wood? Why not metal?"

Bob leaned on the rail next to him. "Because when we ballast down, the wood acts as a natural barrier to corrosion."

Mike nodded, realizing his question was sort of stupid once he'd heard the obvious answer.

"Plus," Bob said, "there's a lot of wear and tear down there, and wood has a lot of give. The Marines tend to bump into things when they come on and go off. The LCACs, the AAVs, and tanks they have would get torn up. Wood is more forgiving than steel."

Mike looked from the hole to the crane behind him. "So the crane lifts stuff from a pier and lowers it through the hole into the well deck and vice versa?"

"Yeah, mainly smaller vehicles and equipment. Right through the Hell Hole. Everything else comes on board via LCAC transport or other cargo craft."

Mike nodded. "Hell Hole, huh?"

Bob chuckled. "Yeah. If a sailor can give a nickname to something, he will." Bob turned away. "Here comes the captain."

Mike pushed off the rail and turned. Rather than a khaki uniform like Bob, the captain wore a blue-gray camouflage. Her hair was a shoulder length. Her frame was athletic but built more like a gym rat than a runner. If he were to guess, she probably did crew in college. Or mixed martial arts. Her height, average.

"Welcome aboard," the captain said and extended her hand. "Commander Sandra Temms."

"Mike Caldwell." he shook her hand. "If you're a commander, why does everyone call you captain?"

"Commander is my rank." Her hand squeezed Mike's a little harder. "Every ship, though, has a captain. Follow?"

Mike didn't answer the increased grip, instead choosing to let go. His observation that she was a gym rat was accurate. "Appreciate you allowing me on board."

Temms nodded. "Orders are orders. Been a bit crazy around here the last few hours. Hopefully you can shed some light on some of the mystery."

Mike smiled. "Hope so."

"So, where's the rest of your team?"

Mike shook his head. "It's just me, Captain."

"I was led to believe—"

"I know, Captain. And I have some explaining to do. If you don't mind, is there a place we can talk in private?"

Temms's right cheek twitched a little but then smiled. "Of course. Let's go up to my cabin."

Mike followed Temms up a few metal ladders and down passageways painted bright white with blue flooring. The Captain's Cabin was on the O-6 level, five decks above where Temms had met Mike and directly behind the ship's pilothouse. The last ladder they climbed had thin white rope wrapped around the rails in fancy twists, marking it as the Captain's Ladder.

At the top, they turned a sharp right and walked into the cabin.

The cabin had a wraparound blue Naugahyde couch in the left corner and a round coffee table with the ship's crest emblazoned on its surface. On the right side of the cabin was a small oak conference table with room for eight people to sit at it. An oak wraparound desk with a computer and several phones on the surface and on the wall behind it sat on the opposite side of the cabin.

"Where do you sleep?"

Temms laughed and pointed at a closed door near the desk. "Through there. But I haven't made my bed yet."

Bob walked in and stood with his hands behind his back.

"Ma'am, Mr. Caldwell's room is ready."

Temms nodded. "Mr. Caldwell, we have you set up in the Marine CO stateroom on the deck below. Ops will take your bag down there for you if you like."

Mike shrugged and handed his bag to Bob. "Here you go."

Bob took it and started to turn away.

"Ops," Temms said, "go ahead and send word to AFRICOM and Fifth Fleet that Mr. Caldwell has arrived and we are awaiting further tasking."

Bob nodded and shut the door behind him.

Temms motioned to the couch. "Please, have a seat."

Mike did. Temms pulled a seat from the conference table and sat across from him.

Temms sighed. "This is one hell of a mess."

"Yes, it is."

"My crew spent six hours pulling a bunch of Arabs off life rafts from a half-sunken ship. We were then ordered to quarantine the survivors and allow no one with the exception of medical personnel near them once on board. Then we were ordered to turn around and gun it toward the West African shore to close the distance on an investigative team being flown out here. Now you show up—alone.

"I've been in the navy eighteen years, grew up a navy brat, and have never seen decisions get made on so little information so quickly as this one. I'd like to know what is going on."

Mike took a few breaths before he started. "It has to do with why that ship, the *al-Phirosh*, sank."

"I figured as much."

Mike kept his voice low. "Do you have a secure satellite phone?"

Temms nodded.

"May I use it?"

"Why?"

"Because my boss wanted to explain this to you once I arrived here."

"And who's your boss?"

"Glenn Cheatum, deputy director for operations of the Central Intelligence Agency."

Temms rocked back in her seat. "CIA. Well great; this is terrorist shit, isn't it?"

"I'll let him explain," Mike said. "The phone please, Captain."

Temms stood up and walked over to her desk. She grabbed a black handset off it and walked back over and handed it to Mike. Mike took the satphone and turned it on and dialed Glenn once he had a signal.

After a few rings, Glenn's gravelly voice came over the speaker. "Deputy Cheatum."

"It's Mike." He placed the satphone on the coffee table and put it on speaker. "I'm on board *Rushmore.* I have Captain Temms here with me."

"Captain," Glenn said, "sorry to conduct business in this manner."

Temms leaned forward over the coffee table. "I appreciate the apology but must warn you, sir, my patience in this matter is wearing thin."

"I understand."

"Now, can you explain to me what's going on?"

"Yes. But I must emphasize this conversation is above top secret: eyes-only-level stuff. You will not repeat what I tell you to anyone."

Temms seemed to swallow a mouthful of frustration and said, "Very well."

"Three days ago a biological attack was executed in the city of Basra in Iraq."

"I haven't seen any reports."

"The long and short of it is the biological weapon used has never been seen before, and its origin is unknown. A lot of people died as a result of it, and to maintain control in the southern part of Iraq and Kuwait, the lid is being kept on what really happened until more can be deduced. In the meantime, the press is being told a dirty bomb was used and the area is radioactively contaminated, to prevent them from slipping in and investigating."

"Won't a dirty bomb cause as much panic as an unknown biological weapon?" Temms said.

"People have been expecting a dirty bomb attack somewhere in the world for a decade now. Now that they have one, it's not a surprise. But tell the world an unknown biological weapon was used, one that causes the people it infects to basically go crazy and kill, and the shit hits the fan. People panic and we've got a worse situation on our hands than the actual weapon. Life gets spooky real quick."

"I see what you mean," Temms said. "But what does Basra have to do with the *al-Phirosh*?"

Glenn cleared his throat. "The *al-Phirosh* set sail from Basra the night of the attack."

Temms rubbed his forehead. "Are you saying what I think you're saying?"

"If you let me finish—"

"Because if you're going to tell me I just exposed my crew to possible biological contamination by picking up those survivors, if you're going to tell me—"

"Captain Temms," a different voice said over the phone. It was lighter and sounded tired compared to Glenn's.

Temms's eyebrows narrowed. "Who is this?"

"Captain, this is the president."

All the color drained from Temms's face. Mike sat back and looked from the captain to the satphone and back to the captain. He couldn't blame Temms for the reaction. Even Mike felt uneasy. He hadn't expected the president to be this personally involved. Which meant Glenn was in the Oval Office, probably with the director and several others of the National Security Council.

Nothing like having the spotlight on you, Mike thought, realizing everyone on the other end would soon be tracking his progress on terminating the survivors.

"Yes, Mr. President?" Temms said, her voice a lot softer than it had been. Nervous.

"I wasn't planning on involving myself in this conversation," the president said. "I hoped Mr. Cheatum could steer you toward your next course of action without too much difficulty. Unfortunately, and rightly so, this unusual situation has raised serious questions with regard to the safety of your crew."

"Yes, Mr. President," Temms said. "My crew is my chief concern, especially if a biological weapon of some kind is involved."

"It is my chief concern as well, which is why what I'm going to explain to you is extremely delicate. It is why Mr. Caldwell is there. It is why much will be asked of you and your crew. And because of it, time is of the essence."

"Yes, Mr. President," Temms said.

"Mr. Caldwell," the president said.

Mike leaned forward, his elbows on his knees. "Yes, sir."

"Would you excuse us? You already know what I am going to tell the captain, and I would like her undivided attention, free of anyone else's presence. For what I am going to ask of her needs to be decided between her and her conscience."

Mike stood and nodded to Temms. "Yes, sir."

Then he turned and walked out of the cabin and shut the door behind him. In the passageway, he leaned against a bulkhead across from the door. The metal was cool and calmed his nerves. He wished he had a drink, but his flask was in his bag.

Twenty or so minutes later, the door opened and Temms stood there, her face slack and haggard. She motioned Mike back in and moved away.

Inside, Mike stood across from her. "Are you okay, Captain?"

"No, I am not." Temms walked behind her desk and sat down. "What you are here for, what you will do, is not something easily accepted."

Mike nodded. "Trust me, I'm still having trouble with it."

Temms rubbed her face with both hands. "Before you do anything, I want to try and at least talk to the shipmaster of the *al-Phirosh*. I want to know what happened, regardless of what you have to do. I need that much, for my sake."

Mike held his hands behind his back. "Of course, Captain. When will you do this?"

"Now. The shipmaster is in the quarantined berthing with the rest of the survivors."

"How many were there?"

"Survivors? Fourteen. Pulled five other bodies out of the water we thought might be alive but were pronounced dead once on board and moved to cold storage. The rest we left in the water to come pick you up. Don't know for sure how many since none of the survivors seem to speak English."

Mike blinked. Fourteen. That would be a lot of souls on his head in a short amount of time. "Out of how many originally?"

"Probably over thirty based on the size of the ship. Those merchants sail with pretty small crews. Don't know the exact number."

Half a crew wiped out. If the same thing broke out on the *Rushmore*, the numbers would be staggering in no time.

"Captain, may I accompany you? I speak Arabic."

Temms nodded and stood. "Let's go. I need an interpreter."

CHAPTER THIRTY-TWO

Mike followed Temms down the Captain's Ladder and the next one after to the O-3 level. Temms pointed and indicated the berthing was just forward of the ladder on the starboard side. Mike nodded and said nothing.

As they approached the berthing, Mike smelled fried shrimp and French fries. He looked over his shoulder down the passageway aft and saw dozens of crewmembers in the same blue camouflage fatigues Temms wore, standing in line.

Temms must have seen what he was looking at and said, "It's the mess line. Fried shrimp is always popular for lunch."

Mike felt his own stomach rumble as he turned back forward. He hadn't had anything to eat since yesterday. Between waking up still drunk and having to sober up quickly and catch his flight, Mike hadn't had time to shove anything down his throat. He hadn't thought to grab something, even a protein bar. The idea of killing people made him thirsty for booze, not hungry for food. Now, though, he wished he'd at least snatched a banana from the continental breakfast at the officers' quarters. Smelling the food now fired his hunger up in spades.

Standing in front of a closed door leading to the berthing was a Marine holding an M16A4. Temms stopped in front of him.

"Captain."

"Corporal." Temms motioned to Mike. "I'm escorting him."

The corporal nodded and stepped aside and opened the thick steel watertight door. "Doc's inside."

"Good," Temms said. "Everything else quiet?"

"So far, ma'am."

They passed through the open door. The corporal shut it after Mike. He watched as it closed and the quick-acting latch lowered, securing the door shut. Being shut inside with a bunch of survivors of an outbreak did not make him feel good.

"Your crew can still eat and joke around even with an armed Marine standing guard outside a berthing a few feet away?" Mike said.

Temms laughed. "They're sailors. We pick up stranded mariners all the time. It's not unusual. They probably figure the guard is there because the survivors are Arab."

"Are we going to put on any special suits?"

"No." Temms stopped and turned to him. "Remember, my people didn't know of any biological weapon when we pulled these guys out of the water. They're in there right now, thinking they're treating some unfortunate merchants. If we walk in with full chem suits on, what effect do you think that's going to have?"

"But you were told to quarantine—"

"Yes but our MOPP level wasn't changed. Quarantine can be for anything from dysentery to Ebola. When no major change to MOPP came with the orders, we assumed this was an isolate-and-tag op. Set positive ventilation, hang the plastic curtains, and check them for parasites and flu. We've done that."

Mike nodded. "I understand."

"We're just going to have to risk exposure. Hell, we've all been exposed already. Except you, I guess. Any objections?"

Mike shook his head. *I went in its prison.* "I'm okay."

Temms resumed walking. They passed a men's bathroom on the left and then went through another door, an aluminum one with a regular knob like in the Captain's Cabin.

"Why the different types of doors?"

Temms's eyebrows arched, as if she didn't understand at first. Then she looked at the doorknob in her hand and nodded. "These are basically just privacy doors. The watertight ones are used for compartmentalization in case of flooding."

"Do merchant ships have watertight doors?"

"Yes." Temms moved closer to him. "You're curious why the ship sank, aren't you?"

Mike nodded. "I can understand the deaths based on what I saw in Iraq. But the sinking still confuses me. It's not as if someone gets infected, goes crazy, and smashes equipment and pokes holes in the sides of ships. All the destruction from the biologic has been person on person."

Temms shrugged. "There are lots of ways for a ship to flood, especially if there's a leak below the waterline."

Mike didn't pursue his sudden curiosity any further, figuring he'd get his answer once they heard the *al-Phirosh*'s master's story. But something about the sinking ate at him, causing him to remain unsettled. How could a hallucinogen sink a ship? If they'd intentionally sunk the ship, that meant they'd tried to sink something with it, and he knew it wasn't a vapor cloud.

Because it's a demon, he thought. *A fucking demon.*

His memory flashed to the prison, the unknown writing, and the man he'd tortured and then killed. Then he shifted to the dream, the insurgent smiling, two holes in his forehead. The sea of bodies. The milk-white eyes. Their hands stretched out. Don't kill me. Please.

"It will kill you," the insurgent had said. "And there will be no mercy in it."

Fuck, he thought. *The sea. The black water. Oil. The tanker. This ship with so many on board. Please God, don't make me kill all these people. Don't put their deaths on my head.*

Mike blinked and shook the thoughts and memories away. He didn't have time for them. And he didn't have his flask handy.

Inside the berthing, Mike saw racks filled with the survivors of the *al-Phirosh*. He followed Temms past a couple of rows of metal beds stacked three high, all occupied. A male and two female corpsmen walked between the racks, treating the men. They hooked up IVs, changed dressings, and provided medications. The room smelled of blood, saltwater, and rubbing alcohol.

They reached the back of the berthing where the *Rushmore*'s doctor, a lieutenant with a bald head Mr. Clean would envy, stood, a stethoscope hanging around his neck.

"Captain," Doc said.

"Doc Morris," Temms said, "this is Mike Caldwell."

Morris looked at Mike. His brown eyes seemed to size Mike up. "Excuse me if I don't shake hands. Just got done washing them for the eighth time."

Mike waved the apology away. "No problem."

"So what brings you on board the *Rushmore*?"

Before Mike could say anything, Temms said, "Mr. Caldwell is an NCIS agent sent by AFRICOM to investigate the sinking of the *al-Phirosh*."

"Ah," Morris said. "I see. Well, no one here's talking about it, in English at least. Hope you speak Arabic."

"I do," Mike said. "Which one is the shipmaster?"

Morris motioned for them to follow. They passed a couple of racks and then stopped. Morris held his hand over a middle bunk.

"This is Shipmaster Yusuf. Haven't gotten a first name yet."

Mike moved closer. The captain was a very common-looking man with a moustache and a slight gut. He was unconscious and snoring loudly.

"Will you revive him?" Mike said.

"He's just sleeping," Morris said. "No drugs."

"Injuries," Mike said.

"None."

Mike nodded and reached out, shook Yusuf by the shoulder. "Captain," he said in Arabic. "Captain Yusuf, please wake up."

Yusuf snorted and blinked his eyes rapidly. "What?"

"Captain Yusuf," Mike said, "can you understand me?"

Yusuf snorted again and his eyes rolled around until they landed on Mike. He stared at Mike for a few seconds and then blinked again and nodded.

"Yes," Yusuf said. "You speak Arabic well."

"Thank you," Mike said. "Do you speak English?"

"Only a few words."

Mike nodded and smiled. "I am glad you made it off your ship alive."

"Has anyone else died?"

"Since being rescued?"

Yusuf nodded.

"No," Mike said. "Should we be expecting any to?"

Yusuf stared at him. Then he shook his head. "I am just worried for my crew."

"They are being treated well here, yes?"

"Yes," Yusuf said. "We were quite lucky."

"You were."

One of the female corpsmen, a short blonde, carried two metal folding chairs to them and set them up for Mike and Temms. Both took a seat. Morris excused himself to check other patients.

Mike pulled out a digital voice recorder and held it up for Yusuf to see. "Captain, I am investigating the sinking of your vessel on behalf of the American and Iraqi governments. For the sake of accurate record keeping, I would like to commit this conversation to audio. Are you acceptable to this proposal?"

Yusuf nodded.

Mike pressed record.

"My name is Mike Caldwell, Captain. As previously stated, I am investigating the circumstances surrounding the sinking of the *al-Phirosh*. Do you mind if I ask your full name?"

"Omar Yusuf, captain of the *al-Phirosh*."

"And what was the cargo of the *al-Phirosh*?"

"Oil."

"How much?"

"Twenty-five-thousand deadweight tons."

"A small tanker," Mike said.

"And old."

"How many crewmen did you set sail with?"

Yusuf looked away and swallowed. "Fifty-five."

Mike looked at Temms and relayed the number in English.

Temms's eyes widened a little. "Fifty-five? Those vessels don't carry a crew that big."

Mike turned back to Yusuf and resumed in Arabic. "That seems like a large number for a vessel of its size. Our understanding is most tankers like yours carry a crew of only twenty-five to thirty, if not less."

Yusuf nodded. "Yes, normally. However, the Iraq Oil Shipping Company, in cooperation with the government, agreed to hire more crew than normal for its ships. As a way of putting more citizens to work. They merely doubled the amount of beds in sleeping spaces."

"I see." Mike relayed the information to Temms, who nodded in acceptance.

"That means forty-one dead." Temms rubbed her jaw. "Not good odds."

"And have you been told how many survived?" Mike said in Arabic, ignoring Temms's last comment.

Yusuf nodded, tears streaming down his temples. "Fourteen."

"A tragedy."

Yusuf said nothing.

Mike waited another moment. "The *al-Phirosh* set sail from Basra a little over three days ago, correct?"

"Yes."

"Your ship was moored when the riots broke out, correct?"

"Yes."

"Your ship was moored when the military helicopters were flying over Basra, ordering all personnel out of the city, correct?"

"Yes."

"Captain, I must ask, why did you get your ship underway after being ordered to evacuate?"

Yusuf wiped his eyes. "Anyone who did not want to set sail was given every opportunity to leave before getting underway. Not many chose to leave."

Tears ran down the side of Yusuf's face. "I thought we were safe at sea."

"I sympathize with your decision. After seeing what happened in Basra, I cannot blame you for leaving."

"After what has happened," Yusuf said, "I wish I would have made everyone leave and never set sail."

Mike leaned forward. "What happened out there, Captain?"

Yusuf swallowed again, harder this time. He took a deep breath and told his story. Mike translated every word for Temms. As Yusuf progressed from the finding of the skeleton to the deaths in the berthing to the loss of his first officer, his words came slower and more labored, as if they stabbed his chest as he uttered them.

When Yusuf reached the point in his story where he and the security detail confronted the walking dead, Mike leaned back and listened, not translating for a long time. He couldn't believe what he heard. Everything up to that point had fit with what had happened at R91 and Basra. The sudden surge of violence. The man-on-man primal attack. The suicide by the last one standing. And then nothing for a few hours until the cycle started once more.

The walking dead, though, caught him completely off guard. And yet, as he heard Yusuf tell his story, he couldn't not believe it. There was such sadness and loss in his words. Mike knew the man spoke the truth, at least what he perceived to be the truth.

Part of Mike, though, fought the ridiculousness of it. He tried to link Yusuf and his security detail's experience to the hallucinogen theory. Exposure led them to imagine dead bodies walking toward them.

But why didn't they attack each other then? Mike thought. It didn't make sense. The whole walking dead thing shot a big old hole in the hallucinogen theory. No one else had reported seeing crazy shit because no one else had survived a direct exposure. This meant if there was a hallucinogen, it was mutating. Or Yusuf was telling the truth.

"You can't kill this one, Mike."

"Hey," Temms said. "You forget about me?"

Mike held up his hand. "I'm just letting him get it all out. I'll tell you the whole thing once he's done."

Temms didn't seem to like that, but she held her tongue and allowed Yusuf to continue his story.

Yusuf eventually reached the end of his tale and stopped talking. Mike rubbed his mouth and turned off the recorder. He tried to think, tried to provide a logical answer for what had happened and what needed to happen next. But he couldn't. All he could do was create images from Yusuf's words. And what he saw was death.

"Jesus," Mike said. He turned to Temms. "I need to talk to you alone."

CHAPTER THIRTY-THREE

Mike stood with Temms in the passageway just outside the quarantined berthing, out of earshot of anyone else. He told Temms what Yusuf had said, choosing his words carefully, not wanting to scare the captain away before he finished. Temms listened but shook her head often.

Once Mike was done, Temms said, "This all sounds like horseshit."

"I know how it sounds, but it isn't horseshit."

"How can you say that? The walking dead. That's ludicrous. Sounds like the good master took too many hits off the hookah."

"Captain, I believe when you spoke with the president in private he may have related to you what happened in Basra."

Temms looked away. "Yeah, he did."

"And so you are aware of the amount of death that occurred there. But not random death. Ordered. A pattern. It started in one place and moved, like riding a wave. Then it stopped. The violence didn't spread to the whole city."

"You and the president and your boss, Cheatum, talked about a biological attack. How the hell can a weapon raise the dead?"

Mike gritted his teeth. Temms was right. From her point of view, based on what she had been told, the whole thing stunk. He could stand there and swear to God and country Yusuf's story was more truth than fiction, but it would get him nowhere. Temms had been told by the president of the United States it had happened one way. Why on earth would she take Mike's word for it right now?

Mike had seen R91, though. He'd been in the prison. And the more he remembered them, the more he knew this wasn't some kind of ancient hallucinogen. There was something else at work here, and he couldn't just hold his tongue and let the possible truth die.

"The biological attack is bullshit," Mike said.

"Excuse me?"

"Bullshit, the whole thing." Mike took a deep breath. "They don't know what it is. They're just using the biological attack to give the whole madness some form of order. But it's crap."

"And how do you know that?"

Mike shrugged. "I've been to ground zero."

"You were in Basra?"

"No, I was at ground zero."

"What are you saying, Mike?"

Mike hesitated a moment and then decided to say the fuck with all the secrecy. The truth needed to be told if anyone was going to survive this.

"Basra wasn't the first outbreak. There was a dig at a construction site outside An Nasiriyah..."

Mike told Temms everything. Everything except the dreams. Those he kept close.

He knew he sounded insane, but getting it all out, baring his soul, felt liberating, as if he could once and for all lift the weight of secrecy and lies off his heart.

"And what was in the prison?" Temms said.

Mike blinked. "What?"

"The prison." Temms's face was hard and unyielding. "What did the man say was in it?"

Mike smirked, hardly able to comprehend that he believed it now. "A demon."

Temms's eyebrows narrowed. "A what?"

"A fucking demon. Hard to believe, huh?"

Temms sighed. "A demon in a box in the desert? Do you expect me to believe a demon is responsible for all this, Mr. Caldwell? Do you know how insane this is?"

Mike shook his head. "I know it's ridiculous, but there is no other answer. Something, whether it's a demon or something else supernatural, was on the *al-Phirosh*. It wasn't a biological weapon and it wasn't a hallucinogen trapped underground until that sewer pipe fell on the slab and freed it. It is some kind of entity that can wreak destruction on whoever it comes in contact with."

"Well, I disagree, Mr. Caldwell."

"Captain—"

"Do you want to know what I think?"

Mike crossed his arms. "Sure."

"I think you've experienced some pretty traumatic stuff in recent days. I think it's affected your rational mind. And I don't think your boss knows how screwed up you are, or he would not have sent you here."

"With all due respect—"

"I also think Captain Yusuf panicked after seeing what was happening in Basra. I think he had a mental breakdown and most of his story is in his head. What happened in Basra was a biological incident, as the president explained, and someone on board the *al-Phirosh* was infected. When Yusuf found out, he freaked and convinced his crew they were all going to die if they didn't abandon ship. He convinced himself something supernatural was on board and told the crew the only way to survive was to sink the ship."

Mike shook his head. "Yusuf wasn't lying. I know when someone is lying to me."

"I didn't say he was. He believes it's the truth. How can you lie when you don't know what's real?"

"What happened on the *al-Phirosh* and what happened in Basra and at site R91 are not coincidences."

"No," Temms said. "They're not. They are all related to the accidental release of a biological specimen probably buried in an old weapons cache. The biological attack story is bullshit; I accept that. The material the box at R91 is constructed of, once examined, will probably be explained as specially developed to contain said weapon. The reason why it spreads to those in close proximity and then stops will probably be due to both rate of decay and airborne diffusion."

Mike shook his head. "I've tried to explain everything with the same rationale. But instead of a weapon, I thought it was some ancient hallucinogen that had been trapped in the box. I believed it caused everyone within a certain distance to see things not really there. Horrors of some kind. And that was why people attacked each other. Like it flicked on a primal switch in the lizard brain or something. But I don't accept that anymore."

"Why, Mr. Caldwell? Are you so desperate for an explanation that you'll grasp on to the irrational answer?"

"Yusuf came face-to-face with it. He saw the dead bodies coming at him. If it were a hallucinogen or biological weapon, he would have gone crazy like all the others who have come in contact with it. But he didn't. Which means there's an entity at work here, hopscotching from place to place."

"If that's true, Mr. Caldwell, if a demon is moving from place to place and wreaking havoc, why didn't it kill the entire crew? Why did it let anyone survive? Why did it let anyone survive in Basra for that matter? Why didn't everyone kill each other like R91? And why, for God's sake, would it kill and then stop only to kill again?"

Mike tried to say something, to come up with anything that made sense. But all possible answers avoided him. He didn't know why it killed only to stop. He didn't know why it let some survive only to move to another place to kill again. And most of all, he didn't understand why it moved. The complete randomness of the whole situation drove him crazy. There had to be an answer, a simple explanation, but it was far from his grasp.

"Do you see what I mean?" Temms said. "Although this mess has been fantastic from the very beginning, indulging in the madness will make it only worse. You are too personally involved in this situation to think logically or make sound decisions. Therefore, I must remove you from it."

Mike's eyes widened. "What?"

"As the captain of this ship, I refuse to allow you to perform your grim task and believe you should rest in your quarters."

"This is not your decision to make. The president—"

"I'm well aware what the president has ordered. But I think everyone is acting emotionally in this matter. I could be wrong but am willing to face punishment for disobeying an order rather than allowing the murder of fourteen innocent people on a hunch."

Mike readied further protest but stopped. His shoulders sagged and he nodded. "It's your ship. But if it makes any difference, I don't think I could have gone through with it."

"I understand." Temms put her hand on Mike's shoulder. "A lot has been asked of you. And by the look of you, you've been ridden pretty hard over the last few days. Go get some sleep."

Mike sighed, feeling like he'd lost a battle. "I'm sticking to my theory."

"Get some sleep and see if you feel the same way."

"I will feel the same way."

"Well, we'll see then. One of three things is going to happen: either someone in that berthing carries the biological weapon inside them and everyone in there will kill each other, or your demon is in there and everyone will kill each other, or nothing will happen. In which case, whatever was on board the *al-Phirosh* sunk to the bottom of the ocean with it. In the meantime, we will keep the survivors quarantined and under armed guard. If anything out of the ordinary happens, we'll reexplore the president's order."

"I hope you're right and nothing happens." Mike slipped his hands in his pockets and exhaled hard. "Things were quiet on the *al-Phirosh* for a long time, and it fooled Yusuf. Don't let it fool you."

Temms nodded. "Go get some sleep."

CHAPTER THIRTY-FOUR

Doc Morris finished his rounds in the quarantined berthing. All the survivors were stable and, with the exception of some cuts and other various wounds, resting comfortably. Confident his corpsmen could manage their needs without any further necessity of his immediate attention, Morris decided to write his report on the five deceased members of the *al-Phirosh* stored in the forward refrigerator on the second deck. It didn't have to be anything too detailed. Most, in all likelihood, had drowned. Basic documentation, though, was required until a thorough autopsy could be performed off the ship.

Before typing the official report Morris had to perform an examination of the deceased. He swung by medical on the way down, grabbed his digital recorder and a fresh pad of paper, and headed to the reefer. He descended ladder after ladder to the second deck. Once there he walked forward down the starboard side. The passageway curved in, following the shape of the bow. Then he took a dogleg left toward the middle of the ship, stepped through a door on the right, and then stood before the big steel door of the reefer.

The second deck smelled of exhaust and gasoline with a faint smell of sewage. The entrances to all the engineering spaces, from the main machinery rooms to the sewage pump rooms to the air-conditioning units, were all on this deck. Morris stood and listened, hearing the knocking of the diesels below him and the humming of the air conditioners one frame over.

Morris liked the engineering spaces. He grew up the son of a mechanic and had a natural affinity for the huge sixteen-cylinder diesels that propelled the *Rushmore*. When he came down, he always paused to listen. Every once in a while, he'd wander down into the actual main spaces and gaze at the engines and imagine what his life would have been like if he hadn't gone to medical school.

Not that he wanted to give up his license so he could go turn wrenches or anything. Morris liked his profession. But the engines reminded him of his dad and that was a nice feeling. His dad had died years ago, and Morris felt closer to him when he was down here.

Morris smiled. *Now back to work,* he thought.

He unlocked the reefer and opened it. Cold air spilled out and enveloped him. It felt good compared to the tropical heat that blanketed the ship. He stepped in. On the floor lay the five bodies, wrapped in plastic and sealed with duct tape. The *Rushmore* didn't have a morgue on board like aircraft carriers and other large navy ships. But the reefer worked well enough as a short-term solution. This unit was kept at just above freezing and would sufficiently maintain the bodies until they could be flown off once they were closer to shore.

Morris squatted next to the first one and pulled out a Gerber knife and sliced the tape. He pulled back the plastic and looked over the body. Then he turned on his recorder and started his examination.

Forty minutes had passed by the time Morris squatted over the fifth body, happy it was the last, and sliced through the tape. He pulled the plastic away and revealed the body to the overhead fluorescent light.

He stood up and gasped. The skin and muscle on the hands and arms had fallen off and collected on the plastic underneath in brown and red powder. The lips dangled by thin strips of tissue.

Morris lifted the recorder to his mouth and started to speak when he saw the dead man blink.

"What the hell?" He stepped back and the recorder slipped from his grasp and hit the deck.

The body sat up, its eyes locked on him, its mouth open in a silent scream.

Morris's adrenaline rocketed and he turned and started to run, when his stomach seized up. He fell to the deck hard, his chest caving in and his muscles twitching. His vision failed and pain exploded in his head, as if a spike had been driven into his brain.

Then it all eased, fading away slowly. Morris's vision returned. It was blurry at first but sharpened. The pressure on his chest relaxed and breaths came easier. His stomach unknotted.

He sat up and looked around him. It took him a second or two to remember he was in the refrigerator. Then he looked at the bodies. All of them were there. His eyes shot to the fifth, the one that had sat up.

Or he thought had sat up. It was lying perfectly still now. But the skin and muscle had indeed fallen from its arms and legs. And now he noticed it had also lost skin on sections of its face.

He moved closer, wanting to examine the body further, when nausea washed over him. He leaned to the side on his hands and knees and vomited. Blood and chunks of tissue shot out of his mouth and splashed onto the slick gray deck. Morris retched and puked again.

After a few more heaves, Morris regained his composure. He rocked back and sat on his legs and looked at what had come out of him.

"Jesus," he said. He didn't know what had caused the seizure and the blackout, but he started to think it was worse than an epileptic fit. He wasn't epileptic but had heard of sudden onset. If he had puked bile, he could have brushed it off as motion sickness brought on by the seizures and strain on his body. But looking at the blood and what was clearly digestive tissue, Morris feared it could be some kind of cancer that had gone undetected.

Before he could question any further what was happening to him, Morris heard ungodly screams outside the refrigerator. He pushed to his feet and walked to the door. The world spun around him and he blinked and swallowed, trying to chase the dizziness away. Once he had, he opened the door.

In the space outside the reefer, an engineer in blue coveralls kicked his steel-toed boot repeatedly into the face of a woman in a similar uniform. Blood covered the floor.

Morris rushed forward and grabbed the guy and pulled him away. He spun him around, ready to deck him, but then saw the look in the man's eyes.

They were dead. Well, not dead but glassed over. The kind of look eyes get when the body dies. Vacant. Empty. As if the personality had drained away to nothing.

The man didn't even seem to see Morris. He just broke Morris's grip and walked in circles around the space. After a second or two, the man reached into his pocket and pulled out a utility knife.

The engineer flicked open the blade and pressed it to his neck.

"Wait—"

But the man sliced his own neck from left to right before Morris could even twitch a muscle. Arterial spray burst from the wound onto Morris and the reefer door behind him. The man dropped to his knees, blood pouring from his neck like a waterfall. Then he fell forward onto his face, the blood pumping out along with the rest of his life.

Morris's body shook. He tried to make sense of everything that had happened to him in the last five minutes, to find order in the chaos, but any rational explanation avoided him. Then, another wave of nausea hit him and he dropped to the ground and puked again.

More screams tore him from his desperate gags. They seemed to echo around him. Morris realized the screams came from above him and from passageways to either side.

"What the hell is happening?" he said.

Morris attempted to push up, to move toward at least one of the screams and see if medical attention was required. He needed to try, to at least prevent one unnecessary death. But the world went black again. And this time his vision didn't return.

CHAPTER THIRTY-FIVE

Mike lay on his bed, eyes open, staring at the ceiling, his thoughts on what had happened and what would happen next, when four shrill blasts followed by a female voice blared over the loudspeaker in his stateroom.

"Security alert, security alert," the female voice said. "Security alert, first and second deck forward of frame twenty. Security Alert Team and Backup Alert Force, report. All hands not involved, stand fast. Security alert."

Mike sat up as the four shrill blasts came again and the female voice repeated the message. He stood up and opened the door and walked into the passageway.

The ship was silent. Then he heard footsteps pounding down metal ladders below him, though soon those faded. He walked down the passageway and found the Captain's Ladder. He climbed it and looked in the cabin, but Temms wasn't there.

Mike moved further down the passageway on the O-6 level, past the Captain's Cabin to a watertight door. The word *PILOTHOUSE* was engraved on blue Bakelite.

He lifted the quick-acting latch and opened the door. On the other side of the door stood a tall man behind a console. Mike saw his hands on a small wheel and assumed he must be the helmsman. To Mike's left stood a woman reading the security alert message out loud into a handheld microphone over the ship's announcing system. Next to her stood a couple of quartermasters bent over a chart plotting fixes.

Mike's eyes shifted from left to right. An officer stood in the middle of the pilothouse, a pair of binoculars to his eyes and looking forward out the windows. Another officer stood nearby, talking on a phone. Then Mike's eyes settled on Temms, sitting in an elevated chair on the starboard side of the pilothouse. She had a wireless handheld radio in front of her mouth and spoke fast into it. Mike couldn't hear her but knew by the shade of red on her face she wasn't happy.

"Sir, we're at security alert," the woman who had been making the announcement said to Mike. "No civilians on the bridge while we're at security alert."

Mike turned to her. "I'm sorry?"

"It's okay," Temms yelled across the pilothouse. "Get over here, Mike."

Mike nodded at the woman, then walked over and stood next to Temms's chair.

"What's going on?" Mike said.

"What's going on is all shit is hitting the fan. That's what's going on."

"An outbreak?" Mike said.

"If you want to call it that."

"Is it happening like on the *al-Phirosh*? Are they attacking each other?"

"This isn't a science experiment." Temms lifted the radio and said, "All teams, this is the captain—report status."

The radio crackled and then a voice said, "SAT 1 moving into position."

Then another voice said, "SAT 2 moving into position."

Finally, a third voice said, "BAF standing by on the turntable."

"SAT 1 and 2, do you hear or see anything?"

"This is SAT 1. Negative. The screams have stopped."

"Negative for SAT 2 as well."

Temms lowered the radio and sighed. Her eyes shifted to Mike. "All hell broke loose about five minutes ago. A couple of spaces around the second deck forward of frame twenty reported hearing screams. Then it seemed to spread. I positioned the SAT teams well outside the possible proximity of a moving infected person."

"You're assuming someone is infected," Mike said. "But has there been anything in the quarantine berthing?"

"Not a peep." Temms shook her head. "The second deck is pretty much engineers. All the entrances to the machinery spaces are down there. No one from the berthing or visiting the berthing would venture down there."

"Not the Marine guards?"

"No reason."

"What about the medical guys?"

Temms started to shake her head again and then stopped. "We pulled five dead bodies from the water with the survivors."

"Yeah, so?"

"We stored them in the forward reefer."

Mike started to ask what that meant and stopped. They had stored the dead in the refrigerator, just like the first incident on the *al-Phirosh*.

"Shit," Temms said.

"Who would have gone down there?" Mike said, feeling suddenly lightheaded.

"Doc Morris. He went down there to start his report on the deceased. As long as we have a dead body on board, the theater commander requires an update on all the peculiars. Call it an intel brief for the dead."

"Because they're going to assume custody of them eventually."

"Right. We get close enough to land and the bodies get flown off. Happens all the time in the gulf, with smugglers and fishermen who drown at sea."

Mike rubbed the back of his neck. "And Doc went down there."

Temms held up a finger and pressed the transmit button on the radio. "Doc, Captain."

Nothing.

"Doc, Captain."

Nothing again.

Temms looked at Mike. "All the officers and senior enlisted on board have one of these radios. They like to call it their 'electronic leash.' Well, he should be answering up. Put two and two together."

Mike swore under his breath. "So, now what?"

"Just like Yusuf," Temms said. "We wait. We've got the area contained. I want to wait a little longer before I order them in to take a look."

Mike nodded. "And then what?"

"I haven't gotten that far."

Mike slipped his hands in his pockets. "If the guys in the quarantine berthing aren't showing any signs—"

"Then we've got something else on our hands. And how we beat it, I don't know. Yusuf scuttled the *al-Phirosh* and that failed."

Mike thought about the situation and possible solutions. Only two sprang to mind. Abandon ship with the survivors of the *al-Phirosh* or abandon ship without them.

"I see the wheels in your head turning," Temms said. "And I know what you're thinking. I'm not ready to go down either route. First, I want to see what's in that area, to see if it matches what supposedly happened on the *al-Phirosh*."

"Understood," Mike said.

The radio crackled again. "Captain, SAT 1. Still no movement or sound."

"Captain, SAT 2. Same here."

"Aye." Temms lowered the radio.

"What about the Marines?" Mike said.

"They're keeping the quarantine berthing locked down."

"From people getting in?"

"From getting out."

Mike rubbed his hands together and waited. After a few more minutes, Temms lifted the radio and said, "SAT 1 and 2, commence sweep of the secured area."

"Aye, Captain," both teams said.

"Apparently this thing incubates," Temms said to Mike. "No one was going nutso when we pulled them from the water. So it has to infect and then develop inside someone before it breaks out."

Mike nodded. "We originally thought of Henry Prince as a carrier with a natural immunity himself. But it's pretty obvious he wasn't special."

"Well, it did pick him. Maybe that's what it does."

Mike smirked. "Sounds like the demon theory."

"If what happened down there even remotely resembles what Yusuf described, I'll be willing to believe anything."

"Not so insane now, huh?"

"Oh, it's still insane. But this isn't exactly a sane situation."

"Captain, SAT 1."

"Go ahead."

"Captain—" The voice broke off. "Captain, it's a damn mess down here. I had to order some of my people out. They couldn't handle it."

Temms closed her eyes. "SAT 2, report."

"It's a massacre," the SAT 2 team leader said. "Blood everywhere. I've counted five dead so far. Jesus, it's Higgins."

The transmission broke off.

"Both teams, pull back to the perimeter." Temms sighed and looked at Mike, her eyes weary. "A lot of people just lost friends down there."

"I'd like to go down there," Mike said.

"Not yet." Temms jumped down from her chair. "Officer of the Deck."

A young officer walked over from the navigation table. "Yes, ma'am."

"We're going to stay at security alert. We may go to GQ if we have to."

"What do you want entered in the deck log?" the OOD said.

Temms chewed her bottom lip. "Just put 'crew riot' and the frame numbers until we can investigate further."

The OOD nodded and walked back to the navigation table.

Temms lifted the radio. "All department heads, this is the captain. Assemble in the wardroom in five minutes."

Then Temms motioned Mike to follow.

Semyaza didn't know how much longer he could go on. He had defeated the soul but again just barely. He had thought he was ready to fight and would not have a problem winning. He was wrong. The soul had fought hard. At one point, Semyaza had almost given up.

He crawled through blood and over bodies to a door. He reached up, his hand shaking, flakes of skin showing on his face, and grabbed the knob and turned. Semyaza pulled himself in and shut the door and looked around.

Another fan room.

Yusuf lay in his rack shaking. He had heard the voice of the female over the loudspeaker and heard the pounding of feet outside. Although he understood hardly any English, he knew what was happening. Knew all too well.

This time, though, he had no control over the situation. Like a rat, he sat trapped in his little metal bed. The rest of his crew around him knew, too. He heard them whispering. They talked of fleeing, making a run for it.

"We need to do something," one of them said. "They will just leave us locked in here to die while they abandon their ship."

"Yes," another said. "They will blame us for what is happening. And then they will sink their ship with us aboard."

Yusuf closed his eyes. He wanted nothing to do with this madness anymore.

"If we are going to act, we must act now," said Mahmoud.

Yusuf's eyes opened. He sat up and looked into the space between racks and saw Mahmoud surrounded by seven other men.

"We can overpower the doctors in here, use them as hostages to force them to let us out," Mahmoud said.

No, Yusuf thought.

"Do you all want to die?" Yusuf said.

Mahmoud's eyes settled on him. "How is that? We are trying to prevent just that."

Yusuf shook his head. "You are all panicking. There is no reason to act this way."

"You heard the woman on the intercom," Mahmoud said. "And I know you heard the sound of people running. It has happened again. They have had an outbreak of violence, just like we had. The dead are walking again."

"I know." Yusuf pushed out of his rack. His ribs ached and he grabbed his side. "But if we add to the chaos, what do you think they will do?"

Mahmoud shrugged. "We will have their people. They will let us go for their safe return."

"And where will we go?"

"They have life rafts. They will give us enough for our numbers. And we will get far away from this place before they all realize they are doomed."

Yusuf shook his head. "I will not allow this."

Mahmoud just stared at him. "You are not our captain anymore, last time I checked."

Yusuf's face slacked. "Mahmoud, do not—"

"It is done." Mahmoud broke his stare and turned his attention back to the men around him. "Tell the others. We move in five minutes. If they want to join us, they will help. Those who cannot because of their injuries, we will carry off."

"Where is Feisal?" Yusuf said. "He will tell you how insane this is."

Mahmoud kept his back to Yusuf. "He died."

Yusuf's stomach folded. "No. He was fine. I saw him. They had—"

"He is dead, Omar. They could not fix him. His wounds were too great."

The others nodded and walked to other sections of the berthing to spread the word. Once they were gone, Mahmoud turned to Yusuf. "I am sorry, Omar, but we have to do this."

Yusuf leaned against the racks and breathed short, shallow breaths. "I pray, for all our sakes, you do not get us all killed. The Americans will not take kindly to Arabs taking hostages on their ship."

"It will work."

Yusuf glared at Mahmoud. "If it does not, all our souls are on you."

Mahmoud reciprocated the glare. "Better to die on our feet than drown in a"—Mahmoud paused and looked at the berthing around him—"cage. Where is the honor in that?"

"We are lucky to be alive."

"Maybe it would have been better to die." Mahmoud smiled. "We tried to get away and it still found us. You know that it is just a matter of time before this ship experiences what we did. I will not experience it again."

Then Mahmoud turned and joined the other men. Yusuf closed his eyes and held his ribs and tried to take deeper breaths. Then he prayed for the safety of what crew he had left.

CHAPTER THIRTY-SIX

Mike stood and leaned against a bulkhead in the wardroom, eating a banana he'd lifted from a fruit tray. The *Rushmore*'s department heads, all either lieutenant commanders or lieutenants, sat at a long dining table sans food. Temms stood before them, hands in her pockets.

"Is everyone here?" Temms said and looked around.

Everyone nodded, but no one said anything. Mike continued to eat, his stomach rumbling as he did. He hadn't realized how hungry he had been until he'd taken his first bite. Now, though, the lightheadedness that had persisted started to subside.

"Okay," Temms said. "Everyone, listen up because I'm going to say this only once. Save your questions until I'm done. We don't have a lot of time."

Mike listened as Temms told her department heads about Captain Yusuf and the crew of the *al-Phirosh* and what had happened to them and how the same thing was now happening on the *Rushmore*. Mike watched their reactions as Temms referred to it as a biological weapon gone awry and briefly covered the events of Basra. Some stared in disbelief. Others just shook their heads. And the rest did nothing except breathe. When Temms got to the part covering the events of the last half hour, a few choked up, especially when she mentioned Doc Morris's fate.

"So now the question is, what do we do next?" Temms said. "The answer is not to abandon and scuttle the ship as Captain Yusuf did. Not yet at least. But we will prepare as if we are going to. So, I want all of you to put your departments into a condition one setting. I'm not going to pass the word for general quarters because I don't want to interfere with the security alert posture. Just get your departments moving via radio. And stay away from the first, second, and third decks forward of frame twenty."

Temms paused and looked over everyone again. "Do you all understand what I'm saying?"

A few said, "Yes, ma'am." Others only nodded. Mike wondered if Temms was just falling into the same trap Yusuf had. The shipmaster had tried several different tactics, including containment, before finally having to abandon ship. Was Temms repeating history?

"Now for the immediate and grisly task," Temms said. "The dead in the secured zone needed to be identified, collected, and disposed of yesterday. Every department is to provide four personnel to execute this and it needs to be done within the hour.

"This will be treated like a CBR attack, not a drill. Everyone involved will be in full chem gear. Gas masks on. Autoinjectors will be worn. DCA will establish the route through the starboard side DECON station. The chief engineer and first lieutenant will coordinate this. Cheng will oversee the movement of bodies to the boat deck. First will take over from there, ensuring bodies are disposed of and working personnel are properly decontaminated once they are no longer needed."

Temms paused for a breath. "Working party personnel will not return to ship's company once complete. They will be isolated in the truck tunnel for further observation to ensure they are not infected. Right now, we're establishing a safe stay time of four hours. Once that time elapses, they will move to troop berthing forward of medical for another forty-eight hours. If no outbreak occurs among them within that time frame, they will return to ship's company."

"What do you mean by disposed of, ma'am?" Lieutenant Schiffer said.

"Returned to the sea." Temms flexed her hands. "I wish there was another way, but we don't have a choice."

"Ma'am, how will we explain this?" Schiffer said. "These people have families—"

"I understand that, Ops." Temms took a deep breath and didn't speak for a moment. "The infection spread on board here by way of a dead body. It started in the refrigerator where the five corpses we pulled from the water were stored. Not in the quarantined berthing. We must assume the dead down there right now are just as capable of spreading this bug. Captain Yusuf did not dispose of his dead. We will. And hopefully, we'll save the ship doing it."

"What about air evacuation?" someone else said. "We're closer to Djibouti. Maybe we can start flying people off as a precaution."

Temms shook her head. "We are on our own until we beat this thing. We can't risk spreading it to another ship, let alone land. If this thing makes it back to the shore, we'll have another Basra; and we can't allow that to happen again."

Everyone sat quietly.

"Anything else?" Temms said.

No one spoke.

"Get your people moving. HMCM is standing by in medical to issue autoinjectors. From there, personnel are to report to the DC shop to receive chem suits and masks. They need to be on the turntable in twenty minutes, ready to go. Now get to work."

Yusuf tried to control his hands, but no matter how much he focused, they would not stop shaking. He stood in the back of the berthing, watching his men. They had delayed their assault to ensure the majority knew the plan and had no objections. None did, other than Yusuf. Two were too injured to speak and Feisal had died. The rest had not taken much time to convince. Mahmoud had painted a desperate picture and they had all bought it.

Ten men stood or lay in their racks, acting nonchalantly as the two ship's nurses walked around and filled out paperwork on clipboards. Then Mahmoud nodded his head and several men moved forward from their racks or from the bulkhead they had been leaning against.

It happened fast. The men swarmed, tackling the male and female nurses. They threw punches to subdue the man. Then they tied his wrists together with strips of sheets and gagged him with pieces of pillowcases.

Yusuf cringed as he watched the speed with which his crew operated. Desperation and fear made deadly instruments of men. But they did not gag both of them before they could scream. The female nurse belted a short wail that could crack glass and it required three men to finally pull her down and force the gag in.

Within seconds, the doors to the berthing swung open and three armed Marines rushed in, rifles raised and leveled. Yusuf watched them fan out and secure the escape routes. All their eyes shifted back and forth, taking the measure of their opponents.

Yusuf looked to his crew and saw panic festering in their eyes. Sweat poured from their faces. Their hands shook. The ones who had wrenched knives away from the nurses held them to the hostages' throats. The blades trembled.

A broad-chested Marine moved toward Mahmoud, the rifle pointed at the rebellion's leader. He spoke English. His voice sounded calm but focused.

Yusuf swallowed. His breathing was fast. The Marine continued to speak, but none of the survivors spoke English. Even if they did, Yusuf knew they were so scared they would not know what to do.

Now the Marine screamed the same words. Mahmoud did not flinch, nor did he break his defiant stare with the Marine.

"Forget the hostages," Mahmoud said. "On my order, drop them and charge the soldiers. They will not shoot."

Yusuf's eyes widened. "Mahmoud, are you insane? These are Marines. They will not hesitate if you charge them."

Mahmoud turned his head and looked at Yusuf and smirked. "We will die like men," he said. "Not like farm animals. Not like our brethren on the *al-Phirosh* who did not get to choose how they died. Here we can die with honor."

The other crewmen seemed to gain strength from those words. Yusuf saw them nod, their hands not as shaky now.

Yusuf could not speak. And yet, he would not know what to say if he could. Although he wanted to live and wanted to see his crew make it safely home, Mahmoud's rationale was compelling. After all, what had happened on his ship had followed them here. Would they escape it a second time?

The Marine barked again. The other Marines also yelled. Mahmoud nodded at Yusuf and turned back toward his opponent.

"Allahu akbar!" Mahmoud screamed. The remaining crew of the *al-Phirosh* repeated the words with death-filled intensity.

"Allahu akbar," Yusuf whispered.

Mahmoud pushed his hostage to the deck and rushed forward, the small knife raised above his head. The others holding hostages did the same. Mahmoud took two steps and his chest exploded in a cloud of red. The rifle shot echoed off the metal racks.

Muzzle flashes erupted around Yusuf in three-shot bursts and all of his men fell to the ground in bloody and bullet-riddled heaps. It ended within a few seconds and not one of the crew lived but Yusuf. Tears ran down his face as he looked over his crew, their eyes staring at the overhead. Strangely, though, the feelings of failure he had felt on the *al-Phirosh*, his belief all of it had been his fault, did not rush back now. Instead, looking over his fallen men, pride swelled within him. They had died like warriors. More importantly, they had chosen when they would die. And because of that, they still had their honor.

Yusuf saw the shame of his actions and regretted not having joined them. For what was he now other than a living reminder of the tragedy of the *al-Phirosh*? Could he go on, haunted by the memory of his crew, and live a normal life?

No, he could not.

Yusuf walked over to the body of Mahmoud and knelt. The Marine who had killed him now yelled, but Yusuf paid him no mind. He closed Mahmoud's eyes and said a small prayer over him. Then he grabbed the knife and sprang, sprinting toward the Marine.

He did not feel any pain when the bullet pierced his chest. Instead, it felt like a hand had pressed his sternum and stopped his forward progress. Then his breaths quit, drowning above water, blood filling his lungs. His vision faded and his legs gave out. Yusuf fell to the deck and died.

Temms had just finished addressing the department heads when the gunfire echoed around them. Then the report came a second later of shots fired in the quarantined berthing. Mike braced himself for crazies to swarm in at any moment. Maybe even the officers in here would succumb. The wardroom was on the same deck and only a few frames aft of the berthing. If it was another outbreak, they would be within the proximity to be affected.

Mike looked at Temms and knew the captain was thinking the same thing because she just stared at the floor as if waiting for the inevitable. After a minute though, nothing happened. The rifle shots had stopped. There were no other sounds of violence.

Then one more solitary shot rang out, and it seemed to wake Temms up. The captain lifted her radio and said, "TAO, Captain; report on shots fired."

"Captain, TAO. Marine security reports attack in quarantined berthing."

"I know; we heard it," Temms said. "What happened?"

"Wait one, sir."

Temms lowered the radio and walked toward the exit. "Fuck waiting."

The other department heads didn't budge. Mike, though, pushed off the counter and followed. Within seconds, they were through the watertight door and then the berthing door. Inside, a fellowship of death greeted them.

Temms seemed to freeze, staring down at the bodies. Mike, though, moved past her and over to a Marine sergeant.

"What happened?" Mike said.

"Who the fuck are you?" the sergeant said.

"I'm the man asking questions," Mike said. "Beyond that you don't need to know anything else. Now what happened?"

The sergeant started to say something else, but Temms finally broke her trance and moved beside Mike. "Yes, Sergeant, what happened?"

The sergeant gritted his teeth. "It got fucked up is what happened. We heard one of the corpsmen scream. We came in and found the whole lot had taken all the corpsmen hostage. I ordered them to stand down repeatedly. Nothing."

"None of them spoke English," Mike said.

"Well, I figured that after the first few tries. But that's not the fucked-up part. After a few seconds, this one"—the sergeant pointed at one of the dead—"started talking to this one." He pointed at the dead body of Captain Yusuf. "Then he yelled 'Allahu akbar' and the rest did the same. They threw their hostages to the deck and charged us."

Mike knelt next to Yusuf. He had a scalpel in his hand. "He charged, too?"

The sergeant nodded. "Last one. After everyone else had been neutralized, this cat walks over and picks up the knife and charges. Craziest shit I've ever seen."

Mike rose. "Suicide by Marine."

"What?" Temms said.

"Like suicide by cop," Mike said. "They wanted to die. They knew the Marines would kill them if they charged."

"Jesus, why?" Temms said.

"Probably heard the security alert and put two and two together. Yusuf thought they had ended it on the *al-Phirosh*. Then they find out it followed them here. I wouldn't want to experience that hell again, would you?"

"No. Who would? But it seems like a hell of a big step. Why not try to escape first?"

"They probably did. They had to know the chances of success were pretty much zero. No, they knew this would be the outcome. It's what they wanted." Mike's memory flashed to the insurgent at R91, begging Mike to kill him. "An honorable death."

Temms shook her head. "It doesn't explain the use of force, though."

The sergeant held up his finger. "Now wait a minute, ma'am. We were within our rights to defend ourselves. Verbal warnings had been given. They held deadly weapons and had already demonstrated a willingness to attack personnel. I wasn't going to let them get within two feet of my Marines."

"You could have subdued them without deadly force," Temms said.

"They outnumbered us. One of my men tries to handcuff one while another slits his throat? No thank you, ma'am."

"Mind your bearing, Sergeant."

The sergeant glared back.

"You will file a report, Sergeant. And seeing that your chain of command isn't on board right now, you'll submit it to me within the hour. But in the meantime, you and your men will move these bodies to the flight deck and the two still breathing in their racks to medical. Now go."

The sergeant turned. "Marines, bag the bodies and move them to the flight deck. Move the lame to medical. Now."

Then he walked off. No one said anything for a few moments.

"Fucking Marines," Temms said.

"They did the right thing," Mike said.

"You're just saying that because they did your job for you."

Mike shook his head. "These men wanted to die. They would have assaulted the Marines if given a chance. Then you would have had hand-to-hand combat in here. Sure, the Marines might have subdued three or four of them, but I'm sure you'd have at least one dead Marine for the effort, maybe two. Instead, your corpsmen are still alive. The Marine guard you posted is still alive. And eleven men who wanted to die are dead. Don't forget, you've still got two crewmen from the *al-Phirosh* too banged up to move. So, it's not like all survivors were killed."

"I'm not going to look at this as some kind of success."

"No, it's a shit sandwich. But it could have been worse. You've got to admit that. Hell, I'm thankful it was something like this rather than another outbreak, or me."

Temms sighed. "What else can I do now? I'm sure as hell not going to put them in a reefer."

Mike nodded. "Do you really think tossing all these bodies over the side is going to do any good?"

Temms shrugged. "Not many other choices to consider, are there?"

Mike stood there, looking at the bodies, thankful he hadn't had to kill them. Even so, it didn't change the fear building in his gut that a far bigger massacre lay just around the corner. He wanted off the boat, but he had no way to leave. And if his dreams were to be believed, he had a date with a demon he still needed to fulfill.

"Well, I hope it works," Mike said.

"So do I," Temms said. "I really don't want to end up like Yusuf over there."

CHAPTER THIRTY-SEVEN

Lieutenant Schiffer descended the ladder from the O-2 level to the O-1 in full chemical suit. His bag of 2-PAM chloride and atropine was strapped to his right thigh. He stopped by the DC shop and picked up his gas mask. Strapping it on, he checked to ensure he had a good seal before lifting his suit's hood up over his head and pulling the strings taut. None of his face or hair was visible now.

Leaving the DC shop, he headed aft down the port passageway. At the end, he passed through a door into the truck tunnel. He proceeded down the tunnel to the turntable, where he was greeted by a Security Alert Team member holding a Beretta, barrel pointed down, safety off.

"Sorry, Ops, only security and working party personnel," the petty officer said.

Schiffer walked up to him and looked down on the shorter man. "I'm on the working party." His voice came out muffled due to the mask.

The petty officer shook his head. "We appreciate your help, but the cheng was pretty specific in his orders."

"I'll talk to the chief engineer."

"Cheng said—"

"This isn't open for debate, Bosun Mate." Schiffer took a deep breath and eased his tone. "Look, I know you're doing your job. But Doc Morris was my friend and I want to help move him. Then I'll get out of the way."

The petty officer looked Schiffer over a moment longer, then nodded his head and stepped to the side. "Okay, Ops."

He opened a watertight door and stood to the side. Schiffer stepped through it and found himself surrounded by plastic sheeting. He heard the door shut behind him. He turned in time to see the latch seal the door against the rubber gasket. No turning back now.

His hands parted the sheeting. A few feet of passageway lay on the other side with another curtain of plastic. Schiffer walked forward and parted the second layer of sheeting.

This time, rather than another contamination barrier, he saw a few members of the working party carrying a body. Its head had been smashed in. An eyeball dangled by the optic nerve, bouncing against its cheek, as they hefted it over a knee knocker on their way out of the space.

One of the cleaners looked up from the puddle of blood. "Yes, sir?" he said, his voice muffled through his gas mask.

"Do you know where Doc Morris was found?"

The guy's eyes narrowed. "No, sir." He turned to a guy sealing a body bag. "Hey, Jimmy. Where'd they find the doc?"

Jimmy looked up from the plastic bag. Schiffer noticed his eyes were red through the lenses of his mask. "Don't know. Maybe the second deck."

Schiffer nodded and moved to a ladder and took it two steps at a time down to the second deck. There, the first person he ran into was the overweight and frustrated chief engineer.

"What are you doing down here?" Cheng said. "Some SAT member called me and said you browbeat him into letting you down here."

Schiffer held up his hands in surrender. "Sorry to be interfering. I just want to help move Doc up to the flight deck."

Cheng started to say something and then stopped. "Forgot how close you two were."

Schiffer looked at the starboard bulkhead. "Yeah."

"Sorry to be the bearer of bad news, but Doc's not here."

Schiffer nodded. "Already took him up. Okay, I'll go pay my respects—"

"No," Cheng said. "He's not here, as in I don't know where he is. We haven't found him yet."

Schiffer opened and closed his mouth a few times without saying anything. Then he managed to say, "But I thought—"

"I know, but he ain't around here. Look for yourself. You'd figure if he was caught up in the shitfest, he'd be lying on the deck with the rest of these poor bastards."

Schiffer took in the scene around him. Talking to Cheng, he'd managed to avoid focusing on it too much. Now that Cheng pointed it out, Schiffer looked down and saw they were surrounded by death. Bodies piled to the side, probably ten to fifteen in all. Blood everywhere.

Then he realized he was standing in blood. Cheng was too, but he wore rubber firefighting boots. Schiffer shifted his gaze back to Cheng and swallowed hard and tried not to look again.

"Why doesn't it bother you?" Schiffer said.

"Oh, it bothers me," Cheng said. "A lot of these boys and gals worked for me. But it ain't the first time I've lost people or seen dead bodies. I was the MPA on *Boxer* when it had its main space fire. Saw thirteen people burned to death. It wasn't any prettier than this."

"But this is different. The fire at least gave an excuse for the deaths. This, though—"

"Ain't no difference. Good people died today. And now we're trying to keep more good people from meeting the same fate. The reason don't matter. It just is. Another damn tragic sea tale."

Schiffer nodded, wishing he could wipe his eyes. "I guess so."

Cheng slapped him on the shoulder. "Come on, let's find Doc, huh?"

"Yeah."

"It is over, Semyaza," Uriel said.

Semyaza did not open his eyes and did not care if the seraph appeared only in voice or in the form of white mist or in his human visage. He reached down deep to withstand the searing pain of Uriel's presence.

"You have come to distract me, to weaken my grip."

"No. I come to tell you it is over. There is no point in this any longer. There never was."

"You said man would be my downfall. I have yet to confront a man who has not tried to flee from me in terror. Maybe that is why I hold on. To see this clay person you said would best me."

"Look at your vessel, Semyaza. Do you not see man has already bested you?"

Semyaza said nothing.

"You will never avoid man, Semyaza. How can you? You see, as long as you exist in this form, your fate and man's are intertwined. You hate them, yet you cannot remain free without them."

"I am not defeated yet. And I will not surrender. I want to see the man who will best me."

"You will," Uriel said. "And when it happens, learn something from it. Perhaps you should take a moment and look in a mirror."

Semyaza felt the scorching heat of the seraph disappear and a slight relief passed through him as a result. Focus. He had to regain his focus. Before he could, though, the doorknob moved.

"Hey, Cheng! We found Doc."

Schiffer spun around and almost slipped and fell in blood. He shuffled toward the excited call, pushing past a couple of people, and saw Cheng walking toward a fan room.

"Mind if I go in first?" Schiffer said.

"Be my guest," Cheng said. "But I'm sending a corpsman right behind you."

Schiffer walked through the door into the dark of the fan room. He pulled out his flashlight and swept the room and found Morris sitting on the deck, leaning against the bulkhead in the back under some exhaust ducting. His eyes were closed and his head faced away.

"Doc, it's me."

Schiffer moved to him and was in the process of kneeling when Morris turned and faced him.

"What the fuck?" Schiffer said and froze halfway between standing and squatting.

Morris's eye sockets locked on him. They were vacant, empty voids. Pieces of skin crumbled and floated off his face like dust stuck in a draft. Morris's rose toward Schiffer, and he saw bone.

Schiffer tried to backpedal and retreat but tripped over the corpsman behind him. He fell and landed on his ass. His tailbone hit steel and he yelped. But he didn't stop moving. He kicked with his feet, pushing himself back across the deck like a crab scrambling away from a predator.

"Sir—what the hell?" the corpsman said. He had stepped to the side after Schiffer tripped over him.

Schiffer motioned to Morris. "Get out of here."

The corpsman looked and gasped. "Oh, shit."

Schiffer jumped to his feet and lunged for the door. As he did, his stomach cramped. He fell and hit the deck. The world went black as his body started convulsing. All around him, he heard screams.

CHAPTER THIRTY-EIGHT

Mike retreated to his room, waiting for the inevitable to happen. It was just a matter of time. He believed wholeheartedly Temms was wrong. Dumping the bodies would fail because what they faced was smarter than they were. It would not let itself just be tossed over the side. It had proved so far to be a survivor. He just hoped they would outlive it.

The flight deck was now covered with bodies wrapped in plastic shrouds. The second deck and surrounding area forward of frame twenty were off limits to him. Not that he wanted to snoop around or anything. He'd seen enough of the results of the outbreak for a lifetime. The one reason he'd been sent to *Rushmore*, to ensure the crew of the *al-Phirosh* died in the event of another outbreak, had resolved itself without need of his presence.

He had nothing to do but wait. Either the ship would make it back to Djibouti without further incident or another attack by the demon would occur and they would abandon ship. For Mike that meant either he'd be stuck on the ship for a month in an imposed quarantine at sea or he'd be jumping in a life raft with the rest of the crew trying to flee the demon.

Or you'll be facing it, Mike thought. He wondered about that. He couldn't imagine a situation where he would voluntarily face it rather than flee with everyone else.

Whatever the outcome, Mike had no job now. So he sat on his bed and pulled his flask from his bag and started drinking.

As the whiskey rolled down his throat, Mike thought of the demon. He swallowed and laughed. Had it gotten so bad that he'd actually accepted the idea that a demon existed and was roaming from place to place? He laughed again and drank more.

Mike screwed the cap shut and set the flask down. He lay and stretched out and closed his eyes. He doubted he would sleep but knew he would need strength for what was coming.

"I don't remember you drinking this much."

Mike's eyes opened. His head lifted. Greg sat on the end of the bed, looking at the bulkhead. Mike sat up.

"You probably don't remember me killing so much, either."

Greg nodded and smiled. "True. I don't."

"Both started after you died."

"So, I'm to blame?"

"No, I am. I showed how good I was at murder when I avenged you. Guess I didn't really consider the consequences of my actions."

"You regret taking your revenge."

"Absolutely not. I just wish it would have ended there."

"Everything happens for a reason, even if we don't like it."

Mike grabbed his flask and took a sip. "You mean like that?"

"It helps you with the demons, I know. They'll always be there, though. What you have to accept is there was a reason for them, all of them."

"And I guess you died for a reason, too, right?"

"Oh, there's no doubt about that."

"Really, and what reason was that?"

"To make you a killer."

Mike almost choked on his whiskey. "That was the grand plan?"

Greg nodded.

"Great, glad there's a plan. Can't wait to see what's next."

"You will soon enough."

Mike took another sip. "Everything happens for a reason, right? Well, what's the point of putting up a good killer against something I can't kill?"

Greg chuckled. "Killing isn't the only quality you possess."

"A hint would be nice."

"You're not a hireling." Greg shook his head. "Sorry, Mike, but you must face the wolf."

Mike blinked and opened his eyes. He lay on his back, looking at the ceiling. He sat up. Greg was gone.

"Fucking dreams," Mike said, grabbing his flask.

A demon, he thought. Something supernatural. Something evil. And if it existed, some kind of hell must, too. Did it wait for him with open arms, ready to embrace a natural born killer?

Mike pondered that for a few minutes. This demon killed a lot of people, too. What did that say about Mike? Was he destined for the same fate?

Staring at him, almost mocking him, was a Bible sitting on the nightstand next to the bed. He lifted it and read the cover. The Ignatius edition. Catholic. Mike thought of his parents and Sunday mornings for the first time in years. When had he last gone to Mass? As a sixteen-year-old? He couldn't remember.

He opened it and inside the cover he found the inscription: "To our son, Come home safely. Love, Mom and Dad." Probably belonged to the Marine CO currently training in the Horn.

Mike flipped past the Old Testament and settled in the Gospel of John. His eyes read down the page to chapter 10, verse 11; and his heart seemed to skip a beat. He read through it twice in his head and the third time out loud to ensure he was reading it right.

"I am the good shepherd. The good shepherd lays down his life for the sheep. He who is a hireling and not a shepherd, whose own the sheep are not, sees the wolf coming and leaves the sheep and flees; and the wolf snatches them and scatters them. He flees because he is a hireling and cares nothing for the sheep."

He slammed the Bible shut and set it on the table, his hands shaking. His eyes never left the leather-bound book though.

"I am not a hireling." Mike lifted his flask again. "I must face the wolf."

On his fourth sip from the flask, the word for security alert was passed again over the intercom. It wasn't the same message as earlier. This time, it extended the secured area to the O-1 level and all decks below it all the way to frame seventy.

Mike closed the flask and threw it on the bed, then headed for the bridge. He passed several people sprinting down ladders.

In the pilothouse, Temms stood in front of the helmsman, listening to reports on her radio. She'd gone stark white and her face looked like it had aged a hundred years since last Mike had seen her a half hour before.

"Captain," Mike said, "what's happening?"

Temms looked at Mike. "It. It's happening again. It started in the same place, but it's spreading rapidly. CIC is getting reports of people hearing screams down both port and starboard sides near the second deck."

Mike nodded. "Looks like option two is on the table."

Temms shook her head. "We can wait it out. It'll stop again. As long as it doesn't spread above the O-1 level."

Mike grabbed Temms by the elbow and walked her to the other side of the pilothouse. "Ma'am, you're doing the same thing Yusuf did."

"What?"

"You're trying to save your ship, no matter the cost. You think you can save it if you can outlast the deaths and discard the bodies. But you're just losing more people than you would if you abandoned ship now. Whatever it is, it is attacking your people. You need to get them off and make sure it doesn't."

Temms moved her mouth, but nothing came out. Then she blinked and nodded. "Yes, yes."

She walked back to the center of the bridge. "Officer of the Deck."

"Yes, ma'am."

"Make this official in the deck log: Commanding Officer ordered all hands abandon ship. Do not pass the word. I'll take care of that over the radio. If this thing understands English, I don't want the order being broadcasted all over the ship."

"Ma'am?"

"You heard me."

"Yes, ma'am." The officer of the deck turned from Temms.

As the OOD made the log entry, Temms lifted her radio and said, "All officers and chief petty officers, this is the captain. This is not a drill. Abandon ship. Security alert teams will maintain boundaries until all other personnel are safely off ship. Also, deploy life rafts one at a time at two-minute intervals, both port and starboard sides. I want safe distances between them in case the biologic makes it on to one of the rafts."

Dozens of voices replied an affirmative over the radio. Temms, satisfied her leadership understood her orders, looked at Mike. "Looks like you need to go down and hitch a ride."

Mike nodded. "I'll go grab my bag."

Mike gathered his belongings and took another shot off the flask, then headed down to the weather decks. As he did, he was passed by personnel running down the passageways and leaping over the metal lips, the knee knockers that marked the bottom of the watertight doorframes. One sailor caught his toe and pitched forward and hit the deck hard. Before anyone could ask him if he was okay, the guy was back on his feet and flying down the passageway again.

The craziness didn't end there. Mike walked by offices where personnel yelled at others to get moving. He saw one guy slapping another, trying to snap the guy out of his panicked state.

The hysteria was even worse on the weather decks. Officers and senior enlisted leadership tried to organize people into parties to deploy on the life rafts. Apparently, everyone had had a life raft number assigned to them upon reporting aboard, but no one seemed to remember which one they belonged on.

Mike looked over the side and saw two rafts in the water on the port side with about three hundred yards between them. The people in the rafts seemed to be doing better than those on board.

At least they're not killing each other out there yet, Mike thought as he remembered Yusuf's tale. Probably relieved to be getting off the ship and away from the madness.

He watched another life raft go into the water and people climb single file down a Jacob's ladder to it. Once full, it cast off while another life raft went in and the process was repeated. By the time ten minutes had passed, five more life rafts had gone in the water. To Mike, the crew seemed to have calmed down and were evacuating pretty orderly.

A few feet away, he saw the officer who appeared in charge of the operation overall and walked over to him to try and get on one of the next few rafts.

"Excuse me," Mike said.

"Mr. Caldwell, right?" the officer said.

"Yeah, how'd you—"

"Captain said you'd be looking for a ride."

"Oh, I see."

"Just hang tight a few minutes. I want to get a few more off and thin this crowd out some. Now that the chaos below has stopped, the crew is moving smoother knowing they have some time."

"It stopped?" Mike said.

"Yeah," the officer said. "About ten minutes ago. No more reports of screams. Captain put the word out over the radio."

Mike was happy to hear the news but more encouraged to know Temms wasn't stopping the evacuation. "I'll be over here."

"Got it."

Mike walked over and leaned against the railing next to the Hell Hole. He stood there for a few minutes, watching the abandon ship operation proceed in a now disciplined manner. Glancing over his shoulder across the Hell Hole, he saw the starboard side mirroring the port.

Good, Mike thought. *Let's hope they get the rest off before this shit starts up again.*

Semyaza opened his eyes and saw gray deck. He pushed himself up and found he'd been lying face down on the floor. He turned over and sat, then looked around. He was in a passageway marked with red piping and white walls. A few feet away from him lay a couple of dead bodies.

Delving into the memory of the vessel, he learned the man was named Robert Schiffer, and he was a ranking officer on board this ship, the *Rushmore.*

You do not have another leap in you, Semyaza thought.

Semyaza shook his head, thinking of Uriel. He knew the great seraph did not speak in figurative language. If he said man would best him, then that is what he meant. He did not mean the shell of a man.

Enough, he thought. He needed to find a place to hide and recover. He did not have time to debate himself.

Semyaza stood and walked down the passageway. He moved around the bodies and to a ladder. He climbed it and found another passageway filled with bodies. They were everywhere. Piled in some places. Blood seemed to cover every inch of wall and floor. He had beheld the carnage so many times already that Semyaza paid no attention to it.

The passageway tapered as he progressed forward. Then he found an open hatch. He climbed through it.

On the other side, he stood in a large open space with two tunnels. One tunnel led up an incline. At the top, he saw daylight and people running around, shouting.

Still panicked from what happened to their friends during the chaos, Semyaza thought and moved toward the other tunnel. He had to avoid people at all costs right now.

The second tunnel led down an incline to an enormous open space that seemed to stretch on forever. He walked down it and started looking for places to hide. As he did, he looked over the wooden walls and floor of the space, knowing this empty cavernous location would not, in all likelihood, provide any good spaces to hide; he wondered why he had come down here in the first place.

Because you have nowhere else to go, he thought.

About half the crew appeared to be over the side and clear when Temms walked out from inside the skin of the ship. The captain consulted with the officer in charge, nodded her head, patted the guy on the back, and then saw Mike and walked over.

"Still waiting for that ride, huh?" Temms said.

Mike smiled. "Told the officer I'd hang tight. It was a madhouse down here not too long ago."

"To be expected. But it looks like we're running smooth now. Only about a hundred more to get off the ship."

"Heard the violence stopped."

"Yeah," Temms said and looked away for a moment. "It spread pretty far though before it did."

Mike nodded. "Sorry, Captain."

Temms looked back at him, her eyes red and glassed over. "Should have done this sooner. I'll have a bunch of ghosts with me for a long time."

"I share that same predicament."

Temms nodded. "I suppose you do."

Mike didn't say anything in response.

"The hell of it," Temms said, "is that we'd just finished dumping all the bodies over the side. Then the chief engineer radioed me and said they'd found Doc alive. Next thing you know, all radio contact down there stops. And then the reports started coming in."

Mike stared at the deck, thinking about what Temms had just said. They'd found Doc and then all hell had broken loose.

"Lost a hell of a lot of good people down there," Temms said. "Chief engineer. The MPA and DCA. Ops, too."

"Schiffer was down there?" Mike said.

Temms nodded. "Yeah, he wanted to help move Doc. They were good friends."

Mike shook his head.

"Hopefully, we can get everyone off before it starts up again," Temms said. "Once we're well clear, I get to call AFRICOM via satphone and give them the green light."

Mike's eyebrows popped up. "Green light?"

"Talked to the president again a few minutes ago and let him know the situation. He was not pleased."

"I imagine not."

"Anyway, once we're clear, a submarine operating off the coast of Somalia is going to come in and plant a MK-48 torpedo under the keel and sink the *Rushmore* to the bottom of the sea."

"At least they're letting you get the crew off."

Temms nodded, but her face was grim. "I had to fight for that much."

"What?"

"Some on the line argued letting the crew off was too risky."

"You're still goddamn Americans."

"Yes," Temms said. "But if it breaks out again on board here or in one of the life rafts, I have a feeling none of us will be allowed to see another sunrise."

"Well," Mike said. "We'll get everyone off and leave this shit behind for the sub to take care of."

Temms nodded. "Oh, your boss wanted me to tell you not to die because he's still got work for you to do."

Mike smirked. "Thanks."

"Sounds like a kind man, that one."

"Yeah, a real teddy bear."

The right corner of Temms's mouth crooked up, but that was it. Then it returned to a grimace. "Well, I'm going to go see how many we've got—"

"Holy shit, it's Ops," someone said.

Mike turned to his right and saw a sailor looking down into the Hell Hole. Mike shifted his gaze and saw Schiffer walking in the well deck below, heading aft, his head hung low, as if he were lost. Then Schiffer looked up at them. His face was covered in blood and his eyes looked empty.

Schiffer scurried off into the darkness of the well deck out of sight.

"Did you see him?" Mike said.

"Yes," Temms said. "We need to go get him. He looks hurt. I'll send—"

Mike held up his hand. "I wouldn't do that just yet."

"What?"

"There's something wrong here." Mike backed away from the Hell Hole. "You said Schiffer was down there when they found Doc Morris. And he was alive. Then everything went to shit."

"Yeah, so?"

"Now we see Schiffer and he's alive. How many survivors have walked out of one of the outbreaks before, on here or the *al-Phirosh*?"

"None."

"Because anyone within a certain proximity ends up killing and then being killed." Mike pointed down into the well deck. "Even if he was the last one standing, he should have killed himself."

"Didn't Yusuf say something about two engineers who felt like they were under a spell and then it broke?" Temms said. "Right before they attacked each other?"

Mike nodded. He'd forgotten about that. "You're right."

"Maybe he just survived long enough to outlast the spell."

"He was at ground zero down there, though. Is it worth the risk?"

Temms gritted her teeth. "I can't in good conscience just pretend I didn't see him."

"No, I suppose you can't."

Mike looked down and swore under his breath. Then he took in the operation around him. There were a lot of life rafts in the water, but there were still plenty of damn people waiting to leave.

And if this shit starts again, we're all dead, Mike thought. *Those people in the rafts, too, if the president does what others want him to do.*

I am not a hireling, Mike thought, and everything crystallized in his mind. *I am a good shepherd protecting the sheep from the wolf.*

"How long to get the rest of the people off?" Mike said.

"Half hour, maybe more," Temms said.

Mike swore to himself again. "I'll go down there."

Temms's eyes widened slightly. "What?"

"You get your people off of here. I'll go down and check on Schiffer. If he is just hurt, I'll bring him back up. If he's, well, if he's something else, I'll take care of it."

"You can't kill this one, Mike."

"I don't think this is something you can take care of in the normal sense."

Mike nodded. "I know. Maybe I can buy you some time. If it focuses on me, it isn't worried about your people. Should give you enough time to get them clear."

"You'd do this?"

"Yeah." Mike remembered Greg, sitting on the edge of the bed, telling him killing wasn't the only quality he possessed. "I don't care if I die."

Temms started to say something and then stopped. She looked around at her people and then back to Mike. "Good luck, Mike."

Mike smiled. "Just get them off."

Temms handed Mike his radio. "Take this. I'll call you when we're all off."

"You sure?"

"I'll get another."

Mike tucked the radio into the back of his pants. "All right, then."

Mike turned and walked toward the truck tunnel leading down to the well deck. As he did, he heard Temms say, "Officer in Charge, CANEX the two-minute separation. Get all these people off now."

CHAPTER THIRTY-NINE

Semyaza knew the humans had seen him through the hole in the ceiling. And he knew they would be sending people to find him. That is what humans did. They saved one another.

He moved away from the hole and down the space, looking for a hatch or a door or anything. He found nothing. The only way out seemed to be the way he came in.

Then Semyaza saw him. He had looked over his shoulder, just briefly, and saw a man walking slowly down the ramp.

They are not sending more because they do not want to lose more, he realized.

He was thankful he did not have to deal with a whole host of people. One man would be easy to take care of.

But do you have the strength? he thought. *If you confront the man, you are not focusing on preserving the vessel.*

Instead, Semyaza turned away and moved toward the aft of the well deck. He needed to avoid all confrontation right now.

As he walked, Semyaza saw a ladder on the side of the space. It ran from about three feet above the deck to a catwalk halfway up the side.

Semyaza moved over to the ladder, grabbed the bottom rung, and pulled up and started climbing.

Mike descended the ramp in the well deck, Beretta in hand and at his side. He moved quickly but cautiously, his eyes sweeping left to right to left, his ears tuning out the ruckus above. Schiffer had to be down here. From what Mike saw, there was only one way in and out, and that was now behind him. The lighting was poor, but enough sunlight passed through the Hell Hole to illuminate a majority of the space.

Then he saw him, almost all the way aft, walking fast. Mike started jogging, the Beretta now held in front of him, both hands in a firing grip.

"Shit," Mike said.

He watched Schiffer cross to the side of the well deck and climb up a ladder. Mike sprinted. By the time he reached the ladder, Schiffer was up and out of sight.

Mike holstered the gun and jumped, grabbing the fourth rung up. He climbed fast despite the pain in his side, made it to the catwalk, pulled himself up into a crouch, and grabbed the gun again. He knelt for a moment, clearing the area around him in case Schiffer had planned to attack him once he reached the top.

Which way did he go? Mike thought. He could have gone aft, but then Mike noticed a small piece of skin on one of the grates. Then another.

Once Mike was satisfied there was no attack coming, he moved forward following the trail.

Semyaza moved down yet another passageway. He looked at a sign on the bulkhead that stated he was on the first deck, starboard side. Then he came across more bodies.

He stepped over them and looked through a couple of doors for a good place to hide. All the rooms were offices. Semyaza knew the ship was in a panicked state, but could he risk hiding in such a public place?

A door opened behind him. Semyaza looked down the passageway and saw the man who had been following him walk through the doorway from the catwalk.

"Lieutenant Schiffer," the man said, "please don't go any farther."

Semyaza saw the gun in the man's hands. He could not risk taking any damage to the vessel. But he had to stop the man from pursuing any further, or he would never rest.

Is it worth the risk? he thought. He admitted he did not have a choice. Either he confronted the man and suffered damage, perhaps serious, or he could scare him away.

Semyaza did not hesitate any longer and reached out.

Mike saw the bodies first, three of them, lying in a giant pool of blood. Then his eyes settled on Schiffer standing on the other side, staring at him, eyes vacant as if no consciousness dwelled on the other side of them.

"Lieutenant Schiffer," Mike said, "please don't go any farther."

Schiffer stared at him. He seemed to be calculating something, weighing his options. Mike didn't like what he saw and knew the lieutenant was not himself anymore. Whether he was changed through exposure or just a vessel for a demon, he didn't know for sure. But he did know Bob Schiffer was gone.

At that moment, Mike decided to shoot Schiffer. This needed to end now, and it needed to end quickly.

As Mike raised his gun, Schiffer extended his right hand in front of him. Mike thought the man had figured out his intentions and was lifting his hand in the "stop" motion, like the corpses from his dreams. Instead, the corpses in front of him moved.

They twitched at first. Then their arms moved, pushing the torsos up. They pulled their legs underneath them into a squat. Then they stood, their heads lolled to the side. Different masks of death covered their faces. One had a serene look, as if death had been welcomed. The other had a permanent sneer, like death had told an unfunny joke. The final had the mask of eternal pain written into its crevices.

Mike took a step back, his unblinking gaze locked on the three corpses standing before him.

"Holy shit." Mike remembered Yusuf's story of the walking dead. The gun shook in his hands.

You can't kill this one, he thought. What the hell could he do?

Schiffer answered his question by throwing the bodies at him. Mike lifted his arm to his face and tried to duck. All three bodies hit him and knocked him to the ground. They landed on every part of him. A head butted his. A knee hit his groin. An elbow nailed his stomach. The wind escaped his lungs, and green dots of light filled his vision.

Mike lay there for a few seconds, catching his breath and blinking until his vision returned to normal. Then he realized three undead bodies blanketed him. He flailed and pushed, knocking the corpses off him and swimming to the surface of dead flesh.

He breathed hard and deep, adrenaline coursing through him. Schiffer was gone. Mike waited to see if the corpses would attack again, but they didn't.

"He controlled them," Mike said. "Jesus Christ, he controlled them."

Mike resisted pursuing any further. What was the point? Then he shook his head. Schiffer was on the move. If he made it to the weather decks…

Not going to happen, he thought. Mike checked his gun and then his hand. He stared at it and concentrated on controlling the shakes, wishing his flask wasn't empty. He forced himself to calm, to regain his composure. After five seconds, his hand steadied.

Another deep breath and Mike moved forward in pursuit of Schiffer. He made it ten feet down the passageway and around a corner, when another body flew at him. Mike raised the Beretta and squeezed one round off, hitting the body in the head. The bullet entered the forehead and blew out the back of the skull.

It kept coming.

Mike squeezed off two more rounds, hitting it in the face.

Still moving, only five feet away.

Mike stopped shooting and grabbed a CO_2 bottle from the bulkhead and swung it and hit the body hard enough to knock it off its forward path. It smacked the bulkhead and collapsed to the deck.

You can't kill this one, Mike, he thought. *No shit.*

He holstered the gun and carried the CO_2 bottle like a staff in both hands. Through a watertight door, Mike saw several more bodies. He slowed and waited for them to spring up and fly at him.

They didn't.

He walked between them, cautiously, sweat dripping from his face, expecting their hands to grasp his ankles at any moment.

They didn't.

Mike breathed easier once he had the bodies safely behind him. Even then, though, thoughts of dead bodies springing to life behind him coursed through his mind.

The passageway hooked left and then right. Mike passed a room with SUPPLY engraved on a brass plaque on the door. As he turned right, Mike stepped over a knee knocker and into another passageway leading past frame fourteen.

Almost at the front of the ship, Mike saw Schiffer sitting on top of a hatch, fiddling with a combination lock. No other bodies lay within sight, so Mike lowered the CO_2 bottle to the deck and drew the Beretta and aimed it at Schiffer's head.

He approached slowly, the gun steady in his hands. When he was within six feet, Schiffer looked up, and it took all of Mike's composure and experience not to scream.

The skin on Schiffer's hands had apparently fallen off or disappeared or whatever skin did when it was no longer needed. So had the muscles and tendons and ligaments. All that remained were the small bones of the hands—the carpals and metacarpals and phalanges.

Mike fired three rounds: one in the forehead and two in the chest. Schiffer responded by scratching at the new wounds briefly before returning to the lock, as if the bullets piercing him had been nothing more than a brief annoyance. Mike went to fire another round but froze, knowing it wouldn't do any good.

You can't kill this one.

He watched the bony digits fiddle with the combination lock as Schiffer's eyes locked on him. Pieces of skin on the man's face had also vanished, exposing muscles around the cheekbones and jaw, as if someone had driven by and flayed certain pieces only to drive off.

"I believe I have run out of escape routes," Schiffer said.

Only it didn't sound like Schiffer. At least not the Schiffer Mike had talked to. The voice was deeper now, almost guttural. As if the person—or thing, if it was a thing—spoke with his stomach instead of a mouth.

Mike kept the gun level and pointed. "Looks that way."

"It also appears your path has come to an end."

Mike shrugged. "Maybe it has."

"It has."

You can't kill this one.

"Well, then, what happens next?"

Schiffer shook his head. "Why are you not afraid?"

"Oh, I'm afraid." Mike had broken out in cold sweats from trying to keep from shaking.

"Why did you not flee then?"

"Not an option."

"Even when the bodies attacked you, you fought them off and still pursued me."

"Is that what you wanted, me to run away?"

"It would have been better for me, yes."

"Why's that?"

"You would not comprehend it."

Mike glanced at his watch and knew he still had to buy more time. "Try me."

Schiffer held his boney right hand up. "This body is not my true form. It is merely a vessel."

"Because you're a demon."

If looks could kill, Schiffer's would have torn Mike's heart out. "I am no demon, human."

"Well, excuse me all to hell."

Schiffer spat and said something in a language Mike had never heard before. More skin fell from his face.

"I am what you clay people call an 'angel.' A Throne to be exact."

Mike's hair wanted to stand on end. He wanted to run, but the fact that he needed more time, that the crew needed more time, cemented him in place.

"Bullshit," Mike said. "Angels don't possess people."

"Not all angels like humans."

"Is that why you were imprisoned?"

Schiffer looked away. "You have seen it?"

"Box under the sand made of weird material and tons of unknown writing carved into the walls. Yeah, I've seen it."

"The writing is angelic. My crimes and punishment carved over and over. A reminder for eternity."

Need to keep him talking, Mike thought. "So, what'd you do?"

"Rebelled." Schiffer looked at his hands and his body. "I sided against mankind. And we lost. I was stripped of my light and imprisoned beneath mankind as punishment. I cannot exist outside of the prison unless I inhabit a human vessel. And I can inhabit a vessel for only a short time before it decomposes."

"And if it decomposes, you go back to prison."

"Or I invade another body and defeat the soul."

Mike lowered his gun, his hands shaking. "So I guess I'm your next vessel."

Schiffer nodded. "You should have run away."

"Why, if you need me?"

"Because each battle weakens me. I have almost lost several fights already. And I am not confident what the outcome with yours will be, you who pursues angels."

"Thanks for the reassurance." Mike squatted and looked at his watch. Only a few more minutes. "Why does everyone kill each other?"

More skin fell from Schiffer's face and arms. All of his teeth were visible. "Part of the punishment. Where I dwell, chaos reigns. When I fight the soul, chaos destroys everyone near. When I am victorious, chaos destroys the host."

Mike sighed. "Sounds like you were better off in prison."

"Man was better off with me in prison." Schiffer closed his eyes. "God chose you above the rest of us, honored you by creating you in His image, allowed you to choose whether you even believe in Him or not. Angels know He exists and when we protested that decision, when we executed our free will not to bow before you, we were punished harsher than your ancestors who fell in the Garden. And now you sit here before me and say it would be better for me in my prison. Well, human, I am no longer cold and alone."

Mike looked around and then back at Schiffer. "You got buddies here?"

"What?"

"Well, you said you're not cold and alone. Don't know what that means, but I got news for you; you're alone. And if temperature has anything to do with it, well, buy a heater."

Schiffer sprang forward and got nose to nose with Mike. "I have been cut off from *God*! Forsaken! Abandoned! You do not know what that feels like because you do not even know if He exists! But I do, and it is a fate worse than hell!"

Mike refused to blink even though his insides softened like jelly. "And do you feel God now, demon?"

Schiffer gritted his teeth and Mike saw all of them rub together.

"Your soul will soon feel me, human."

"So, you're real. And heaven's real. And hell—"

"Is real."

It's real, Mike thought. *And what happens to a natural-born killer when he dies?*

Mike remembered the people he had killed and wondered how he would be judged as a result. Was he righteous or just a devil with a gun? Knowing now there was more than his conscience to battle scared the hell out of him. But he could change it, right? He could be the good shepherd from now on.

"You can't judge yourself." Gunny Lowe's voice echoed in his head. *"But you will be judged."*

Mike's radio crackled. "Mike, it's Temms. All personnel are clear of the ship."

Schiffer looked at the radio and then back to Mike. "What did he say?"

Mike smiled, relief pumping through his veins. "Everyone's off the ship. Well, everyone but me. Looks like I'm your last stop."

Schiffer backed away and fell on his ass. "Gone?"

Mike nodded. "Yep."

"It is over." Schiffer buried his face in his boney hands. "That is why you came down here? To distract me?"

"Well, I came to keep you from making everyone go bat-shit crazy and kill each other. I didn't understand the whole body-jumping thing at the time. Figured I could occupy you long enough for them to get off."

Schiffer lifted his head. Almost all the skin on his face was gone. "You chose to sacrifice yourself to save them."

Mike shrugged. "Didn't look at it that way. I can't kill you, so I kill myself to win."

"But you came nonetheless."

"I don't care if I die or not. Those people do. If some demon kills me, so what? I've been dying on the inside for a long time."

Schiffer chuckled. "My name is Semyaza, human."

"Mike." He felt suddenly uncomfortable at the laughter. "What's so funny?"

"Besides the fact that you are the first human I have ever talked to? Someone told me man would best me, defeat me. I assumed it would be an actual battle. Flesh against flesh. I did not expect a man to willingly give himself to me, so to speak."

Mike nodded. "I see. So does that mean you're giving up?"

"I could take your body but I'd have nowhere to go. Stuck at sea with no other possible vessels after you and this one rapidly decomposing. I am doomed, Mike."

Mike didn't say anything.

"I finally see what makes you humans so special."

"What's that?" Mike said.

"Your ignorance."

Now Mike chuckled.

"You laugh, but it is true. Your ignorance is what allows you to make sacrifices. Angels do not die for one another because we do not die. Therefore, we do not sacrifice for one another. We follow orders. We can make choices, but faith does not matter to us. In my case, pride was my downfall because I was not willing to have faith in man. I refused to sacrifice position for you.

"If humans knew without a doubt their souls lived beyond their flesh, would people still willingly take that leap? Would they still sacrifice what is sacred, or would they become more reckless with their mortal possessions? If you knew what I know, I doubt you would have risked your life for all those people because you would know that there is more beyond this realm."

Mike rubbed his head, trying to comprehend everything he'd just heard.

Semyaza chuckled again. "Do not try to understand it all. Just know I refused to sacrifice my position in favor of man. I thought man was nothing more than an animated ball of clay. I see now you are more complex. You sacrifice for the good of others. Faith does not matter to angels, but trust does. I wish I had maintained my trust. My loyalty. For that, I am sorry."

Mike only nodded.

Semyaza looked at his hands and flexed his fingers. "I am tired of this existence, Mike. And I think I am going to surrender it now."

"Okay." Sweat dripped from Mike's face.

"I would put that gun out of arm's reach. When I release my grip, chaos will reign for a few moments until I am away from here. I would hate to have shared this conversation with you only to see you kill yourself."

Mike nodded and flipped the safety on the Beretta and slid it across the deck away from him.

"Good-bye," Semyaza said.

Mike said half a syllable, when his world went dark.

CHAPTER FORTY

The trance broke and Mike found himself kneeling in front of a bulkhead, his hands braced on it, and his head reared back as if prepared to head butt the steel.

Dizzy, exhausted, and drained, Mike pushed off the wall and landed on his ass and sucked in a deep lungful of air. To his right he saw Schiffer slumped over; all of the flesh and muscle had dissolved into powder on the deck around his skeleton.

"It's over." Mike wiped the sweat from his face with both hands. "I hope."

He found the radio on the deck a few feet away. He crawled over and picked it up and cued it. "Captain Temms."

"Mike?"

"Yeah."

"Jesus, we figured you were dead when you didn't respond."

"I was in the middle of something."

Temms paused on the other end and then said, "Is it over?"

"Yeah, I think so."

"How do you know?"

"Long story."

"What was it?"

Mike glanced at the skeleton. "Long story. I'd say it's probably safe to come on board but would wait awhile longer. I'll stay here and see what happens."

"All right, Mike. We'll stay a few hundred yards off the ship."

"Okay." Mike sat up quickly. "Hey, that sub isn't getting ready to sink me is it?"

"No," Temms said. "We haven't called it in yet. I'll take care of it."

"Don't sink my ass."

Temms laughed. "We'll do our best."

Mike set the radio down.

"It doesn't matter how many I kill," Mike said, looking at Schiffer's remains.

For the first time in a long time, the weight of so many ghosts on his shoulders lifted. He sighed and closed his eyes.

Semyaza found himself teetering on the edge of a cliff above a dark chasm. Around him, the blackness of damnation watched in silence. He looked down at himself and found he had been given his true form back.

"You look surprised, Semyaza."

He found Uriel standing at his side, appearing in the human form he had chosen earlier.

"This is not my prison."

"No," Uriel said. "It is not."

"What is happening, Uriel?"

"I told you man would best you."

"Yes, you did. But you also said I would return to my prison."

Uriel shrugged. "Things have changed."

"What do you mean?"

"You were penitent, Semyaza. At last you recognized the folly of your pride. You have earned your freedom from your prison and will be judged."

Semyaza tried to say something but could not. "I… I…you mean, I am being damned?"

Uriel nodded. "I am sorry, Semyaza. You have earned judgment, but you have also earned your place in hell."

"I understand." Semyaza wept. "Thank you, Uriel."

"You are welcome."

"If I could go back and change what I did—"

"I know; I know. I just wish your brethren would see things the same way. Unfortunately, they have even harsher punishments in store for them."

Semyaza said nothing.

"Farewell, Semyaza."

"For good?"

"For good."

"Well, then, farewell."

Uriel's human form dissolved and transformed into a swirling ball of fire. It swooped in and wrapped around Semyaza. The Firmament radiated through Uriel and burned Semyaza to his core. Then the mighty seraph cast the fallen angel into the dark chasm for eternity.

The night came and went, and everything remained quiet. Mike had moved from the death spaces to the wardroom, where he passed out on the sofa in the lounge. The next morning, the crew of the *Rushmore* started moving back on board. Mike helped as long as he could until his body just gave out. Temms ordered him to bed and Mike concurred, after he got his bag back.

In his room, Mike slept for a full day.

When he woke up, all the bodies had been returned to the sea; and the ship was en route for Djibouti. It would have to remain in quarantine off the coast for a week rather than a month. Temms had told the president it had been a biological specimen and Mike had successfully found the carrier and disposed of it. A couple of days without further outbreaks seemed to convince the president the crisis had ended.

Mike decided it was time to tell his side of things to Glenn. But when he called him, he couldn't force himself to recount the story, as if he'd imagined all of it and didn't trust what he believed.

"I know you're holding out on me," Glenn said.

Mike stood on the forecastle and watched the sun dipping near the horizon over the African coast. The salt air never smelled so good to him.

"I don't even know where to begin," Mike said. "It's all pretty unbelievable."

"Tell it to me when you get back to Langley. Get your thoughts in order. Write it down if you have to."

"Langley? No desk job, right?"

"No desk job."

Mike took a deep breath. "I'm not killing any more people. I'm done with that unless it's in the line of duty. No more assassinations."

Glenn was silent for a moment. "We'll talk when you get home."

"As soon as I'm allowed to set foot on Djibouti soil, I'll hitch a ride home."

"Before you do," Glenn said, "I want you to take a short detour to Iraq."

"I thought—"

"Go to site R91. I want you to see what's there."

Mike shook his head. "Glenn, I've already been there. I can tell you what's at R91."

"Go to R91 and see what's there."

The line went dead.

Mike looked at his phone and then the sea and wondered what the hell his boss was playing at.

CHAPTER FORTY-ONE

Mike stood at site R91 under a blistering sun and in a whipping wind that pelted him with sand. All around him, earth-moving equipment groaned and roared, lifting soil and burying large pipes in the ground. The yells of crews interrupted the grind of machinery, barking orders in both English and Arabic.

In front of him was the pit that Semyaza's prison had been in. Now a large sewer line sat there. It had not fallen in like the piece that had freed the angel. Instead, it had been placed there, the branch of several lines coming together.

"What the hell happened?" Mike said. "Where did it go?"

Glenn had told him to come to R91 and see what was there. What he saw was one missing prison, gone, erased from the face of the earth.

"Can I help you?"

Mike turned and saw an Iraqi in a hard hat with safety glasses on staring at him. Sweat had soaked through almost every inch of the man's clothing. On his vest he wore a nametag: A. Haddad.

"Uh, yeah. Are you the foreman?"

Haddad nodded. "I have taken the place of the late Henry Prince."

"Smart to hire an Iraqi."

"The company felt it would help eliminate some of the information lost in translation."

Mike smirked. "I was here not long ago investigating the massacre." Mike pulled out his identification for Jeremiah Hosselkus. "There was a strange tomb down in this pit last time I was here. What happened to it?"

Haddad inspected his ID before saying anything. "It's gone."

"I can see that." Mike looked back down in the pit. "Did the Department of Antiquities excavate it?"

Haddad looked at him a little longer. "How much do you know about what was down there?"

Mike hesitated, then figured what the hell. "I was in it. Basically a box constructed out of this weird material. Like nothing you ever saw before. Strange writing carved into—"

The words stuck in Mike's throat as he noticed a tattoo on the foreman's chest. It wasn't noticeable at first. But when Haddad shifted his weight to his other foot, the collar of his shirt opened a little more, revealing the writing just under his collarbone.

Haddad caught what Mike stared at and closed his shirt. "I am afraid you must leave now. Employees only."

Mike shook his head. "You're one of them."

"I do not know what you are talking about."

"Bullshit." Mike got close, almost nose to nose. "I was here when your little group attacked. And they had those same tattoos. Just like the writing on the walls of that prison that has mysteriously disappeared. So you tell me what I want to know, or I'll take care of you right now."

"Arrest me? On what charge? Too many tattoos?"

Mike smiled, the old reflexes kicking in. "Who said arrest?"

The foreman's face slackened and his eyebrows drooped. "You would not."

"I was here that night, and it wouldn't be the first time I've taken care of one of your kind." He didn't want to kill, but inflicting some pain wasn't sounding so bad. "Now tell me what happened to the prison."

Haddad looked away, biting his bottom lip.

"Tell me." Mike fingered the Spyderco in his pocket. "Now."

"It disappeared."

"It what?"

"Disappeared. Vanished. As if Allah's breath blew it away."

"And the angel inside?"

"The what?"

"The demon, damn it. I know what was in it. Is it gone?"

Haddad shrugged. Mike gazed down in the pit.

"You have seen it, have you not?" Haddad said.

"Why do you say that?"

The foreman pointed at him. "You have a look on your face, like you are relieved."

"You're not relieved?" Mike said. "I thought that was the whole point of your little gang."

Haddad nodded. "I was raised on stories about my duty as a guardian. I did what was required of me." The foreman pointed at him. "You, though, were a witness to it, were you not?"

"I don't know what you're talking about." Mike smiled. "And I'm going to do some checking on you, friend. If I find out you were involved in that attack that night, this won't be the last time you see me."

Mike turned and walked away, leaving thc foreman stammering. He headed for his car, ready to put all the supernatural shit behind him. Ready to go to Langley.

Ready to do some real work.

A secret order at war with itself.
A Syrian official who wants to set the Middle East ablaze.
And all of them want nothing more than one unlucky CIA agent…

Read on for a sneak peek of the sequel,

GUARDIAN

on sale January 27, 2015,
from Harper Voyager Impulse!

An Excerpt from

GUARDIAN

CHAPTER ONE

Mike Caldwell hadn't killed anyone in a couple of weeks. Hadn't wanted to, either.

Until now.

He sat in his Lincoln Town Car in the makeshift lot at construction site R91 outside Ur in Iraq, the A/C blasting. He chased dark thoughts away and tried to gain a handhold on calm.

Go back to site R91, he thought. *See what happened. And I did. Just like Glenn said. What do I discover? The prison's gone. Up and pulled a disappearing act. Oh, and the site foreman also happens to be a tattooed asshole member of that wonderful group that tried to kill you not too long ago.*

Speaking of which, A. Haddad, the site foreman, stood by a backhoe thirty feet away, talking on a cell phone, staring at Mike.

Probably calling his buddies. Which meant he better get moving. *They might be after you. Come at you in numbers. And you're all alone out here.*

But the dark winds swirled around him with greater velocity. Mike considered throwing caution to the wind. He rubbed his fingers and licked his lips. He wanted his flask. Longed for the burn.

You're a killer. It's what you're good at.

The old thoughts bounced around his head as the blackness pushed in on him. Haddad stood there in the infernal Iraqi sun, never breaking his stare. Daring Mike to add him to his closet full of ghosts.

Mike had made peace with his past. Locked the ghosts of his victims away. They would always haunt him, but he believed he could bear them. As long as he didn't add to their grim population. But now, looking at Haddad, part of him wanted to bump up the total. Stuff one more in the closet of death that was his head.

Enough. He licked his lips and looked away. He typed the foreman's first initial and surname into his cell phone and pressed save. He wished he could have gotten a first name, but it hadn't come up before the conversation turned sour. All he could do was grab the name and initial off the foreman's nametag and make a promise to find out his role in the attack on R91.

Now leave.

But he didn't want to leave. He wanted to get back out and walk up to Haddad and put a round through each eye. One for Lowe and one for Greengrass.

Not now, he thought. *You're burned. Get moving.*

Mike shifted into drive and floored it. He'd had enough of R91 for several lifetimes. The rear tires spun, creating a cloud of sand. The Lincoln roared from the lot onto the main road leading from Ur to An Nasiriyah. He cranked the stereo and blasted Stevie Ray Vaughn through the speakers.

Just when he thought he'd put the last bit of craziness behind him, he learned not only that the prison had vanished into thin air, but that the guardians still circled the site. They knew the prison had disappeared, too. Haddad had said as much. But they were still here. Why?

Doesn't matter, he thought. *Ponder it when you're in safe country and no longer outnumbered. Because you have no idea who else is out here besides Haddad.*

Just because there wasn't a prison to guard anymore didn't mean the desert-dwelling assholes wouldn't try something stupid. It wouldn't be the first time. How many times had they been wrong so far? Well, one: they thought they'd been guarding a demon.

But it wasn't any run of the mill demon, Mike thought. It was something more. One of Satan's very own. The assholes had it big-time wrong on that front. Not an Arabic folklore version of a demon at all. Nope, a fucking fallen angel.

Two, they hadn't even known the exact location of the prison. Just knew it was buried near Ur. So they protected a whole swath of land for God knows how many years. And the one time it did need protecting,

when the construction crew dug it up and opened it by accident, they were nowhere to be found.

But it was all over now. Semyaza was gone. The prison had mysteriously disappeared. What did it matter anymore if Haddad belonged to the Ancient Order of Dumb Fucks or the Masons?

Mike's thoughts drifted to Greengrass and Lowe. Good men. Great Marines. The former now severely wounded and the latter dead, thanks to Haddad and his buddies. Maybe Mike wouldn't stop with Haddad. If he found out enough about the guardians...

Should have just killed him, Mike thought, his grip on the wheel tightening. Maybe not kill—just a good throttling. Beat him within an inch of his life. Something to relieve the anger until he found out more information on the guardians. Let Haddad know how lucky he was to be alive, at least for now. He could have exacted a little revenge for Lowe and Greengrass at the same time.

Mike considered turning around. Only for a second or two. He needed to keep his priorities straight and *numero uno* on the list was getting out of Iraq and back to Langley.

"Fuck it." Mike pegged out the volume. Stevie's long solo in "Texas Flood" reverberated around him. "Get back to work and put this shit behind you for now."

The back window exploded into hundreds of pieces. Little bits of safety glass raked his right ear and the back of his neck. Mike swung the wheel hard left, swerving out of the line of the next rifle burst. He took

a quick glance in the rearview. A dark blue Renault barreled down on him. An Arab with an AK-47 stood up through the sunroof, firing on full auto. Haddad's friends.

You took too long getting the fuck out of here, he thought. *Doom on me.*

Mike swerved right and then accelerated back to the left, cutting serpentine trails down the road. The pursuit driver, though, was experienced and matched his movements, keeping the Renault close enough for the gunner to unleash another dozen rounds. Most of them connected, blasting out the left rear window. Glass flew; other rounds pierced the door and ripped up the passenger seat, sending leather upholstery soaring around the cabin.

"Motherfucker!" Mike risked taking one hand off the wheel to grab his cell phone. He made sure it was still on with the GPS locator active. He texted code 9-9-9 to Glenn. Then he slipped the phone under his seat before grabbing the wheel again.

Another burst erupted behind him, only to stop a second later. Mike glanced in the rearview. The gunner was reloading.

Mike straightened the car, straddling both lanes of the lonesome road. He eased off the gas as the Renault closed on his rear. The gunner had a fresh clip in and the rifle ready to fire.

He slammed on the brakes. The driver of the Renault wasn't quick enough, ramming the back bumper and trunk. The collision rocked Mike forward, and

his head smacked the steering wheel. He blinked stars away and didn't linger on the pain coursing from his forehead to the back of his skull. Instead, he floored it.

The Town Car accelerated past fifty kilometers per hour. Mike checked the rearview. The Renault's front end was smashed to hell. The driver stabbed at the airbag. The left side of the bumper dangled and dragged up underneath the engine, both headlights destroyed and the grill cracked. But it was still drivable. And its driver gained ground fast after puncturing the airbag.

The Town Car raced past sixty-five. Mike tucked his Beretta under his left thigh. When he passed eighty, he lowered the driver's window.

Ninety.

He yanked up on the emergency brake and turned the steering wheel hard to the left. The Town Car skidded and spun, the tires screeching across the asphalt. Mike watched the pursuer as his car completed the 180-degree turn.

The Renault tried to brake to avoid hitting him, but its closing speed was too great. As a result, the driver had to swerve, swinging to Mike's left.

Mike leveled the Beretta out the window and fired rapidly. He wasn't a good shot with his left hand, but he unloaded enough rounds to hit the gunner twice in the chest and once in the throat before the car passed behind him.

The main threat dead, Mike shifted into reverse and accelerated. He tucked the Beretta back under his

thigh and looked over his right shoulder while steering with his left hand. The Town Car slammed into the Renault's left side, smashing the door panel and shredding the right front tire.

Mike didn't let up, gunning the engine and pushing the Renault off the road and into a sand-laden ditch. The wheels spun as the driver tried his best to free the car from the soil. All he did, though, was dig the tires in deeper.

Beretta in hand, Mike bolted out of the Town Car, moving fast in a semicrouch. He kept the gun level on the driver as he swept around to his side, sites fixed on the man's head.

"Take your hand off the wheel and foot off the gas," Mike shouted in Arabic. "Now!"

The driver looked at him. Blood poured from cuts on his forehead and formed small streams running down around his eyes and nose into a thick beard. He was young, probably no more than thirty. Mike saw the top of a tattooed letter on his chest in the V of a button-down shirt.

"Do it now."

The driver let go of the wheel. The revving engine eased down. A look of defeat spread across the man's face.

"Get out of the car." Mike made quick scans of the road in front of and behind him. No traffic. No other pursuers. "Let's go."

The driver moved his left hand down slowly and activated the handle, opening the door. He raised his

left hand again and stepped out of the car. Mike could tell it wasn't the first time he'd had a gun on him or had been ordered out of a car.

"Good. Now turn around and put your hands on the hood."

The man did as ordered. When his palms were flat on the crinkled left fender, Mike moved up behind him and patted him down with his left hand. No weapons.

Mike stepped back, the Beretta trained on the back of the driver's head. "I know who you are. You're a Guardian of the Prison, right?"

The driver said nothing.

"A lot of good you guys are now. Last time I checked, the prison's gone. So either you're guarding sand or you were waiting for me."

The driver shrugged. "Maybe."

"Yeah, maybe." Mike wanted to put a bullet in the man's skull but restrained himself. He needed information. "What do you want with me? You pissed I killed some of your buddies that night of the raid?"

"I am only following orders."

"Orders, huh? Does Haddad give you the orders? Is he the boss man?"

No response.

"Guess I'll just have to go and ask him myself. I have ways of getting answers. Since you're not willing talk, maybe he will."

"I do not think so."

"Think what?"

"I do not think you will talk to Haddad."

"Well, that's a nice thought for you. Too bad it won't happen that way."

"No, it will. In fact, I do not think you will ever see Haddad again."

Mike started to speak but stopped. Something wasn't right. He'd lost control of the situation. He wasn't sure how, but his gut tingled. It felt bad.

He scanned the desert over the driver's shoulder. Just sand and scrub. A whole lot of nothing.

There. A dark shape a few hundred yards away down the road. Facing him.

Shit, Mike thought. He wanted to duck, to jump to the ground behind the car for cover. But his left shoulder exploded in a sudden burst of fire and pain. The impact knocked him back three feet and down. The Beretta fell from his hand.

The concussion of the sniper shot echoed around him. The burn spread into his chest and neck. Decent caliber round. He glanced at his shoulder, and bloody pulp stared back. No, it was only shredded bits of his shirt covered in blood.

Fuck, it hurt. Mike moaned and grabbed his shoulder, probing the wound. Good entry. Clean shot. Didn't feel like the clavicle was broken. Though, he was sure the shoulder blade was dust.

He rolled onto his side and pushed up to his knees with his right hand. His gun. He had to get his gun. The world blurred and spun around him. His heart hammered, pumping blood as fast as it could, trying

to keep him conscious. It wasn't working too well, though. He fell back down to his side, barely able to stay conscious.

My gun, he thought. *Find it.*

"Do not move any further."

The blurry shape of the driver stood over him. He saw his own Beretta pointed at him. Not good.

Mike forced deep mouthfuls of air into his lungs and tried to ignore the pain. *Stay awake,* he thought. *Don't fucking pass out.*

He didn't think he could follow his own orders. His head begged him to lie down. The fire burning in his shoulder activated a flood of endorphins coursing through his body. The natural reaction to trauma.

You survived a confrontation with a fallen angel. Don't let these camel jockeys get the better of you.

The motivational thoughts didn't help. His consciousness was shutting down. Time to sleep. Mike fluttered his eyes and rested his head in the sand. He exhaled long and deep. His shoulder didn't hurt as much now.

Another shape appeared next to the driver. This one was silhouetted by the sun. All Mike could make out through his rapid blinks was a sniper rifle in its hands.

Fucking sniper, he thought. *Probably jumped out of the car after it rear-ended me. Should have covered that contingency. Always assume there's more than one shooter. Stupid mistake.*

The two conversed in Arabic, but Mike couldn't make out the words. He closed his eyes and tried to pray. He couldn't think of anything to say. If they wanted him dead, he would be by now. No, they wanted him for something else.

Might as well get some sleep, he thought and passed out.

CHAPTER TWO

Glenn Cheatum stood at his desk, looking down at a brief he'd prepared to present to the director, when his cell phone vibrated on his hip. He grabbed it without tearing his gaze from the paper. Deep musings on the chances of civil unrest in Lebanon. Fucking scintillating stuff. Once he finished the last line, he glanced at the phone.

Not a call, a text message. From Mike.

He read the text: 9-9-9.

"Shit."

Glenn called Mike.

Pick up, pick up, pick up.

It rang five times before going to voicemail.

"Fuck."

Glenn hung up and clipped the phone back on his belt and left his office. It took him three minutes to reach the Operations Center in the CIA Headquarters

at Langley, Virginia. When he walked in, silence greeted him.

Four people sat at computers, monitoring operations around the world. Not a busy day. Most days, the center buzzed with life. Today, though, nothing much was going on in CIA land.

Glenn approached the guy closest to him, sitting at a flat-screen monitor watching video surveillance from the Kingdom of Saud. "What's your name?"

"Who's asking?" the guy said before he turned around. When he did, his eyes widened and his plump cheeks deflated. "Oh, shit, sorry, Deputy."

"Don't worry about it. What's your name?"

"Terry Kolchak."

"Terry, who owns Iraq today?"

"I do, along with Kuwait and Saudi Arabia."

Glenn nodded and put a hand on Terry's thick shoulder. "Any air assets up over southeastern Iraq?"

"Yeah, we have a Global Hawk north of Basra near the border."

"Reroute it to Ur."

"Ur?"

"Outside An Nasiriyah. North."

"Any specific location?"

"I'm going to give you an asset number, and you should be able to pull up a GPS squawking. The coordinates it gives is where I need the bird to go."

"No problem. What's the number?"

Glenn released Terry's shoulder and pulled up Mike's info on his phone. "700316."

Terry punched in the numbers. "Got it." He hummed.

"What?"

"Well, it's an unknown subject. Never seen an asset come up as unknown."

"That's for me to worry about. Copy?"

"Yes, Deputy."

Good, Glenn thought, thankful Mike was smart and knew to leave his phone on. "How long before we've got video?"

"Seven minutes, give or take."

"I want it on the big screen."

While Glenn waited, he pondered what might have happened. The code 9-9-9 was for an agent in duress. Mike had gone to site R91 on Glenn's orders. The military had handed the site back over to the construction company. Work had resumed. The area should have been safe.

Should have been.

"Global Hawk on station, Deputy," Terry said.

Glenn fished a pack of cherry antacids from his pocket and popped one in his mouth and ground it between his back molars while watching the live feed from the UAV. The real-time color imagery from the drone was displayed on the giant digital screen at the front of the Operations Center. It circled a couple of hundred feet above a black Lincoln Town Car and a blue Renault, both shot up and beat to shit.

Fuck, Glenn thought.

"Geez," Terry said. His pale face had turned a slight pink. "Hope no one was hurt."

You and me both, Glenn thought. He stared at the footage for a few more seconds. No bodies. No cars other than Mike's and the pursuit vehicle. Whoever had him now had left in a different car for sure. And Glenn had to assume they had Mike because his agent would never have left his phone behind.

You went to R91 like I told you to. Someone saw you there, remembered you from the attack last month. Wanted some payback or to finish the job.

It was the only thing that made sense. Glenn doubted it was a foreign agency or a terrorist group. No, it had to be someone familiar with R91. The only group outside coalition forces and Iraqi regulars to visit the site in the last few weeks was the little band that had attacked it.

What had Mike called them? Guardians of the Prison, or some shit like that?

He still couldn't fully swallow the whole tale. Mike had been serious when recanting the events at R91, and Glenn admitted something strange had happened, including the prison disappearing. But he had a hard time accepting whatever was in the prison was supernatural in origin or worth protecting by a bunch of desert dwellers for thousands of years. More likely the prison had been temporal and excavated by looters and sold on the black market. Nothing supernatural about that.

Of course, he didn't know what Mike meant by supernatural because Mike was going to tell him the whole story once he got back to Langley. All he'd told

Glenn so far was it wasn't a weaponized hallucinogen or any other chemical agent. Getting that much out of him had taken a direct order. The rest Mike had to tell him in person, where he'd have a better chance of convincing him it was all true. If Mike had tried over the phone, he thought Glenn would have him committed or killed for being insane.

I still might, Glenn thought. *First I need to get you back to Langley alive to hear it.*

Glenn ran through possible plans. He had zero CIA assets available in the immediate area. The closest ones he wasn't willing to divert off of current operations. Not to mention he would have to admit to having a rogue agent working in-country. The chain of command would go ape shit and arrest Glenn for conducting illegal operations. Glenn would end up in jail and Mike would end up dead.

He could call in the Iraqi military. But then he'd still have to explain to his boss what was going on without giving away Mike's identity and their relationship. Not an option.

Shit. No, Glenn needed to handle this on his own if he or Mike stood a chance of coming out of this unharmed and free of prosecution. Free of the pokey.

So how do I save our asses?

"Thanks, Terry. Break off the bird and return it to its normal operation."

"What happened, Deputy?"

Glenn shrugged. "Don't know. Probably chasing a ghost."

"None of our people were involved in this, were they?"

"No."

"But the GPS for the asset number—"

Glenn clamped down on Terry's shoulder and squeezed while fixing the fat man with his gaze. "Is no longer your concern, Terry. Do you understand?"

Terry nodded, his cheeks jiggling.

"Smart move." Glenn let go, straightened his jacket and tie, and focused on the screen. Two destroyed cars and one missing rogue agent. Wonderful. "You do good work here."

Glenn turned from the screen and walked over to a nearby empty console. He lifted a phone and punched a number.

"Special Activities Director," the voice said. "This is a secured line."

"Steve, it's Glenn."

"Deputy, what can I do for you?"

Always formal. "I need a favor."

"This have anything to do with you redirecting a UAV over Ur?"

"Word travels fast, I see."

"When the deputy director walks into the Operations Center and diverts a UAV without any explanation, people notice."

"Guess I should come down here more often."

"So, does this have something to do with why you're there?"

"Yeah, it does."

"You know I don't have any assets in Ur. Wonder why you're so interested in that area, being there's no CIA there."

"The asset doesn't belong to you or Clandestine Service."

"Are you going to tell me who he does belong to?"

Glenn gritted his teeth. Although Steve Ogden, as the SAD, worked for the director of the National Clandestine Service and the NCS reported to Glenn, the two came into the CIA at almost the same time and therefore were equals experience-wise. Steve was formal, but he wasn't against busting Glenn's chops from time to time. Even so, Steve was solid and damn good at keeping his mouth shut. Basically, the only guy at Langley Glenn knew he could trust right now.

But would he back a rogue player? Glenn thought. *Time to find out because you don't have any other angle.*

"He's my guy. Mike Caldwell."

A moment or two of silence passed.

"I'll meet you in your office, Glenn."

Click.

Glenn hung up and sighed. Shit. This wasn't going to be easy.

Steve was already in his office and sitting in front of his desk when Glenn walked in. The man was over fifty but still had the body of a linebacker and every inch of it filled the chair. Before Glenn could say anything, Steve launched in on him.

"Mike Caldwell resigned earlier this year."

"This needs to stay quiet, Steve." Glenn eased into his chair. "And no, he didn't. Well, he did, sort of. I made it look that way."

"He's working for you, huh? Doing projects outside the scope of Special Activities and the Clandestine Service?"

"You don't want to know the details. Most of it isn't legal, so you want to keep your knowledge limited. He's working projects for me, yes, which puts my nuts in an even tighter vice than they normally would be. That's all I want to say about it for your sake."

"And DNCS has no idea?"

"Nor does the director. No one does but you and me now."

"What happened to him?"

"Got snatched. Don't know by whom or where he's been taken."

"Why not just write him off? No one knows he's there but us. Wash your hands and it all goes away. Sounds like the best play if you want to stay out of jail."

Glenn swallowed a mouthful of spit. "Because he's my guy. And you couldn't do it, either, so don't suggest it again."

Steve rubbed his chin. "You're putting me in a tight spot, Glenn. I can't pull resources to help someone who doesn't technically work for us anymore."

"I know." As special activities director, Steve oversaw all US HUMINT operations in hostile areas. His

were the operations Glenn had not wanted to jeopardize. "I'm not asking you to do that."

"Then what are you asking?"

"Mossad's doing a snatch-and-grab op in Iraq, right? In An Nasiriyah. Coordinating through you to keep the locals calm."

"Yes, I briefed that to DNCS two weeks ago. It goes down tomorrow. Some fucking Kraut arms runner funneling shit to Hezbollah and Hamas. He should have relayed that to you—"

Glenn waved him off. "He did. I need the lead Mossad agent's contact info."

"You're going to need to get Mossad's approval to change their operation."

"Won't work. No, I need to talk to the lead agent in the field. I need him to redirect efforts to find Mike. And I need to keep this all between you, me, and the wall."

"And what makes you think I'll give it?"

Glenn leaned back and fixed Steve with his gaze. "You will."

Steve waved a finger. "Don't try that dead-eyes shit with me, Glenn. We've known each other too damn long for that to work. My reflection scares me more than you do."

"Right." Glenn chuckled. "What was I thinking?"

"Even if you convince the Mossad agent, he'll still inform his controllers."

"No, he won't."

"And how do you know that?"

"Because I know him. We go back a ways. He's their most senior clandestine agent and director of Metsada. I just don't have his contact info in the field. You do. So I need you to help me out."

"What are you going to tell the director about the UAV?"

"Say I chased a hunch and found nothing."

"You think he'll buy that shit?"

"After I saved his ass from the presidential fire over Basra? Yes, he'll buy whatever I sell him. Plus, who gives a shit? So I diverted a UAV for a few minutes. Not like I assassinated anyone."

Steve's right eyebrow flicked up. He steepled his fingers together and rested them under his chin. Glenn watched him, knowing the thoughts racing through his counterpart's head, weighing what he should do versus what he would do.

"Come on, Steve," Glenn said. "I need help on this one. You know it would take a lot to ask a favor like this. Besides saving my ass from a congressional inquiry and certain jail time, you'd be saving the CIA's rep and brother agent."

"The perception is he resigned and perception is reality."

"He's an operator. Don't hold his status against him."

After another minute of silence, Steve said, "You're going to owe me a ton for this, Glenn."

Glenn smiled. "I wouldn't expect anything less."

CHAPTER THREE

Mike felt like he floated in the calm waters of a lake on a dark starless night. Everything seemed still and peaceful and somehow right. Then something blew by him in the darkness. He searched, looking, and found only a shroud of black enveloping him.

It blew by him again. He spun and felt something surging up his legs and torso. Something moving, swirling. It constricted as it covered every inch of him. He couldn't move. Couldn't scream.

But he could hear. Flies buzzing. Locusts singing. They bit at his skin. First in random intervals. Then all at the same time. Biting and ripping while their wings beat the air louder and louder and louder…

Mike fluttered his eyes and breathed deep, grateful to be awake from the nightmare. Then he realized he

was lying on a metal table, staring at the framing of an old drop ceiling sans fiberglass tiles. Any feelings of gratefulness vanished.

He tried to sit up but couldn't. Lifting his head, he found his naked body strapped to the table. Leather belts wrapped his ankles and his waist and his chest, pinning his arms against his sides.

Not good.

The hole in his shoulder had a big gauze pad covering it. Surgical tape held it in place. As he wriggled, no pain emanated from the wound.

Local anesthetic, Mike thought. They wanted him alive, that was for sure. But why?

He let the question go. The more important thing to do now was try to get the hell out of Dodge. Easier said than done, though.

Mike glanced around him. The room was fairly large, like an open work bay or schoolroom with no furniture. Only the table he lay on and another table next to him. This one was smaller, metal, and covered with—

"Oh, shit."

Spread out on a white rag was a needle for the local anesthetic, a rubber mouth bit for biting down, and a silver amputation saw.

Maybe it's not for you, he thought. *Why would they keep you alive only to cut your ass up? How about we get out of here before we get an answer to that question?* Some things are best left unknown.

Only he wasn't going anywhere fast. Unable to move anything but his head, Mike quickly accepted the fact

he was at the mercy of his captors. Unless he could manage to become Houdini right quick. Fat chance. Maybe, when someone showed up, they might slack a strap or two. Maybe just enough to get a hand free. Then he might be able to escape. But until that happened, Mike had no choice but to play the waiting game.

Preserve your strength, he thought. *Sharpen your mind. Relax.*

Then he looked at the saw again and all motivation died.

He tried his best to focus on the ceiling. His will lasted about five seconds before his eyes were locked on the gleaming serrated blade. Christ, what did they have planned for him?

A door creaked open behind him. Mike forced himself to remain cool and collected. Footsteps grew closer and the skinny frame of an Arab with a short, well-trimmed beard appeared next to him. He wore a light khaki shirt with the collar open. Mike noticed the curve of a tattoo arcing over the top of his sternum. The two locked eyes.

"Greetings, Mr. Hosselkus," he said in Arabic. "I hope you are comfortable."

Hosselkus. So they had only the alias from his wallet. Nothing else. He tried to find the positive in anything he could. Hopefully, they hadn't snagged his cell phone from the car.

"The table's a bit chilly," Mike said. "I swear I'm a grower, not a shower."

"I apologize for the inconvenience, but nothing can be done about that." He leaned over and inspected the dressing on his shoulder. "I think you will find our treatment of your injury, though, more than hospitable."

"Sure. And since you're being so kind, why don't you let me go?"

"No."

"That's a shame." Mike jerked his chin at the man's tattoo. "So, you guardians got a personal grudge with me, huh?"

The man smiled. His teeth were straight and perfectly white. "No grudge at all. In fact, you have become very important to us. Hence the reason we have gone to such great lengths to ensure your wound heals properly. Your health is our great concern."

Mike wasn't digging the vibe coming off this guy. Part of him wished the stranger would just straight up say he wanted Mike dead or something. This whole concern for his comfort was creeping Mike out.

"You mind telling me why I'm so important?"

The smile faded. "Oh, I think you know."

Mike thought about it for a moment. It took only a moment. Only one thing connected him to the guardians and the prison they'd done such a shitty job protecting.

"Your demon." Mike shook his head. "But it's gone. I thought that was a good thing."

"It is. But it was not the only one."

Mike swallowed, remembering his face-to-face encounter with Semyaza. Oh, how lucky he'd been to survive—only to die naked on a metal table. *God has a sense of humor.*

"So, there are more," Mike said. "What's that got to do with me?"

"We do not know where the other prisons are." He straightened up and walked over to the table with the saw on it. "The one outside Ur was well known to us, discovered by our ancestors by accident long ago. They ensured it remained hidden after one of them received a vision—"

"A vision?"

"Yes, an angel instructed him to never open the prison. That a monstrous demon dwelled in the darkness, bound in chains. It became his and his tribe's task to guard it, to prevent an outsider from ever freeing the beast within."

"And you failed."

The man picked up the saw and turned it in his hand. He touched his thumb to one of its teeth as if checking its sharpness. The light reflected off the polished blade and Mike bit his tongue.

Shut up, he thought. *Being a smart-ass is not a wise play at this juncture.*

"Yes, we failed." The man put the saw down and Mike breathed a little easier. "But you did not. You confronted it on the navy ship and survived. Which means it let you live. Which means it found something in you worth leaving alone."

"How do you know about the ship?"

The smile again. "We have our own sources of intelligence."

"Pretty fancy for a bunch of tattooed tribesmen."

"We were once a tribe. Over the years, well, we have become more of an organization."

Mike didn't like the sound of that. They knew a lot of crap they shouldn't. How big were they?

"It wasn't what you thought it was, by the way."

Dumb fucks. "You seem to have access to trivial information, but when it comes to the most important, like where specifically the prison was and what was actually in it, you suck."

"Jinn, demon, fallen angel. They have had many names throughout time. They are more accurately known as the 'Fallen.'"

Maybe not so dumb, Mike thought and regretted losing his cool. *Don't play this guy's game.*

"Anyway," the man said, "the entity is gone, as is its prison. But there are still more Fallen out there. More prisons, too."

"How do you know?"

"The vision. The man who received it so long ago was told of a war in heaven. Four angels, leaders of Satan's four great legions, were bound in these prisons under the creatures they refused to serve: Us. Humans. The vision, though, did not specify the locations. Nor would my ancestor have understood where they were, since the known world at the time was so small."

"You think they're spread out around the world?"

"It is logical to think so. But we are not certain. We do have some theories, though."

"And you want to find them?"

"Yes."

"And do what?"

"Well, guard them of course. That is our appointed task." He opened the top button of his shirt and exposed the tattoo some more. "That is why we are marked. A reminder of our purpose in life."

Mike swallowed saliva pooling in the back of his throat. "So where do I come in?"

The man moved away from the table, turning his back to Mike. "We believe you are marked, too."

"I don't have any tattoos."

"Not that kind of mark."

"Semyaza never touched me."

The man spun around. "You know its name?"

"Yeah, it told me."

"You conversed?"

"There wasn't much else to do."

"Why did it not kill you?"

Mike stared at the ceiling, not wanting to explain that Semyaza had seen the goodness of man through his actions. "He realized he couldn't stay free forever."

"He surrendered?"

"So to speak."

"Amazing." The man moved close to him again and leaned over him. His breath smelled of mint. "Do

you know you are the only person to have survived an encounter with one?"

"I know now. And that makes me special, huh?"

"Very."

"But how am I marked?"

"Since you are the only one to survive a direct encounter, we believe you may have a trace—call it a residual essence—from the entity."

"You planning to make fallen angel cologne or something?"

The man smiled. "No. We are planning to locate the remaining prisons."

"With my supernatural essence."

"So to speak."

"Like a divining rod? How do you know it'll work?"

"We do not."

Mike sighed. "So, you're swinging at balls in the dark."

"I do not understand this expression."

"You're taking a chance, hoping I'll start glowing or something when I'm close to one."

"Perhaps."

"You're fucking nuts."

The man's smile disappeared. "You think you are very clever, Mr. Caldwell."

Mike's veins froze. He knew his real name. *Shit, shit, shit.*

"Oh, yes, I am well aware of your true identity," the man continued. "Michael Caldwell. Clandestine field agent for the Central Intelligence Agency. Until

recently, when you resigned. Yet here you are, still working covertly. Interesting."

The man has top secret information, Mike thought. *Which means he has a source inside the agency. Which means his organization is serious and possibly powerful. Double shit.*

"I said we have our own sources of intelligence." The man clapped his hands together. "And we have narrowed down where the other prisons may be within a few dozen square miles. If we take you to one and our plan works, all is the better. And if it does not, then we kill you."

Mike swallowed another mouthful of spit. "Guess I don't have much of a choice right now."

"No, you do not."

"Well, seeing that I'm not going anywhere fast, would it be possible to get some clothes and just handcuff me to the wall or something?"

The man shook his head. "I am afraid not. Because you will no doubt attempt escape at the first possible opportunity, we must take certain precautions to ensure you do not flee."

"How about some clothes, then? This table is a bit cold."

"Again, I am sorry." The man turned to the door. "Gazzar!"

The door opened and another man, this one portly with a long beard, walked in. He took up station at the table with the equipment on it. His eyes settled on Mike's legs.

"As I said," the man said, "we must take certain precautions."

Despite his best efforts, Mike felt his hands start to shake slightly at his sides. "What kind of precautions?"

"Gazzar is going to amputate your legs just above the knees."

ABOUT THE AUTHOR

ERIK WILLIAMS is a former naval officer and current defense contractor (but he's not allowed to talk about it). He is the author of the novel *Demon* and numerous other small press works and short stories. He currently lives in San Diego with his wife and three daughters. When he's not at his day job, he can usually be found changing diapers or coveting carbohydrates. At some point in his life, he was told by a few people he had potential. Recently, he told himself he's the bee's knees. Follow him on Twitter @TheErikWilliams.